"In *Stamped: An Anti-travel Nov*[...] tells the stories of American expa[...] or remake themselves in the far-flung corners of Asia. His narrative voice—steady, visual, and evocative—is complemented by his keen ear for dialogue. In this impressive debut, Guillermo has given notice that he is a writer to watch."

—Peter Bacho, winner of the American Book Award, a Governor's Writers Award, and the Murray Morgan Prize

"Kawika Guillermo's novel teaches the reader how to engage the world and reveals the very best about being a traveler rather than a tourist. We follow not only a vivid visual adventure across Asia, but also a linguistic journey into understanding new language and a definition of 'we' that is inclusive and empowering and revealing."

—Shawn Hsu Wong, author of *Homebase* and *American Knees*

"Kawika Guillermo has just crafted a brutal, sexy, and intelligent first novel, a deftly interwoven tapestry of colliding histories and desires. Guillermo's characters are insiders who suddenly find themselves on the outside in an Asia that has little time to coddle their fantasies. Stranded within the false privileges of race and empire, they struggle, survive, and are transformed by encounters with their speculative Others that are both horrifying and fascinating. Guillermo's novel is a thoughtful and unflinching look at the inescapable consequences of history on even seemingly 'innocent' relationships."

—Lawrence Chua, author of *Gold by the Inch*

Stamped

STAMPED

AN ANTI-TRAVEL NOVEL

Kawika Guillermo

Westphalia Press
An Imprint of the Policy Studies Organization
Washington, DC
2018

Several excerpts from this novel first appeared, in different form, in the following publications: "That Sarcastic 90s Mando-Pop" in *The Cimarron Review,* "Just to Spite the Recession" in *Word Riot,* "Don't Proceed" in *The Kartika Review,* "Red Is the Color," in *Tayo Literary Magazine,* "Leaving the Womb" in *Hawai'i Pacific Review,* "What Fell Beneath the Tracks" in *Liar's League Hong Kong,* and "The Imperialist's Salon" in *Open Road Review.*

Cover art by the students of Northbridge School in Phnom Penh (led by Anna Malgorzata De Nogales-Sudra). All images designed and edited by Kawika Guillermo and Dom Chung.

STAMPED
All Rights Reserved © 2018 by Policy Studies Organization

Westphalia Press
An imprint of Policy Studies Organization
1527 New Hampshire Ave., NW
Washington, D.C. 20036
info@ipsonet.org

ISBN-10: 1-63391-694-4
ISBN-13: 978-1-63391-694-4

Daniel Gutierrez-Sandoval, Executive Director
PSO and Westphalia Press

Updated material and comments on this edition
can be found at the Westphalia Press website:
www.westphaliapress.org

For Y-Dang & Kai Basilio Troeung

In remembrance of my grandmother,
Prisca Guillermo, who passed not long
after my birth, and whose absence left me
crossing ocean, body, and imagination.

Contents

ONE

Flaneurs

ThinkTravel! Blogbook

Post Date: 2007 MAR 6

User: SkyFaralan

The plan is to travel until the pain runs you over. But Bangkok was the worst place to start. It's just too easy here, in the land of smiles. Instead of a long, pathetic decay, you find food so cheap you couldn't possibly starve. People so beautiful you couldn't possibly be lonely. A police-force strictly for foreigners. A hotel room for seven dollars. Cheap massages that taunt your hopes of perishing in a blaze of hardcore travel glory. And because you are as brown as the fried cricket snacks that tantalize every street stall, you get to stroll into historic temples through the locals-only line. You can slide into an American coffee shop and shoot the breeze with ladyboys about their foreigner clients. You laugh at them, the white men, calling them big, hairy gorillas. Here, the rules of the game have changed. Your race card has turned wild.

Conscientiously objecting to every facile bit of American life, you started leaving from an early age. First you left your religion, then your background, then your family, your girl, your sex. Then, when there was nothing left to leave, you came to Southeast Asia with five hundred dollars from your leaving-life. It seemed one step better than genuflection: this going someplace you haven't yet been, a spot in the mind, dark and stuffed down the horizon's edge.

And I go with you, or you with me, sauntering along Bangkok's dull dark canals, fueled with the night's gifts, pretending we are Khajit thieves hovering our tails to cat-walk upon

3

exposed supine sexpats caressing young brown men in white briefs. We have no idea where we are because the street names on the tourist map are covered by cartoonish coconut drinks. The light-rail train roars overhead. You've stepped into a glob of elephant feces, soft and wet. The man leading the creature gives you bamboo but refuses to tell us how much it costs to feed the elephant.

So like good backpackers we ditch the animal, we toss the map, and just go. We pass a temple's silhouette. We use the light from the gold mountain as our only landmark, wishing to find ourselves lost. The streets seem unusually clean, making the city unusually boring, making us wonder if this could even be called slum diving.

An alley swallows us in a steam cloud, saturating our clothing with the smell of pork-buns. A dilapidated building has caught on fire. Men in tank tops stand around watching the ash float about in bits of winged red light. Monks hum a wistful chant. An old firetruck plugs into a hydrant but no water comes out. And there is some strange insect on your right hand, green and splintery. You blow on it, and it moves up your arm and into your shirt. It dies, perhaps, near your arm-pit.

This traveling with pretend-you thing seems to be working because it's been hours since I thought about real-her. You're tired of it by now. The inner-turmoil of a first-world depression that seems morbid in the face of Bangkok's tarpaulin rooftops; a luxurious, shameful struggle. So why is she still there, in the mind's projection screen, when your real eyes stare at real eyes staring back at you? That must be your unrelenting lust that you feel bursting open like a crushed lantern, its flame spreading to every unknown corner of the earth.

How do you proceed, how do you do this thing, called travel?

First, don't go too fast, remember to stay close to the street lamps. That's common sense. Ok, now cross that bridge. Now look over the dull waters, thick like melted rubber. Focus on it: its darkness, its blackness, not like the blue sea in Hawai'i, not like the fountains of The Bellagio. Stop that—now stick in your sandal, swath your toe, but don't fall into the muck. Don't wonder what she would think of all this. In that moat you will find it: a nothing. A big nothing, stuck within the ruinous figures that make up a backpacker's wet-dreams, picture-perfect in its unknowable poverty. If you were a different traveler you could take a dozen pictures, perhaps, and catch some gaseous yellow light.

Next—flap forward, stop thinking, and Look! Look at the gated temples with sleeping security guards. Look at that night market full of fresh eggplants and pig carcasses. Smell pungent fruit co-mingling with the scent of petrol from cackling motorbikes. Try to separate their aromas as you approach the stall. Don't think! Focus on that noxious smell of durian, the way it calms you, brings you into a mellow inflection. Listen to cooking oil pop as the smell of spices from a Thai curry stall—lemongrass, lime leaves, shallots—mixes with the spices from a Chinese noodle stall—garlic, ginger, green onion. Learn the smells, this is real shit right here. The smell of squid, fish, and clams. Don't think, you fuck. Ram your nose in there, that unusual, Bangkok, Asian, Thailand, metro-imperial fish. Now, listen to your stomach cry a newborn's wail.

While you're up and at it, be on the lookout for a malleable body to grasp onto, one that really suits you. Enviously watch two clean-shaven men settle in a nest of discarded McDonalds bags, warming each other from the icy stares outside.

5

Forget yourself, you are only your passport: Skyler Faralan. Twenty years old. American. Your face, brown and pale at the same time. Your sunken dark eyes that scream "get me the fuck out of here." Past that, a single stamp: Thailand, entry, 30 days. Then empty blue pages that unfold like an undotted sea.

Spend the night watching revelers trample in and out of the Khao San clubs. Read Balzac in a steamy cloud of Pad Thai. Sit on your damp motel bed. Choke down the smoke from a pyre of paper money. Share words with someone graspable. Knock on a door, make sure you have permission to enter. If not, offer nothing—small nothings—to those lost ghosts.

Arthur refused to get a taxi; only yuppies did that. It didn't seem to matter that taxis in Shanghai were cheaper than Seattle bus tokens.

He paced down the sizzling concrete letting beads of sweat leak through his polyester Megadeth shirt. He pushed the umbrellaed baby carriage quickly so the breeze would calm Joey, his eleven-month old son, now waking from a nap with a sliver of drool webbing down his blue onesie. Ahead of him, his wife Vanessa paused at a pedestrian walkway, waiting for the light to turn, fanning her dark blouse to keep it from sticking to her skin. Arthur caught up to her at the crosswalk and waited next to a tall woman who carried a tiny leashed dog, its body hair shaved, its head hair dressed like a crème puff. Nice dog, Arthur wanted to tell her, but he couldn't remember the Mandarin word for 'dog.' It didn't matter. Like Vanessa, the woman was also absorbed in a cell phone call.

"Joey," Arthur called to his son beneath the shaded carriage. "Joey, look. Doggy. Do-gy."

The baby's brown eyes surveyed the fashion-forward puppy. Rather than clap his hands, like babies in commercials, Joey chewed on a cloud-patterned blanket. Nearly a year old, the child was already bored with the new Asian faces in shopping malls and metro stations. Even after traveling six thousand miles from home to see, for the first time, his mother's people, the child remained unimpressed.

Arthur gripped the carriage and squatted to the boy's eye level. "Doggy," Arthur repeated. "Say doggy." His son's eyes moved, not to him or the puppy, but to those hitched chains of tiny gold lotus flowers strewing from his mother's sequined skirt like jellyfish tentacles. Arthur reached in his backpack for a bag of popcorn chicken and shook it vigorously.

"Chi, chi," Vanessa said in-between cell phone calls. As soon as the light changed, she charged across the pedestrian walkway, her unflappable stroll shuffling through Shanghai's skyscraper canyon.

Arthur hadn't prepared for how difficult China would be. When he and Vanessa went to Puerto Vallarta for their honeymoon, at least he could read Spanish words aloud, even if he couldn't understand them. But reading Chinese characters seemed as mysterious as reading palms. Banners and state-sponsored advertisements branded Shanghai as an international city, and yet the only local who seemed to speak English was the hotel concierge.

Arthur booked it toward Vanessa, letting the carriage hiccup on the tiled sidewalk and dip into a hole where the asphalt had worn away. His five-pound Sony camera swung from his neck, which carried a hundred something photos of the city's skyline covered in various levels of pollution.

Vanessa turned left, away from the taser-shaped towers of downtown. Arthur shouted, "Mind telling me where we're off to now?" He raced past an arm-in-arm elderly couple, the carriage dribbling over the yellow tube-shaped tiles meant to guide the blind. He saw her draw into a long queue outside of a restaurant doorway made of crisscrossing fake wood. A restaurant! Arthur thought. The dots came together—Vanessa's mother, who they had come to China to meet, was in Nanjing, a three-hour train ride from Shanghai, but her schoolmates worked in Shanghai. Perhaps he would finally meet them? Would they speak any English, or was this to be an exchange of pure smiles and nods?

That's why he loved her, he told himself, she always kept him guessing.

Vanessa was six people ahead in line, and a man just next to Arthur stood babbling on his cell phone, his feet positioned at a forty-five degree angle, a perfect slant to slowly cut in front of him.

"Hon!" he shouted at Vanessa. She was already near the counter, her black chiffon blouse tossing in waves as the restaurant's overhead air conditioning blasted the heat off her.

"Hon!" he called, wiping sweat from his face.

She pointed Arthur out to the waitress and waved him over. "They're already here," she said, pulling the baby carriage from Arthur's grip. She hoisted the carriage up and maneuvered her stick-figure body between tray tables and buffet lines, leaning the carriage back to avoid a shimmering glass chandelier.

After detouring through the bathroom and wine displays, Arthur sat down at a banquet table full of Vanessa's old friends: young urban elite who looked like advertisement models for whiskeys and stainless-steel watches. Steam from the boiling pot at the table's center blanketed their faces, making their rapid Mandarin sound like the *kkssshhh* of a fuzzed-out television channel. A woman next to him welcomed him in English, offering him a smile bordered by a ruby red lipstick that matched her ruby red tulle shirt and ruby red puffed pants. According to Vanessa, this look was a modern version of the Cheongsam, the body-hugging one piece made fashionable in 1920s Shanghai. But Arthur could see only pajamas.

"Baby so cute," the ruby red woman told him as she took Joey into her lap, nuzzling the child's nose against her own.

"Eyes so round!" she exclaimed, holding the child up into the haze of rollicking steam coming from the pots of boiling soup. "Nose so straight. Skin white as rice. Blonde hair!" She passed the child to a muscular man with curvy pomaded hair.

"Ta da zhang zenme gao?" the woman asked Arthur. He smiled at her, shrugging. She added: "You learn Chinese?"

"I'm American," he said. "We're monolingual."

"Mono ..."

"That means we only speak one language."

"Really?" She poured him a cup of tea, flakes of rose petals tapering along the liquid arch. "Try coming to Nanjing, where I live. You will learn Chinese fast."

The glass cup burned Arthur's fingers. "Actually," he said. "I just remembered a Chinese word. *Gou.*" He gave the word a thick drawl.

"Gou? It means dog. Tai bang le." She sipped from her cup. "That's what we say to children who do well! Ni keye xue."

"Yes." Arthur looked to Vanessa for an explanation, but his wife had moved across the table to chat with a woman whose hair stood up in a stale bouffant. He drew back to let a waiter set plate after plate of unthawed meat. Behind the hotpot steam, Arthur heard Vanessa laugh with such flamboyance that she seemed to be mocking someone, and they were all having a riot out of it. How different she seemed, he thought, when she was with her own people. Outgoing, likable, popular. And funny. When was she ever funny around his friends? He scratched at a newly formed rash near his fleshy paunch.

"Arty!" Vanessa called to him. "They want to see your comics. Hurry up. Kuai le!"

That was Arthur's cue to reveal his portfolio of comic book drawings: laminated monographs he brought to show Vanessa's parents that he possessed some kind of ambition. Vanessa's friends passed around his drawings of hoody-wearing tree creatures, unable to comment in Arthur's own language. When the ruby red woman received it, she smiled and said "hen you yisi" before standing to fetch a dumpling from across the table. Vanessa shared a joke in Mandarin with a man next to her. Perhaps it was about the way Arthur still kept superhero action figures. Or how he never really learned to use chopsticks. Or how losing at video games made him leave bite marks on his Xbox controllers and fist-shaped holes in the wall. They laughed at something, their necks arched back, gripping onto each other's arms.

"I know something else in Mandarin too," Arthur said, interrupting them. "Wo yao zhenzhu naicha."

"Ah!" the ruby red woman exclaimed as she pulled a

11

steaming cluster of slim enoki mushrooms. "You mean that you want milk tea with rice balls."

"Yes!" he shouted, barely hearing himself above the laughter across the table. "I! Really! Love! Milk! Tea!"

"Cute!" the ruby woman said, patting the mushrooms onto Arthur's plate.

"Xie xie," he told her, meaning thank you, and followed that with a slight bow. A waiter ladled out soup laced with the scent of crab. Somewhere beneath the soup's steam a child laughed. He saw a group of three women marveling at an object. No, wait, that was not Joey. Just another puppy. Also a blonde.

Mandarin overtook the room, shoving Arthur into reticence as he sat spinning his golden wedding band on the table's smooth white cloth. He looked over the English beer menu to find only Carlsbergs and Buds. His lips smacked for a stein. Or a warm stout. Or an IPA just out of a cask. The absence of real beer brought a tinge of fear, that instinctual longing that comes with low blood sugar. He closed his eyes and listened to a thread of pleasant singing that wavered toward him from the restaurant speakers. It stirred his ears, hooked him onto a melody, made him reminisce on his 90s middle school years. He thought of Alanis Morissette, Fiona Apple, that brazen and honest voice that seemed so rare in the laser-noises that came in the 2000s. The old beat, playful, but too soft to tap along with. The singer seemed just slightly ahead of it, as if the words had to pierce through the instruments. But this voice sang in a graceful, colorful Mandarin. The woman's words were not pleading but sharing, a whisper floating in the air. He felt a taste in his mouth, dark, dripping.

"Arty!" Vanessa was trying to feed him, her manicured fingers brandishing a pair of wooden chopsticks. The steam from the boiling pot crawled over her blouse like white ropes as she held her chopsticks with one hand, her other hand cupping a piece of red meat to catch the morsels of hot soup dripping off. The ruby red woman next to him held her mouth to keep from laughing.

"Arty, are you daydreaming again?" Vanessa asked.

"I'm ok," he said. "Where's Joey?"

Vanessa said something to her friends in Mandarin. She started laughing first, and the rest followed. Arthur smiled and scratched his rash.

After dinner Vanessa hailed a cab before Arthur could tell her no. To keep his mind off the money he was wasting, he kept his eyes on the television screen embedded into the passenger-side seat, where massage artists hovered above floral embroidered couches. He turned off the screen, just in case there was a surcharge, and watched Shanghai's buildings from outside the cab window. Three days ago, when they first arrived in China, he was enthralled by the purple lights from the lotus-skyscraper spilling into the streets, coloring the pedestrian walkway, Nanjing Road, with the constant glimpse of an early sunrise. Lotus flowers, symbols of good luck, of youth, of a readiness that blooms and spores at the same time, of a beauty that comes from mud. But now the tower looked tacky, as uninspired as the swanky haircuts on Shanghai puppies. What youthful naiveté, Arthur thought. What chintzy sell-out. What an artless city of art.

The driver shouted on his cell phone in that impossible language. "Kidneys!" Arthur imagined the driver saying. "Fresh kidneys! I got a foreigner here with fresh kidneys, any takers? Or how about clean, pollution-free lungs? Get'em while they're hot!"

"You like my friend, huh?" Vanessa said. That familiar tone. "You like looking at her?"

"Aw, god, V."

"You're too late. She's going back to Nanjing tomorrow." She pulled yuan from her purse, always ready to pay. "But you have no chance with her anyway. I've known her forever, since middle-school. You know what happens in all-girls schools?"

"What?"

She glared at him with dark beaming eyes, the demeaning look that once turned him on. Those irises rolled away from him. "It's only girls. *Only girls.* Don't you like to imagine it? You like to think we need you, don't you?"

"Only girls, as in, girl on girl?" Arthur asked. "Come on, seriously?" She had never said anything like that before. Perhaps she needed attention. He kissed her scalp, tasting the Alterna hair spray that always gave him an allergic reaction, reddening his lips. She picked up Joey, her long hair bouncing as she burped raspberries onto the child's stomach.

"How about I just leave you for her?" she said. Joey squealed in laughter. "She and I raise Joey together. You would like that, huh? You can go back to America, land of freedom, and screw other women."

Arthur gave a surrendered sigh and stared out the window. Vanessa had made similar suggestions before, especially when she was drinking, her face red and excited with an indulgent spirit—indulging her anger onto him. She continued without abandon: "I can do it! We're not like you guys. Call one 'gay,' one 'straight.' Giving names. Don't need names, don't even talk about it. Just do it."

"What does that mean?"

Her long straight figure sprawled out, her legs parting to expose her knees above the black skirt, those tiny gold lotus blossoms clinking against each other like window chimes. Joey lit up at the sound and reached out to grab them.

"Ni yao ma?" Vanessa cooed at the child. Joey nodded in response. "Tai bang le!" Vanessa said, with a single clap. She snapped the chains off her dress and placed them on the baby's stomach. "Can you believe it?" she exclaimed. "Joey understands Chinese!"

Arthur gave a nod of approval. Ni meant "you," he was fairly sure. And ma was like a question mark. But the other word, yao, recalled nothing.

In the morning Arthur woke to the sunlight of an empty bed. As usual, Vanessa had stepped out early to have her first and only full meal for the day. He spread his arms out, yawning, excited to be left alone, away from the polluted oven air outside. He spent an hour in bed screwing around on his laptop, looking up movie reviews and the local news in Seattle, and eventually found himself running a search for Mandarin female singers, hoping to find the Chinese song he had heard at dinner. He found far too many, so he limited his search to 90s Mando-pop. Another hour passed as he downloaded songs and synced them to his iPod. Only then, when he was plugged in and ready to peruse this new, fascinating genre, did he realize that Vanessa's clothes and luggage were gone. He reached to his side—no stroller. No pacifier. No baby blanket.

A sound spurt from his laptop:

Wo buyao anwen

Wo buyao xisheng!

It was during Arthur's twenty-first birthday barhop, just before he fainted at the strip club from popping too many oxygen capsules, that he decided to get out of Portland. The next month he quit his job at the grocery and moved to Seattle's Capitol Hill, a district of rusted urban apartments and group housing that everyone complained was too upscale. The only place he could afford was a studio in an alley bordering Roy Street, an energetic avenue where rainbow flags flapped over Catholic churches. Drag bars like Linda's and Pal's, famous for Madonna impersonators, were a mere block away. He often walked near Julia's outdoor U-shaped bar, passing the hand-in-hand gays, never nodding to them but smiling. A year later, he walked the same street hand-in-hand with Vanessa. Without much effort he had become one of those white men holding hands with an Asian woman: the queer district's least queer sight.

They had met on OkCupid.com, a site he preferred over other dating sites like plentyoffish.com, since he could adjust his preferences accordingly, vetting out any religious women. He was not prejudiced, he had just spent his teenage years learning to distrust religions, and his new free-thinking self could never let him carry a relationship with a Bible thumper.

Excluding all religious people left only sex-positive women whose profiles used a hodgepodge of mysterious acronyms. From BDSM and NSA to obscure aberrations like ABR (adult breastfeeding relationship) and TPE (total power exchange), which Arthur had to translate using an online *kink*tionary. Worse were the dates with these women. The overwrought vocabulary, it turned out, was more than just an internet convention. The sex-positives talked about "ggg" experiences and all the things that made them uncomfortable. While one woman praised the steampunk art scene, another rolled her eyes and claimed that lavapunk was the new deal. Scattered throughout such talks were terms like "swag," "meme," and "intersectional."

Too many failed dates with sex-positive women left Arthur desperate to try the other group of non-religious candidates: Asian women. Specifically, new Chinese immigrants. They were easy to find: "SAFs" was their only acronym, Single Asian Females. And Vanessa, an accountant for a logging company, was his first and only SAF.

She did not seem to waver in choosing him; she showed up to the Broadway drag queen bar wearing glasses and sweatpants, as if they were already married. He explained that he was a "level one administrative assistant" (read: data entry) at a small-platform software company. He asked her about music, but she had never heard of the bands he liked. He mentioned baseball, but she knew only the Yankees. He mentioned politics, but she did not even know who the Vice President was. Even when he called Budweiser "fucking pisswater," he had to teach her that the word "fuck" wasn't always to curse someone, but could be used humorously, like in an Offspring song.

"Who?"

"You have to at least know The Offspring," Arthur said. "You have to know them, everyone knows them." He said it quietly. For most Seattleites, The Offspring were, officially, a shitty band.

Vanessa shook her head. "You have their music? Maybe I can try a listen."

He took her to his undecorated apartment only a block away. Sitting on the stained futon Arthur had found on the sidewalk, they listened to his favorite Offspring song, "Gotta Keep-em Separated." She did not seem put off by any of it—perhaps China wasn't all money and glitz.

"Wowow!" She exclaimed after the song was over. "This is so good! *Fuck* yeah!"

Over the next few weeks Arthur fell into a soft, shameless love. Two months later they were married, and weeks later, on their honeymoon, Vanessa discovered she was pregnant.

One week after Joey's birth, Arthur turned twenty-two.

At the hotel's front desk, Arthur pleaded to a receptionist wearing blue-rimmed glasses, who spoke a spattering of English.

"No. Mei you," the receptionist said. "That woman. She is gone now. With her baby."

"But she's coming back," Arthur said, nodding his head as if to affect her answer.

He would have called Vanessa, and gotten this all cleared up, but SIM cards in China did not work with his locked American phone. He tried to look up where Nanjing was on the hotel wifi, but google maps was blocked by Chinese government censors. That's where she would run. Nanjing, where her family was, where her old schoolmates were. Where the woman in ruby red still lived.

Arthur zipped out of the hotel, dragging his roller bag along the tiled sidewalks. At the main road he worked up the bravery to flag down a cab.

"Train station!" he yelled at a cab driver through a cracked-open window. The driver shrugged at him. "Train station!" Arthur repeated until the cab blew away at the green light.

He wandered into an alley of hair salons and noodle shops. He retraced his steps and found himself in a backstreet of Chinese medicine vendors. God dammit—he had no idea where he was. The afternoon heat upon him, he walked aimlessly, dragging his jumpy roller-bag, looking for a sign pointing to an air conditioned metro station. Asian things were supposed to be small. Bonsai trees and all that. But the main streets of Shanghai felt larger than American freeways, large enough to support tanks. After merely two blocks his shirt had bunched up his stomach, drenched in sweat. He could feel wetness dripping from his nose, chin, and ears. He passed abandoned dogs, some trailing him, some limping, their hair in skinned patches with hanging chewed-off fur.

He found a sign that read "subway" in English and followed it underground, bumping his roller bag down the stairway until the handle snapped off. He cursed, freely, since no one would understand him anyway, and lugged the bag by the bottom, searching the underground hallways for any sign of a subway train. After circling the area twice, he thought that perhaps, for Chinese people, a "subway" was merely an underground pass.

He collapsed at the corner of another hallway, letting his broken luggage drift into the tiled wall. He stared at the plane of concrete squares. Stained white tiles stood in a large family across the ceiling, chipped and broken. On the ground, brown and tan tiles decayed from the white gunk that built up in the cracks like calcified plaque.

"Houchezhan," Arthur whispered to himself. That was it. *Train Station*. He remembered the phrase from the Chinese survival pamphlet he had read on the airplane. "Hou" meant train, but also meant fire. When trains ran on coal they must have looked like dragons blowing smoke through the mountains. "Che" was car. "Zhan" was station. "Houchezhan." Arthur repeated the phrase, not letting it slip away.

During their first six months of marriage, Arthur loved Vanessa's cultural quirks. He loved her collection of unplayed and untuned musical instruments: trombones, guitars, flutes, and oboes. He loved the orderliness of their Fremont apartment, which coincidentally overlooked Aoki, the city's most popular Asian restaurant. He loved that his co-workers had to take their shoes off before entering his place. He loved that she could learn enough Spanish in two weeks to guide him around Mexico for their honeymoon. He loved that when she became pregnant, she told him, "Never mind the money. My father will send enough. We will actually be richer now." He loved that she never once brought up a green card, and whenever someone else did, she would tell them: "Why should I want to live in this country?"

Perhaps it was the pregnancy that changed their relationship, or perhaps it was the post-honeymoon boredom. He blamed it on China's culture of fear. Her fear of drugs kept him from ever seeing his meth-recovering sister in Eugene. Her fear of disease kept him from his HIV-positive uncle. As her fears manifested into aggressive insults, his number of female friends began to dwindle until there remained only one last remaining threat: Stephanie, one of his sister's ex-roommates, a woman too busy with children to incite Vanessa's competitive edge.

Or perhaps his American culture had made her change. When they first met, she loved going out to movies at non-profit Seattle theaters, to jazz performances, to Shakespeare in the park. But when their nights out were so stalked by the fear that his eyes would follow another woman's skirt, they stopped going out entirely. If anyone asked about Arthur's sudden absence, he blamed fatherhood.

When Vanessa's father died of lung cancer and the money stopped coming, Arthur suggested moving to China, claiming he had always wanted to go there. Arthur's parents were even poorer than him, and their house smelled of cigarettes and "white trash," as Vanessa put it. So that left Vanessa's family in Nanjing, who Arthur had never expected to actually meet.

When the taxi dropped him off at the train station, Arthur felt victorious, like he had beat a level in a video game. He waddled through the hallways with his knees bent to drag his broken luggage. The lines at the ticket booths spread across the station in all directions, merging into a mountain of black hair. Where were the distinctions? Who was in line, who was in the crowd, and who was just standing around on their cell phones?

Arthur found something like a line and stood in it. Instantly someone cut in front of him. Then an entire family pushed their way past him like he was a stray animal. Well isn't that different? But the family was not alone—one of them carried a bright blue flag. A tour group came in a rush of smiles, squeezing him out the exit doors. He tried again in another line, this time widening his legs to keep people from passing him. Near the middle of the line he used his luggage to create a demarcation. Nearer the front he brushed people aside, treating the queue like a contact sport. Another man cut, his head seemingly lost in a newspaper. Arthur whispered, "go ahead you stupid asshole," hoping, just a little bit, that the man understood English. Despite being a Northwest leftist from perhaps the most liberal city in the United States, Arthur found himself seriously wondering how much more orderly and respectful the Chinese would be if everyone carried a gun.

The train was cleaner than Arthur imagined, though it didn't occur to him that it was his first time ever on a train. Vendors ambled up and down the aisles selling ramen, juice, and fermented eggs. As the engine drifted to a slow start, an intercom announcement came in a Beijing-accented Mandarin with stressed "r"s and "j"s. Arthur translated it to the only Mandarin he really knew: "wo xiang zhenzhu nai cha," *I like tapioca milk tea*. He imagined the entire announcement was about this.

"I really like Milk Tea! Do you like Milk Tea too? I like Milk Tea with tapioca. What do you think? Does anyone else like Milk Tea?"

Beyond the city, the train reached 200 mph, sailing passed rows of concrete apartment blocks still under construction, with massive cranes perched upon each tower. The train blew past coal factories with gigantic haystacks frothing bubbles of smoke. How did he end up like this, here, in this place, chasing his wife and child? Were American women too boring for him? When high school ended, there was little to do but bask lazily about, waiting for a friend to drive him to one of the McMenamins micro-brew movie theaters. Arthur had worked a ten-hour a week service job at the Fred Meyer, suffering an invisible anguish and not knowing why. He lived with two friends from high school, their apartment burdened with festoons of in-box action figures, superhero-designed kitchenware, and lichen-infested ceilings. He moved to Seattle, ultimately, to do something, to do anything.

Two years after leaving Portland, he returned triumphant, with a gorgeous exotic woman armed with a discernible taste for fine wine and sushi. And Vanessa's figure, in her white wedding dress, dropped jaws. So gorgeous even without make up. So youthful that no one believed she was thirty-five. He joked that he had married to "cash out while he was high." Two years in Seattle and he was still a data entry worker and a part time secretary, still under the title "Level One Administrative Assistant." He made almost nothing, was known to nobody, had achieved nothing.

But he had a wife.

In the crowd leaving the exit gate, Arthur thought he saw her—a woman the same height as Vanessa, with the same wavy black hair. The lithe shadowy figure held a child in one arm, and the arm of another woman in the other. She was on her cell phone, and disappeared in the crowd.

"Ni de piao!" the female checker shouted at him as he tried to exit the revolving gate, her voice grating his ears. Arthur pleaded with her in English as she kept her arm held out toward his chest. "Ni de piao!" she repeated, so loud it seemed to scratch the air apart. He tried to dive under her, beneath the partition, but her white gloves clutched his arm. He wrenched her away but she took hold of his broken roller-bag. He sprinted ahead without it.

Words tore out of his lungs: "That's my son!"

The train station did not let out into a large sprawling metropolis, but to a lake, grayed out by the haze of pollution settled over the buildings just like Seattle's overcast sky. Searching for the woman, he let the crowd lift him into the line for the ferry. A sign in English read that the boat came once every ten minutes, from 8 am to 8 pm. Arthur had no watch, and no other leads. Fuck it. The rotor started as soon as he stepped on.

At the first stop Arthur flew through the crowd, scanned the dock, and sprinted up a small hill path. He looked for her from atop the hill, but saw only the edges of the island, bordered by small bridges, stone walls, and temples.

Signposted arrows directed him toward the best vantage points for scenic picture-taking. Near the lights of a temple, the ferry docked near the city's ancient stone wall. Its light flicked off.

He paced around the island as if he would find some clue. His frisson of energy subsided. A bridge led to the lights of the city on the other side: Nanjing, where even fewer people spoke English. How could he get a taxi? How expensive were the hotels? Who could he call? On this island, the air was cool, and he was alone, with the stillness of the lake.

He sat on a bench watching the lights glint from the city's skyscrapers, then slowly disappear into the dark pollution haze. No stars, just a thick blank tapestry. He thought for a moment that he could hear the people in the city talking in that jargony language, picking mushrooms from hot pot, and wearing Cheongsams like it was still 1920. It was easy to watch with this lake-sized spot of elbowroom.

The vending machines provided the only light besides the city skyline. He rested with his iPod in a bed of grass, listening to the Chinese pop princesses he had downloaded the night before, that playful music sung in a sarcastic voice. He imagined Joey speaking Mandarin. Growing up, being admired by all the cute Chinese girls for his Western eyes and hair, finding everything so much easier than he would have, were he raised in America. The free healthcare, the rising stocks. A youth without guns or drugs. Just the feeling of being special wherever he went.

Sunlight came, revealing a sallow mist that seeped from the hills and crept onto the lake. Translucent clouds spread languorously upon the iron-colored waters, surrounding Arthur completely, a cold enfolding. His iPod had lasted the night, and he could still hear the music of that Mando-pop singer. Her voice whispered to him, cutting just ahead of the beat. One day, he decided, he would understand whatever it was she was trying to say.

ThinkTravel! Blogbook

Post Date: 2007 MAR 25

User: SkyFaralan

On the overflowing banks of the Mekong River, you bask in a sleepy, laid-back paradise of four-dollar motel beds, shiny glasses of coconut shakes, and free plates of green curry from nearby Wats. You spend the day by the Mekong, watching its heavy brown creep. Every now and then a local tries to sell you cigarettes. Sometimes you feed the stray cats.

Laos is known for being the poorest country in Southeast Asia. But you're poor too, so you can handle that. Vientiane is the most boring city in Laos, so the foreigners around here say. But you're boring too, which is why you're here.

Since there's nothing to do in Laos, nothing is exactly what you do.

There are no set opening times, no set closing times. All depends on one's mood. You pass four pharmacies right next to each other, none of them open. But the condom and Viagra dispensers bordering them work fine.

Animals walk the streets living off scraps and goodwill. Dogs, cats, roosters, chickens. They all seem indifferent to you as they pass, as if you don't belong in their animal metropolis.

But the people never stop staring at you: the drivers, the tourists, the NGO workers too. You are a white farang as well as a brown among other brown people. And though this fact creates confusion everywhere, it carries some potential. You walk into a bar without anyone trying to sell you drugs. You walk through the gates of Pha That Luang without being mauled by touts. You meet an Australian in a Hawaiian shirt who just assumes you are from Manila. When you tell a local, a tourist, a guide, that you're American, they nod their head. But you can see it in their eyes. Something about you remains unacceptable.

"From where in South America?" asks some white Australian guy who owns a house in the Philippines, and who bounces a young Filipino man on his lap, occasionally stroking his crotch. The Filipino looks so much like you, you could have been switched at birth.

"You mean you're half-American," says Philip, a lanky American man wearing thin glasses. He graduated top of his class in computer engineering. He calls Chinese people backwards. He only intended to stay in Laos for a couple of days, but now he can't imagine leaving. He told his boss that the communist Lao government wouldn't permit him to leave. That was two years ago. When Philip asks "What is your exact ethnic composition?" you abruptly open yourself to where you are. How shall you compose yourself here, you unknown ethnic? A self not yet compost but composable, as if composing a letter, not something born, but invented.

From the Guidebook: "The only substance that really keeps the malaria-ridden mosquitoes away is alcohol."

From a Korean traveler: "I come here for the Mama bars. That's where women take young men to their hotel rooms."

From a Filipino man on the bus after you tell him that your grandfather refused to pass his language onto his descendants: "I would do the same."

From Philip: "In Beijing, all the Chinamen crouch down to slurp from bowls of rice-soup. They must be the race closest linked to animals."

From a young Polish man, after spending a week in intense meditation at Wat Mahadhatu: "I feel great."

From Ben the American, who curls his dreadlocks: "Everywhere I go, people scream at me: 'Hey ladyboy! What's your name?' All because I walk around in a dress."

You: "Why do you wear a dress?"

Ben: "It fits into my backpack easier."

From a Lao woman at the Mama and Hound pub, after you tell her in a fake accent that your name is Nico, and that you're a poor student from the Philippines with very little cash: "I will pay you forty dollars."

In the morning she nabs the hotel bill and buys you breakfast at a shaded street stall. Someone pours red soup into a bowl of vegetables and hands it to you. She watches you eat, perhaps the same way she watches her son and daughter eat. Who is taking care of them? How did she get the money? Why does she need you to lean against her while you eat?

You tell her she's the second person you've ever made it with. She balks and digs another fiver from her purse.

She let smoke seep from her mouth and creep into her eyes, her nostrils, her hair, until it settled upon her shoulders and covered the plastic table. She spat the residue into a dark mound of dirt and washed the taste out of her mouth with a Tiger beer. She hated the taste, but being enveloped in smoke comforted her: she, a girl of twenty-one from Florida who sat alone, having never sat alone at a restaurant before, not before she left America. Now here she was, alone in Penang's Georgetown, watching a Malaysian cover band play a jazzy version of 'American Girl' while a local man sporting a mullet mimicked the words in an interpretive dance. At the words "she was an American Girl," the man pointed to Melanie.

She tried to drown out the music by reading from the hand-sized Bible she had picked up at Incheon airport. She had intended to read the entire thing from front to back, but for some reason, she skipped the Torah and went straight for the steamy Song of Solomon:

> Your temples behind your veil
>
> are like the halves of a pomegranate.

Melanie annotated the text with a red pen: *Could the woman be wearing a veil?*

> Your breasts are like two fawns,

> like twin fawns of a gazelle
>
> that browse among the lilies.

That line demanded another cigarette. She lit and spit. Melanie wasn't a smoker, not really, but no one bothered a smoker. Perhaps it was the pyre of herbs and ash that she held in her hand, the power of those joss statues at the colorful Buddhist temples, that fire lighting the scent of incense wafting through Little India, mixed with clove, frankincense, and sandalwood. A pleasant fire, not like the fire at Camp Aurora's cabin confessionals, where as a teenager she had to walk upon jagged coals, dark with heat and melted skin, while her father sat watching, a silver cross hanging from his tight necklace—the cross he started wearing after her mother, high on painkillers, set fire to their apartment.

Melanie's dessert arrived and she lifted her heavy camera to capture the diamond-shaped pink- and white-layered cake. Her photo blog was full of more sweets than scenery. The first bite tasted of gelatin and coconut.

Mmmm ... creamy goodness. Good Lord, I love you.

A man sat at the table directly across from her. She felt a strange impulse to bristle the back of his head. When he turned around to smile at her (as they do) she saw a tamed 20s-something black man in a striped blue collared shirt. She held up her Bible to scare him off. That did it. He turned around, lighting a cigarette of his own. She kept to her book, keeping him in her purview as he flirted with a Malay bargirl in hot pants. Something about him drew her. Perhaps it was the polite smile on his face, or, more likely, his V-neck shirt that left exposed a tuft of untamed hair. Or the way he laughed, which suggested he must have been good at sex. A whole body laugh, with stomach muscles unafraid to flex. The waitress left and the man snuck another glance at Melanie, slightly scratching his chin. It seemed inevitable that they would hook up. They were too foreign in this land, their bodies too optimal in their own.

He sat next to her and introduced himself as Winston. And Winston came complete with a triangle smile, a permanent five o'clock shadow, and peppery hair shaped like the pages of a tossed-open book. He spoke with a puzzling accent, sometimes British, sometimes American, sometimes Australian, as if he had been raised in an expat bar. Winston claimed to have traveled all over Asia, funded by his father's sugar, pineapple, and coffee plantations in the Philippines.

When it was Melanie's turn to give her life-story, she gave the most abridged version: "I'm taking a break," she said, blowing smoke. "I teach English in Korea." No need to say that she had fled the country after being caught banging (or getting banged) on bar stools, on pool tables, on camera, and in her students' homes. The endless clubbing of Busan, the soju bottles she tossed from her sixteenth story window, the Korean men she picked up from the street and brought home, all of it was captured and exposed in a Korean newspaper, which made its way online. Then her blonde hair and tight tank tops brought on the eyes, those stares shoving her out of the country. As if somehow Jesus Christ himself had followed her across the sea and found her morals lacking.

"Let me guess," Winston said, pointing his index finger at her, boggling it up and down, "you're not too long out of the womb?"

"Excuse me?" she said, puffing smoke at a mosquito.

"You know what I mean. The *womb*," folding his legs, "Where you were forced to act like the same person by friends, family and every boozer who said they loved you." He skipped his empty beer mug across the table, letting it quiver back and forth before asking for another.

Melanie remembered the canals near her home in Fort Lauderdale. The harbor of white yachts. What lies beyond good and evil? she thought. Boredom, that's what. "I been away for almost a year now," she said. "They all think I'm on a mission. For God."

"That's hypocritical. Religious people are so dim-witted. Rip off that religious band-aid early. You're still young."

She shrugged. "Gives me a good excuse to keep using my daddy's credit card." In truth, Melanie hadn't used the card in months, paranoid that her father might use the bank statements to track her down. But her funds were running low fast.

"How old are you?" Winston asked, jutted chin. "I'm just curious if you really have it all. Blonde hair, thin, white, and young to boot. What are you doing with all that?" He sipped from his newly replaced mug and she noticed a scar across the right side of his face. She could not tell if it was from a knife, pimples, or a burn.

"Yesterday was my birthday, actually," she said. "I managed to dodge turning older on an airplane in the sky this year. So yeah, still a year younger I reckon."

The band played another Tom Petty song. The dancing man pointed to Melanie at the words "Mary Jane."

"I gotta ask," Winston said, pulling his chair toward her. "Why come here? Doesn't Malaysia seem like a scary Muslim place?"

"I ain't that particular." She stubbed out her cigarette and felt his gaze stroking her white lace tanga panties, sticking out from her jeans. She felt that old drive clinging to her. "Just headin' south."

"The usual route. I'm heading south too, toward Kuala Lumpur. When are you going?"

"Whenever."

"Me too."

When he crept closer, to whisper in her ear, she looked down, at her breasts, imagining two fawns nipping at rosy petals.

On the way to his hotel they came across a pyre of charred white paper spun in small puffs of wind. Four Chinese bar workers wearing matching black outfits crouched beside the fire. Melanie ensnared a piece of burning paper beneath her twine sandals, and saw Chinese characters followed by a large print of "$1,000,0," the last two zeros burnt in a slightly yellow tint.

"This an auspicious day today?" Winston asked an elderly Chinese woman observing the fire. Her gaze grasped at them with marble-eyes: "Hell money. I believe in ghosts. I have seen them once—when?—when I was little."

"Sorry, don't believe in ghosts," Winston said firmly.

"I have seen one."

"Well, on second thought," Winston asserted. "It doesn't matter whether you believe in them or not, what matters is if they're really there. And they're not."

With the fire still blazing, the working girls lined back into the karaoke bar, where the sounds of a falsetto singer squeezed through the doorway. The fire burned in bright embers, and the passing motorbikes swerved to avoid the growing pile of ash. Down the street another pile of paper burned, its growing darkness encircled by small candles. Further down the road, two more pyres throbbed ash. From thousands of miles away, Melanie could hear her father grunting. Demons, he would say. They're worshipping demons.

They passed pile after pile of lit demonic hell-money until they reached Love Lane, the old red-light district now filled with Reggae themed bars. Winston's hotel was in an old Peranakan mansion, and his bright villa had old paintings of Chinese scholars on the walls, which Melanie could only see through the small rays of light peeking through the bathroom window. She caressed him on the King-sized mattress, their sex concealed by the used towels and bedsheets he used to block the windows from the other villas. While facing the wall, Melanie could make out a pattern of downward brush strokes. A waterfall, covered in light fog. Her hand disappeared beneath his forest of pubic hair, grabbing at his dick, as lame as a charred bundle of paper money. She turned onto her elbows and felt him slapping his cock on her ass to wake it up, while she stared at the wall-art of a Confucian disciple holding a scroll. She was so close to the man's thick beard that she saw only a horde of minuscule downward strokes.

Winston plopped in front of her. "It's the medication," he said.

"It's fine," she said. "What about me?"

"You? You can stay here with me if you want." He turned his back to her with the pillow bunched beneath his neck. "No need to pull from daddy's pockets anymore."

She turned to her side, away from him. She knew there was scriptural precedent for her station, but of all the unsatisfied biblical women that popped into her head— Hannah, Esther, and of course the holy virgin—she went to sleep imagining herself playing the Queen of Sheba in a glittering royal veil.

For three days Melanie stayed with him, kindling the hope that he would be good in bed. After another night of falling short, they woke early to catch the train to Kuala Lumpur. Mel's heavy rolling luggage made the only sound as they paced through the Hindu temples on China Street. They had counted on the outdoor buffets for breakfast, but the only movement in Little India was that of a stray dog following closely behind them with its mouth gaped in curious hunger. The only food at the train station was the small triangle-sandwiches made of glossy eggs and ham. The globs of moist eggs tasted just like the ones Melanie ate in Korean convenience stores at four in the morning, after two or three bottles of green-tea soju.

A massive yellow train pulled in. Melanie found her leather seat sizzling in the rays of the morning sun. The other Malays, Chinese, and Tamils fit snugly into the train and Winston unconsciously shoved her further into the singed seat. Halfway to the next stop her white blouse clung to her skin, and she had to continually re-adjust her neckline to not offend the women in their veils. As she turned her body against the sun, her thin denim shorts worked up her legs, bunching up in sweat. Her skin shone with the high glaze of the sunshine and her feet seemed to expand in her sandal's tight twine.

"There's no food anywhere!" Winston groaned, his arms reaching up into his green shoulder-bag on the upper racks. With his arms stretched, the locals could spot the foreigner's ass-crack and hairy navel.

"No, no food," said a man in the seat directly behind Melanie. The man's skin seemed so ideal, that sort of brown tint that Melanie used to go for on Miami Beach. She turned to him and his eyes flinched upward. Sweat had loosened her tank top, exposing her cleavage. She turned around, covering herself, rubbing the thin material into her sweat to help it cling to her skin.

"It is Ramadan," the man's wife said, her eyes concealed behind apple-sized sunglasses. "We do not eat until the sun sets. Unless you are very, very naughty. Then it is ok."

Melanie looked the woman over, struck by her kind smile and her floral-designed headdress. The woman's exceptionally light skin seemed more Chinese than Malay, though it was difficult to tell with the veil. Followers of a hateful religion, her father would say. We must not be overcome by evil. Remember, only through Christ.

"Bollocks," Winston growled, finding nothing edible in his bag. He sat down. "And what if you are very, very hungry?"

"Then," the woman said. "You hide snacks in your room and hope no one finds out."

Melanie suppressed a laugh.

"This makes my day," Winston moaned. "No water, no food. Sounds downright pleasant in *one of the hottest places on earth*." He looked at Melanie. "Doing everything in secret, afraid of being seen as an infidel, the morality police arresting you. Real pleasant country."

Melanie remembered her first day-long fast, holding hands in prayer circles with the school counselors, then being served massive amounts of water, orange juice and yogurt in the Camp Aurora cabins. Years later, after learning just how much sugar juice and yogurt really contained, she had her own "detox" fast for five days with only water. The hunger pains ceased after the second day and the thought of mastication disgusted her. By day four she could not help rubbing her tongue against her front teeth, which began to feel like heavy ivory. On day five she finally gave in, unable to avoid the cookies and cream cheesecake her father had bought to entice her back to health.

Winston kept talking, perhaps to Melanie, perhaps to himself, perhaps to the couple who had provoked him: "If there was no God, the upperclass would still invent him to keep workers passive. Kings have no power without this God delusion. To raise a child with religion is nothing but child abuse. You couldn't choose to worship God any more than these folks could choose Ramadan." He was talking to Melanie now. She found her fingers clutching the train cushion, the water from her eyes mixing with the sweat dripping off her nostril. Wiping her face on her shoulder, she took the Bible from her shoulder bag and started reading. So far, it hadn't failed to shut Winston up.

This time Winton snatched the book from her. He flipped to that part in Isiah about gutting Babylonians:

"Whoever is captured will be thrust through;

all who are caught will fall by the sword.

Their infants will be dashed to pieces before their eyes;

their houses will be looted and their wives violated."

"Infants!" Winston said, clapping the book shut. "Need I say more?"

Thrust through, Melanie thought, thinking of his limp dick. She put her hands in her lap, feeling the sun warm her. She squinted from the sun's glare, did not pray but thought of prayer: how her friends clung their hands together in circles, each warm hand squeezing the other, passing the prayer on. One Thanksgiving, she deliberately stood next to her blonde-haired cousin, his hands like a workman's, a carpenter's, a welder's. Hard and soft, big like a smothering pillow. His hand rubbed hers only slightly, just enough to keep her into it. When the prayer came to him, he said, "Lord, thank you for this day. Thank you for the trees and the amazing, loving, caring family you have given me."

Just squeeze, she thought.

"Thank you for planning to give me that used F-150, with the dark blue exterior."

Squeeze, please just squeeze.

"But seriously, Lord, thank you for providing us everything we need every day of our lives and for the blessings you have bestowed."

Just fucking squeeze!

Then she felt it. That hard, full-second tightening that shook her core. A squeeze that made her tongue clap against the roof of her mouth, clinging to her hand like fire on wood. For his squeeze, it was worth standing in those prayer circles whispering sweet blessings to the ceiling. "Dear God," she would say next.

The sun finally moved above the train and outside of her space, but her skin was stuck against the seat's arms. Winston ate greedily from a bag of pink prawn crackers. Rather than tear her arm from the faux-leather armrest, she left her arm fused to the seat as she watched the Malaysian forest pass, thick with knee-high water. Her eyes followed a stream, slow but still moving in a curve, as if being sucked into an underground vortex. As her eyes adjusted to the forest's colors, she could spot a mosque within the trees, surrounded by green and gold spires hiding in the landscape.

Once they settled into a hotel in Kuala Lumpur, Winston took her to his friend's outdoor duck restaurant on Jalan Alor, a street food area in the foreigner's district. Melanie sat on a beanbag watching the flood of shoppers who streamed between the five shopping malls of Bukit Bintang, the women dressed in long colorful veils, some in patterns mimicking Coach and Louis Vuitton designs, and others covered from head to toe in thin black burkas, their only exposed flesh those stunning eyes. What would that be like? Melanie wondered. To have no one know you— to have nothing but a silhouette? Strangely, and against all of her American upbringing, she felt herself envying those women. Once upon a time she had enjoyed giving young men hard-ons, letting them sneak a peek or suck back whisks of her scent (really just her shampoo). Then she felt guilty for it, sinning by leading them on. Then she felt wrecked with the guilt of her own pleasure, a Lilith grinding on easily misled boyhood saints. Now each pair of eyes peering at her felt like a Bible verse. Within each a promise, a judgment, a secret she no longer cared to discover.

One of the burqa bodies walked just in front of her, side-by-side with her husband who had a thick beard and wore a collared polo sporting some British soccer club. Pink nail polish glowed from the woman's toes, half concealed in jaded purple sandals. Her eyes were bright in purple mascara, an off-tone complemented by the studded jewels lining the top of her forehead. When the woman's eyes met hers, Melanie felt naked. The woman could be frowning at her—gawking, sneering, or perhaps, smiling.

Remember. Only through Christ.

"Nothing like eating chicken rice and duck every day," Winston said, his fork deep in a marinated thigh.

"You are the first American girl I meet," said the husky Thai owner, who Winston called Boon. He leaned over the arms of his wooden chair. "Don't you think we Muslims are all terrorists in Malaysia?" Winston joined him laughing. "I have nothing attached to my stomach, look!" The man pulled up his shirt, exposing hilly curves. Melanie looked away.

"She's been Debbie Downer all day," Winston said as if Melanie wasn't there. "Her club's been shit this year."

"She a Manchester girl?"

"*American* football."

"The last game was gut wrenching," Melanie said, finally on a topic she knew well. "All the glory should have been ours. Now we're freaking oh and three."

"It's apparently a big deal," Winston sneered. "Two U.S. states, competing."

Boon nodded, his turn to look stern and unamused. "Wow Winston. This one is *really* American, isn't she? I thought maybe she was Russian and you were just trying to fetch me a high price!"

The boys were crushed by laughter, holding each other. Melanie smiled faintly, then shifted her attention to the rows of plastic tables that seemed to stretch for miles. She didn't mind people thinking she was hollow. Her friends in Florida were so much worse. If it wasn't their skin tones they were gabbing about it was Paris Hilton. Being hollow, in that place, was the only way to earn respect. And being a hollow American girl in Malaysia, Melanie could sit back and watch the other tables: the older men with long beards laughing gaily with their hands upon their filled stomachs; the women drinking chai with their legs crossed; the backpackers blowing hookah smoke beneath red lanterns. Melanie noticed the couple next to her, whispering to each other. She held her breath as the man's hand crept up his girlfriend's skinny leg, slowly tracing the leg-ladder of her long black robe, until the woman beat him away in flirtatious kicks.

"Boon's going to take us out," Winston told her, his teeth gnashing the juice out of a roasted cherry tomato. "Could get expensive."

The corner ATM inside the Petronas Towers glowed like radioactive metal. Her father's platinum debit card wiggled into the machine and she entered the password feeling as if she were posting a letter asking for forgiveness, crawling back from the long journey to take her rightful place in that heaven-bound hollow. Luke 15:11, Prodigal Son.

The screen read, "Insufficient funds."

He had frozen the account. She hadn't told him where she was, or responded to any of his emails. Maybe this was his letter to her, to cut her from his domain. Was it simply to get her attention? Perhaps he found out that she had gone to a Muslim country—in a sense, she had joined the other side. Or had he too seen the pictures of her caressing that Czech woman in South Korea?

Melanie imagined how she might repent without also feeling like a coward. Perhaps, like all good Christians, she just needed to experience a moment of true desperation and struggle. There were those who had borne through it, who had sat and smiled and kept the same friends. Who just got by squeezing hands. Just as there were those Muslims who ate Chinese food on Ramadan.

She heard Winston behind her, chewing on a lamb skewer and eyeing the Indian girl at the info booth. "Finished?" he asked.

"Babe," she said, holding Winston's hand. There was no mincing words—she needed help.

"Of course," he said with a slim smile, motivated, she felt, by compassion. "And don't think of it as borrowing." He offered her the kebab. "Here. This will keep you from having a hangover tomorrow."

Winston and Boon brought her to a fashion boutique where she met Malt, a well-groomed Malay Australian club owner who dressed her in a studded leather jacket, and a matching striped hat and dark jeans—a significant shift from her backpacker's apparel of a tank top and denim shorts. The four of them took the elevator to a hotel skybar lit by the alabaster whites of the Petronas Twin Towers, a photogenic image that reflected off the swimming pool in the center of the bar. They slipped through packs of the city's youth sipping on sugary cocktails, and sat on a couch overlooking the towers, a space that proudly declared "700 DOLLARS TO SIT HERE." Malt ordered a bottle of Scotch single malt whiskey, the source of his invented name.

Winston griped about the censorship of internet pornography, his feet dipped beneath the indoor pool. "Even boning this all-American girl," he pointed to Melanie, "could get the Malaysian moral police on us. They asked us for a marriage certificate at the hotel today, believe that? I had to pay a bribe—heathen fee, I call it."

Melanie took a sip of club and lime, dipping her toes in the pool, letting her toe-ripples refract the Petronas Towers in sharp spikes of white light. She watched a woman walking through the bar, talking into a cellphone tucked neatly into her pink headscarf. The woman's hands were occupied: a shopping bag in one hand, a nearly burnt out cigarette in another.

"I wish I could unlearn some Malay words," Boon said, kicking his naked left foot in the tub. "Just using the word for 'porn' could get me deported!"

"So goddamn repressed," Winston sneered. "No sexual progress in a millennia. An entire country still in the womb."

"We have our ways," Malt said, the same triangle smile as Winston, "to do what we want."

If it weren't for her money problems, Melanie would probably have gone for Malt. His hair, combed back and sculpted like a dark crème, needed her hand to ruffle through it. She took a breath as a bearded waiter appeared next to her, offering her a martini glass. At first just her legs reacted, shivering away from him, but then his dark wide eyes met hers and her whole body jumped in a single spasm. She saw water splash onto the waiter just before feeling herself submerge into the pool, her feet jolting with nothing to support them.

She cursed in air bubbles. Too embarrassed to swim up, she pulled at her hair, those blonde roots. She floated there, letting the chlorine seep into her new leather jacket, too expensive to fathom. Somehow she had retreated into that place again, of wanting to crawl into anonymity. From beneath the water's surface she saw the Petronas towers, two shining beacons radiating a dazzling whiteness onto the entire city, whose base was a conclave of investment banks and luxury brands. She surfaced, keeping her back to the sounds of claps and whistles.

"What's wrong?" Malt asked, gripping her hand. "Are you ok?"

She took his hand. That familiar cling.

"Just still in the womb," Winston said.

Back at the hotel, Melanie took a quick shower and collapsed on the bed, hoping to shut out the night's events.

Barely asleep, she felt Winston's hand crawling against her stomach, as it had every night before, and she could feel those vibrations in her breath, like new blood lassoing from her body around her brain. When his hand moved down her stomach she clutched it there, keeping it from moving below her waist. Refused, the hand moved upwards, cupping her breast in a gropy massage. She bit her lip but lowered the hand. It crept back up again.

"Stop," she said simply.

"Look," he said. "I'm hard. Look."

His hand lay flat against her breast, and she saw herself wishing it would do more. *Just fucking squeeze* she heard herself think. But the hand lay motionless. She glanced down at him, saw that whatever pressure he had managed to build was gone.

The silence wailed on until it was broken by the crash of a thrown ashtray.

"This is *my* hotel room," Winston shouted, standing up to hide his dick. The blanket shifted and her roller bag tilted off the bed, flinging pink elephant souvenirs onto the tiled floor. "Sex with white women is shit anyway. They just sit there like a corpse, as if it's my honor to fuck you. Christians with their fucking *guilt*." She found herself unable to defend herself. "These are mine anyway." He jammed her new clothes, still dripping wet, into his backpack. "I paid for them."

He left the door wide open. His footsteps pattered down the hallway. The shower faucet dripped in small 'poit's. She saw herself crying into the pillow, the mattress, even the strange shell-patterned blanket that smelled of laundry detergent. The hotel was paid for only one night, and after that she had no cash, no cards, no friends, nothing. Perhaps this was what her father wanted her to experience. Struggle, freedom, moment of grace. And next up: forgiveness. She clasped her hands. Bits of water and mascara ran from her nose, smudging onto the white pillow. She heard her father's voice, telling her to come home. She saw the white suburbs of Florida, the white churches, the white yachts.

Somehow she had flung her Bible across the room, its thin pages tearing against the wall. She didn't expect herself to run to the book as she did, and cradle its torn pages as if she could resuscitate it. The loose binding fell apart in her hands and the pages collapsed between her fingers into a crunched-up pile. She gathered pages and found the passage in Song of Solomon that she had marked up with a red pen.

Could the woman be wearing a veil? Melanie had written into the page. Was it really so hard to believe? She tried to imagine the woman, but no image came. Then she tried Solomon, then the entire fleet of prophets and saints.

Acid climbed up her stomach. Holy shit, Melanie thought. None of them looked like me. Not one. Brown. Black. Veiled. Bearded. Their faces materialized clearly in her mind as pages slipped from her hands.

ThinkTravel! Blogbook

Post Date: 2007 APR 20

User: SkyFaralan

You wake up dry-heaving into a small plastic vomit bag. It's only hour four of the thirty-three hour bus ride from Luang Prabang to Hanoi. You adjust the scarf around your neck, covering your mouth from the exhaust wafting in from the rear windows.

Hour six: you watch a sickly man, beaten by the potholes in the road like a dusty drape, vomit upon a younger man's face.

Hour twenty-one: you cross streams with men pissing on the roadside.

Hour twenty-six: the driver parks at a motel and splits with a young prostitute, leaving everyone on the bus sitting in staid darkness.

Hour thirty-three: you stagger off the bus into a parking lot full of motorbikes without a clue where you are, with no map to guide you. Billboards ask you to invest in The Bank for Investment of Capital in Vietnam, or InvestCo, or Saigon Investment. You pass a lake, a bridge, and find an expat-run bookstore full of bootlegged copies of the last Harry Potter book. The bookseller points you to the tourist district. Every other store you pass sells construction materials. Cars and motorbikes line up at the traffic lights, revving their engines at pedestrians crossing the street. The adrenaline hits you like a hammer every time you cross, and all you can think is: I'm going to die.

The thought calms your body. You catch yourself daydreaming, only to wake to the nightmare of your own heartbeat.

Each of the six beds inside your hostel dorm is taken by an American traveling alone, harrowed by guilt. You join their lines for confession at the war museum, aptly named The Museum of American Imperial Aggression. You kneel in front of unclaimed dog-tags. You notice how many people on the street are missing limbs. You pass a tour group of Saigonese wearing T-shirts that say: I love America and I want to be Americanized.

One of you, Florence, small and chipper, doesn't carry any guilt-ridden death wish, she assures you. She's the daughter of Chinese-Vietnamese refugees, and she wants only to take photos of your travels, "to construct an image of the guilty American backpacker." None of you even carry a camera, so you don't mind.

Matthew, from San Diego, talks of spending the summer on a sail boat, riding from America to Manila. Bearded, beer-drinking, sunglasses, balding. He wouldn't mind a death tinged with eternal mystery.

Terry, a lanky Mormon, takes you down every rakish alleyway. He has traveled to Africa, India, Indonesia, and now here. He smokes pot like a champ, but covers his face when Florence tries to capture it with her camera. His family would never forgive him, he says. Terry doesn't know how much he hates himself, because suicide is a sin, but you know why he is the first to suggest cat-walking from one rooftop bar to another.

You tell them your name is Cecil and that you're from Kentucky. Travelers don't know shit about Kentucky, including you. None of them ask why you've come, why you careen across freeways like a man marching into a quick and blurry end.

When the midnight curfew comes you all stay out to spite them, luxuriating in your American privilege, unobstructed even in this communist country. To hide from the police, the nightclubs lock everyone in with their alcohol and their flashing lights until 5am. When you arrive at the Uncle Ho club they have already locked it down. You rattle on the iron gates to no avail. You press your ears against the cold rims and hear the house music inside. Nearby, Terry smokes hash with two policemen on the sidewalk.

Searching for your own ends, you find only reminders of ongoing war. You Americans, the generation of terror, find there is nothing exceptional about your suicidal tendencies. What continues to stare you in the face in every ground you desecrate with your American bodies is that, ultimately, you got what you wanted. They are like you.

A crowd of disfigured and misshapen people await you at the entrance to the War Remnants Museum. You hide from them beneath museum fans. Inside are collages of disfigured people, of death tolls, of victims from the Mỹ Lai massacre, B52 carpet bombers and Agent Orange. The last tourist monument sports images of fat Frenchmen standing atop their Vietnamese servants, being fanned, carried about and served hand and foot by their colonial coolies. As you leave the museum, locals try to fan you and carry you about on their motorcycles. The four of you, strangers until the day before, separate here, each on different motorbikes. Yours is driven by a cackling woman with only one hand who swerves in and out of oncoming traffic. She slides over the sidewalk, sending needles down your spine. Vegetation slaps your face and neck. For the first time in your life you scream in terror.

Money jitters out of your hand and into hers. You squeeze onto the sidewalk and squat, leveling your head onto a plastic chair.

That feeling of panic, that adrenaline rush, yanking you from your body. For a moment, you were no one and everyone. For a moment, free from yourself.

Thursday 23:00

Sophea raced out of her tuk-tuk and inside The Palace Resort Hotel, scraping her right calf on a metal "No Sex Tourism" sign nailed just next to the entrance. She limped into the lobby, trailing a thin stream of crimson. The two clerks at the front desk squinted their eyes in concern as she lost control of her own voice, shouting when she did not mean to. "I need to call the police!" she stammered. "Those pieces of shit stole my fucking bag!"

The clerks spoke to each other in Khmer. Sophea only understood bits and pieces.

"Was it a member of the hotel staff?" the squat one asked, his face unreadable.

"What was inside the bag?" asked the other.

"It was two men on a motorbike," said Yunho, just behind her. "They cut her bag and drove off with it." He nudged her with a black hair clip that had fallen from her head. She took it and strapped her hair back, feeling the dry streak of blue hair dye that she had combed in that morning.

"Her smartphone was inside," Yunho said slowly, in case they weren't familiar with smartphones yet. "It has her information in it."

"*And* they stole my money," Sophea said. She looked to her hands as if the purse would reappear. It was a one of a kind find, with pink and blue fades on top, black on the bottom, silver lining on the strap. "And the keys to my apartment building," she added.

"No passports?"

She shook her head and noticed for the first time two large paintings of Apsaras hanging just beside the front desk, their faces blotched in red and orange paint. Their circular breasts hung over the heads of the hotel clerks like flexed muscles. Their legs were slightly crossed, as if bowing after a moving performance.

"No credit cards?"

"Can you just call the police!?" she screeched, wishing she could claw through their prim black suits. "They're getting away!"

"How did it happen?"

Sophea shook her head, unable to relive it. She remembered drinking cocktails on the riverside with Yunho, watching Cambodian children chase bubbles on the grassy edge of the embankment. The children's confidence was so infectious she hadn't thought twice about walking down that dark alley, even when Yunho suggested taking a tuk-tuk, even as they passed mounds of garbage in plastic bags filling the streets, ridden with flies. Then she insisted cutting through that unlit marketplace, if only to prove to Yunho that Phnom Penh was far safer than its reputation. Then the child who approached her, casing her, his eyes unlike the other children, asking for nothing. Then the putters of a motorbike slowing down, stalking her. Then the snapping of scissors, cutting loose her thin-strapped purse before it ripped from her shoulder. Then the roar of the bike's engine as she stood immobile, paralyzed in disbelief.

She left Yunho in the lobby and shot up to the hotel room, dropping the keys twice before getting that door open and going straight for the room's safe, triple-counting the money and bank cards. She sat in bed, gripping the covers, sitting up straight to mind her posture, of all things. She imagined tearing through the hotel staff, lining them up against that lobby wall of blue-lit water drips, interrogating them one by one. She saw herself in the mirror: her dark purple fingernails, her salon-styled wavy blue-streaked black hair, her woven anklets. All of it copped from Cambodian markets. All of it conspired to mark her as a spoiled American backpacker. And with her hammy thighs three times the size of the Cambodian girls in her office—no wonder the Apsaras liked to mock her. Of course the thieves would steal from her—of course!

As she unstrapped her anklets she found a trail of light red blood bee-lining about the hotel room, leading to her scratched leg. She started bunching hotel towels to soak up the blood when Yunho opened the door.

"The police are not coming," he said in a barely audible tone. "They are not working now. I cannot believe this. The police. Not working? Is that possible?"

She paced about the room not knowing whether to sob or punch through the wall. "They must be in on it. Those fuckers at the front desk, they planned everything!"

"All the money is here, yes?" He sat with his legs crossed on the bed full of scattered bills and documents. "You have your passport, and your extra set of keys, right?"

"I know it was THEM!" She would have collapsed then if not for her pacing back and forth, from the bathroom to the drapes and back again.

"We can do nothing anyway." He arched on the bed, using his bunched up T-shirts as a pillow. "The police will not help us. The hotel people told me, if we fill out a police report, they will ask for money. How much is it? I asked. They just said, it is not cheap." He started stacking the Cambodian riel, the sharp sea-blues of the harbors, the faces of a Bodhisattva at Angkor Wat, the King's scrutinizing stare.

Her hands flexed in and out of fists. She closed her eyes and remembered seeing weapons somewhere. Just that morning, before they left the hotel. Inside the gift shop. Next to the scarves and Buddha carvings. Large handmade forks and knives. Chef's knives, pairing knives, cleavers, switchblades. All handmade from Cambodian steel. The stuff of Angkor warriors guarding the gates of Wat Bayon. Perhaps the shop was still open. If not, there was always large pieces of wood. And stone Buddha statues that could leave a bitch black, bruised, or bludgeoned.

She opened her eyes, looked at her hands. For a moment, calm had blanketed her body.

Friday 6:00

Sophea rechecked the items in her safe at least a dozen times before daylight covered the disheveled hotel room with glints of a red-yellow desert hue. She thought of calling in late, but feared that abandoning her post would stain her reputation at the NGO. Even in crisis, she would never become one of those flakey two-week volunteer tourists.

She walked through the barrage of tuk-tuk drivers outside the hotel, shielding herself with her purple sunglasses, feeling every eye monitoring her moves. Passing tourists on the street, she could not help but look at their slim purses, handbags, and satchels. Opportunities for bag-snatchers everywhere. Holding her own leather backpack bundled around her torso, she waited in line at the only ATM booth in town, and a pop! noise came from one of the sputtering motorbikes inching forward in congested traffic. A muscle jumped along her neck, punctuating the flow of blood along her arms.

She left the ATM line and headed straight into the French colonial mansion where her NGO, the State Violence Monitors, held office in an old library. When Pol Pots' soldiers had taken Phnom Penh they ransacked the mansion unrecognizable, and there were still cut wires where chandeliers once hung. The only furniture left from its colonial days was restocked bookshelves and a grandfather clock weathered in layers of darkening brown, still doling out time and memory.

She couldn't get to her desk without repeating her story to her coworkers. The slowing down motorbike, the heaps of trash in the alley, the inadequacy of the police. She recited the story to Vicky, the French Cambodian woman who smelled of jasmine massage oil.

"You gotta be careful," Vicky said. "Man, what an unnerving scenario, right?"

She recited the story again to Shantala, the other Cambodian American, one of the founders of the NGO who came from Boston. She simply shrugged away Sophea's tourist squabbles. "You were asking for it."

The more recent volunteer from Hawaii came in late, his angular body sliding between the computers and desks as he sat next to her. His name was Skyler, but Shantala called him "muscles," as he was frequently asked to lift pieces of equipment and weaponry that their NGO bought off the black market to gather for evidence in criminal cases and UN investigations. Skyler also offered Sophea little sympathy, and like the others he just reminded her how lucky she was to be in a country where she wasn't stabbed or shot. "You did all the right things," Skyler said. "Except for being a young woman walking at night in a third world country. Try not to do that again."

Two weeks ago she had picked Skyler off the streets, as she liked to put it, transforming him from a narcissistic tourist into a contributing NGO volunteer. She worked with him closely, making posters, event calendars, online infographs, and flowcharts.

"Do you think they're eye-fucking your photos right now?" Skyler said with a sly sneer.

The tourist photos. The ones taken at the Tuol Sleng prison. Did the thieves think she was just an ordinary tourist? How could they know that she had taken those pictures not to gawk at the disappeared, but to mourn for them? Members of her own family—cousins, grandparents, uncles—had disappeared, their lives reduced to picturesque skulls that only told stories of barbarism. The thieves would swipe through pictures of her parents who had escaped to America as children. They would find images of her brothers. Bulky, tattooed versions of themselves. And then pictures of her, kissing at the camera while dancing at the Heart of Darkness nightclub, the first in her family to return to Cambodia, a full-bodied American. The thieves would see her giving peace signs next to Angkor Wat, her getting the words "Khmer Girl" stamped on her wrist inside a tourist booth, her cutting up spices for a cooking class where she made fish amok, her posing with a tall Korean man, Yunho, in his high-rise condo. Yunho kissing her cheek. Yunho taking a post-coital nap, wrapped in hotel bedsheets.

Shantala was right. Sophea was asking for it. With reflexes alone, she could load a gun or unbuckle a man's belt. So why did she do nothing when they ripped her bag from her? There was no impulse to give chase, nothing but first-world fear. She should have pushed the motorcycle over. Should have let it crush their legs. Should have slammed the driver's head against the pavement.

"Muscles!" Shantala called to Skyler, who promptly turned around, excited to leave his desk. "I need you." Shantala pointed outside to a truck packed with munitions.

Sophea sat staring at her computer screen, amazed at her own imagination. She felt the thief's hair, felt the pavement, heard the crack of bone, witnessed the staved-in skull.

A message popped up:

[Please re-enter your email password.]

She did. Rejection. She tried again. Then again, keeping the inevitable at bay, as if shaking a key in a stubborn lock. She slammed her hands on the desk. She tried again.

The thieves had her email. How did they even know what a smartphone was, let alone how to crack into it? They could be reading her bank details. Her social media. Her blogs about her brother's wedding, where she posed with all her white American girlfriends, drunk on tequila and sick on shrimp. Or, God, all those messages she sent to Yunho over that travel dating site. The ones where she said she couldn't wait to ...

She searched for a way to recover her accounts and found an official statement from the email host:

Because we provide free software, we are not responsible for compromised email accounts.

Sophea sank her head into her hands, trying not to cry. In that darkness he appeared to her, that child who had scouted her on the street, the one who distracted her just long enough for the thieves to cut her bag. She could go after him. She could swipe him off the street, gag the hapless waif, refuse to feed him until he gave up every thieving worm in his soon to be dead squatter family.

"Be careful!" Shantala screamed at Skyler, her voice echoing through the bookstacks. "There are explosives in that crate! You drop it, then there's no more you. Got it?"

"Just pumping iron!" Skyler responded, bobbing the crate up and down to tempt the fates. Though Shantala called him Muscles, the boy was scrawny and had weaker arms than Sophea.

Sophea tried her password one last time before the system locked her out. Now the thieves had access to everything. Did it matter to them that her life in America was itself trauma-inducing? Her father in and out of jail. Her mother always gone to God-knows-where. Her brothers dispersed into the Mid-West, unable to afford Silicon Valley's encroaching empire. Would the thieves have guessed that her name, Sophea, was no misspelling, but was a Cambodian name? And would they care how difficult that was to explain to every single person who treated her as if she—*she* were mistaken, in spelling her own name? No. They had stolen from her all the same. To them she was like any other tourist, just more brown.

"That's an epic amount of weapons," Skyler said from behind Sophea as he squeezed passed her desk. "Usually those crates are just full of photographs. What a haul. We could start a fucking war with all that scrap. Kind of funny, storing it in a library."

"They got into my email," Sophea whispered, her voice a ragged gasp. "The thieves. I kept everything in there. Every time I had a new password, I sent it to myself by email. My bank accounts. My credit cards."

"I'm sorry," he said. "Sorry that you can't go to the police, like in any other country in Asia. You know what we should do? We should start a new NGO, a police NGO. Call it 'the American Broforce.'"

"You were lucky," Shantala said, peering at their work from behind a bookshelf. "Get this—last year, I get my apartment broken into, my laptop, my five-hundred dollar camera, both gone. And at the station I had to wait six hours just to report it, then pay them a bribe. In the end, they were completely useless."

"But can you imagine what American police would do in Cambodia?" Skyler said. "We'd bust heads, put the fear of 'Merica right into 'em."

"God!" Shantala moaned through the bookcase, "Fuck, I

would rather lose my purse every month than wish American police on anyone!"

Vicky's voice came from behind a shelve of books on Cambodian culture: "You have to be careful with how you narrate these kind of things," she said. "The outside world only sees crime and danger. We can't be a part of that story."

Sophea kept silent, trying to think of a way out of this story that the entire world knew but she had ignored. Poverty created downcast people in need, women with time on their hands to embroider Apsaras onto bamboo coasters. But the ones truly rising above their station were also the ones who could snap the band of a purse in one swift sweep, who could break into a smartphone, steal email passwords, blackmail, hack, and manipulate. The skills NGOs dared not teach.

In the work-silence, her colleagues began avoiding her. Hours passed. She started shedding tears, slamming on the keyboard. In the evening she felt Skyler slide behind her to leave for the day, his hand patting her shoulder like she was a bullied child.

"Maybe we should get drunk tonight," Skyler said. "Go to the riverside, get a massage, find some sexy local boys? Maybe end the night with some happy pizza?"

"I hate them," she said. "I hate them."

'Hate.' A bold accessory she had seen in shop windows, but never dared try on.

"I'm sorry," Skyler responded. "Just—take care of yourself, ya hear?"

Sophea dagger-stared him, stabbing that cliché line right in its fake-heart. Once out the door, he didn't turn back.

Alone, she submerged herself into the repetitive process of online recovery, trying to log in, getting cut out again, searching for other routes. The sun set. The security officers woke up from their long naps and disappeared. She successfully changed her passcodes, only to find that someone else had logged in under her identity. She was kicked out of her email when they changed the codes again, this time with new phone numbers, new back-up emails. Security walls were fortified with new questions to identify her. Questions about a dog she never had. Questions about her family.

Security Question #2:
What is your grandmother's name?

"I don't know it," she whispered to herself in the dark library. "I don't know it because I never knew who she was. I don't know because you, this place, you fucking killed her." She thought of the child who had scouted her. The boy's vicious smile. His feet without shoes.

She was alone, all alone in an old mansion abandoned to its English and French tomes. In every room stood the remnants of an ongoing battle, the tools of slavery, thievery, consent. And in the basement were all the ammunitions one could ever need to start a war.

Dehumidifier machines hummed in the basement equipment room. Skyler had made no attempt to hide them—those crates of weapons confiscated from illegal firing ranges. Though the ranges were banned over a decade ago, the government did little to enforce it, and tourists were still free to play Rambo on the outskirts of Phnom Penh, firing bazookas, shooting machine guns, and chucking hand grenades. The NGO's mission was a lost cause. The

Chinese had supplied so many munitions to the Pol Pot regime, and the American's to the Lon Nol regime, that the stockpiles would never end. And neither would the tourists.

She used a crowbar to pry open one of the two crates. The stash was out of a war movie: Kalashnikov rifles, shotguns, bullets, knives, ammunition. She touched the weapons, felt their iron, their sanded wood, their heaviness. Then she found small round objects padded with styrofoam. She lifted one that looked like the turtle-shell ashtrays sold in the tourist market. She knew it was what she wanted when she felt its abnormal weight.

Above her, the grandfather clock chimed its hourly slogan.

Friday 20:00

A dull pain beat in her right calf as she passed the "No Sex Tourism" sign inside The Palace Resort Hotel. She looked down to where a small stem of dried blood led from her red band aid to her black sandals.

In the elevator to Yunho's room she jiggled a new purse that she had picked up from a street stall, a cheap Louis Vuitton knock off. She felt the round weapon in it bounce, imagined it was an alien embryo gestating for her mad purpose. She clapped the dust off her hands before knocking on the door. Yunho answered wearing a dark blue hotel robe that enclosed his thin frame.

"Passwords still not work?" he asked as he hugged her, rubbing her back. She shook her head and he kissed her with his unshaven face.

She took her laptop from her leather backpack. "Nothing."

There he went, in a cross-legged lean-in, drilling away on her computer. Sophea opened the curtains, revealing the bruised evening sky.

"Keep it shut!" Yunho snapped. "They rob hotel rooms too you know."

She drew the drapes and ordered a long island from room service. White towels bunched beside the bed, patches encrusted with blood. "Why didn't the maid come yet?"

"How can you trust a maid in this country?"

"Go anywhere today?"

"To the pool. You know there are North Koreans here? Just, swimming. Sun-bathing North Koreans."

"I thought you had a meeting."

"Cancelled," he said, eyes on the screen.

She had never seen his distressed side. When they met after finding each other online, she liked him instantly because he wasn't a tourist. He had come to Cambodia to do something with his life, even if that something was translating for a construction company. She liked him more on their first date at the Foreign Correspondent's Club because his eyes never wandered to the Cambodian servers, though even she could not help gawk at their beauty. She liked him even more when she said the Pol Pot regime committed a genocide and he nodded in agreement. She really liked him when she explained her name was pronounced "So-Pee-ah, with a hard P sound," and he never got it wrong again. And he liked that she had bigger hips than those youthful club girls. He even called her his little Apsara, and she, a tad uneasy, let him.

Room service arrived with her long island, decorated with tiki stirrers and olives. Sophea downed the drink and ordered another before the server left. She sat on the bed and took out the needle and thread from her purse, cupping the grenade inside. So, she thought. This was what it felt like to be pushed out of sanity, to a level of desperation that only her parents could have understood.

"Want to hear something?" Yunho said with a slight smile. "I was so angry about what happened, all day, I started to imagine crazy things. I thought, maybe we should hire gangsters to find them. Put them in prison. Of course, that would make life so hard for them, maybe forever. Crazy, right? How quickly your mind can go that far."

She said nothing and aimed thread through a needle.

"Ok, I can see the information they used." Yunho tapped on the laptop screen. "It looks like they changed every account to their phone number."

"It's a Cambodian phone number," Sophea said, looping the thread. "I checked already."

"Well I looked on the Cambodia tourist forums. This number has been used before. You call them and they give you the number to a bank account in the UK. Some people, they sent one-thousand dollars to get their account back. But one person sent only two-hundred."

"You sure?" Sophea paused. "Why only two hundred?"

Yunho drilled into the keys with a growing intensity. Using his loud clacking as cover, Sophea used her scissors to pierce through the fake Louis Vuitton bag, then carve a small hole.

"Here it is. The woman who only paid two hundred. She is a local Cambodian. So she got local's price. Two hundred. It is one-thousand for foreigners. I cannot believe it. In Korea, if I forget my wallet, someone always contacts me about it. Here someone steals something, then demands more!"

Sophea wove the black thread around her clenched fist, circling it six times before making a triple knot to keep the loop secure. She looked at the weapon inside the purse. This is crazy, she thought. Who had she become? She had thrown a few punches before, knew how to point a pistol. In high school she always kept a baseball bat in her trunk, and let everyone in the neighborhood know it. She only took it out once, when one day some scumbag felt up her breast in a shopping mall, and her two brothers dragged him through an emergency exit, while she went to fetch the weapon. By the time she returned her brothers were already retreating, yelling back at the man's bloodied face, "No one fucks with a refugee!"

"What's so funny?" Yunho asked, giving a quizzical glance.

"Nothing." She continued looping the thread. "Call the number. I want to talk to them."

"Ok." Yunho dialed on the laptop. "Your family was in the genocide, yes? You should tell them that. Tell them how your name is pronounced. Tell them your story. You are Cambodian, maybe they'll give you the local's price."

Her story. The first time she heard it was when her father was in prison and social services came to check on her. Her brothers had recited the story slowly, with a quiet gravitas. Pol Pot, the missing relatives, the killing fields. Years later she told the same story at her high school graduation, where she was selected to speak not because her grades were good (she barely passed) but because the school wanted the other parents to revel in the school's diversity. "While all my friends could talk about their grandparents, and their cousins, I only had pictures of disappeared people." She told her story for a school that taught her America had saved her, even though it had dropped an unfathomable amount of bombs on her people. And yet there she was, the refugee daughter, fed from America's spoils, repeating a story that would not stop defining every inch of her life.

Keeping her back to Yunho, she wrapped the black thread around the pin of the grenade. She had read online that the weapon would make a loud noise when it was about to blow. She twisted the safety clip and snapped it off. No sound. Damn device was so old, it might not even detonate.

"Ok, I am calling the number now." Yunho turned the laptop toward her, with a big blue screen displaying a telephone. The laptop rang in a cat's *purrrrr*.

"Don't forget, your story," he said.

As a child she had learned to shape gratitude with her mouth. She had packed, puckered, tucked, brushed, angled, and twisted her mouth until the right expression formed. One that read energy, happiness, gratitude. To her the shape was disturbing. To the world, it was a smile. She was meant to smile until the very air was saturated with optimism.

Purrrrr.

By high school, she had worn that smile for so long that the nerves felt frozen in place. Her lips had become firm, staid. It was like waking up with her mouth bent sideways. Eventually it became too painful to stretch it back into place. The smile was inflexible. Even as she learned more facts about the genocide, about the numbers and faces who could have been her relatives, her smile remained, hiding the numbers that never stopped mounting.

Purrrrr.

Those numbers, the counting of every breath of life. Those numbers she kept not in her mouth but in between her cupped hands. She grasped them despite the smile. She took them with her to graduation, to dinner tables, to midnight dance parties. And every now and then the numbers spilled out from between her fingers, whenever she clenched them into fists.

"Hello?"

The voice from the laptop sounded like a Cambodian well versed in English. She could hear whispers in the background.

"Hello?" the voice repeated. "Is this A-man-da? We have your phone, Amanda."

"Tell him," Yunho whispered. "Tell him who you are. About your family."

"Is this Mike?" said the voice. Perhaps he was reading from a list. "Mike Smith? Or Sophia? Is this Sophia?"

The man said "Sophia," So-fee-a, with a soft "p."

"You have no fucking clue who I am," Sophea said, the words bubbling out of her as she leaned into the laptop. "I am the person who is going to find you. Then I am going to kill you. Then I am going to kill your family. Your wives and your sisters and your children. To me you are just worms squirming in the dirt of this fucking country."

Silence. The voice returned: "You must pay one-thousand dollars."

She slammed the laptop shut. The audio buzzed with the sound of a lost connection.

Friday 23:00

The night had an unreal air. The grenade in her purse had seemed light at first, but now it weighed her arm down, and stuck from the fake black leather in a bulbous swell. The leg pain from her broken skin made her wobble as she walked along the dark alleyway near the riverside. She tugged the black thread from her purse and felt it tighten around her wrist. The weight from her bag grew heavier, as if at any moment it could give, and her wrist would pull the pin, the surprisingly buttery thread making her a lethal clutz.

Go ahead, snatch it, she thought. You stupid twats. You snatch it, you keep whatever's inside. You fucking worms. Steal from a refugee, and that will be that—no more you.

Yunho would never understand her anger. After the phone call, he had just stared at the closed laptop in silence, while she drank another long island and dressed the part of a weak, clueless tourist, with jean shorts and a black "I Survived Cambodia" T-shirt. He didn't know the kind of woman she was, that she was once a wildcard. Her mother taught her that Cambodians were the most beautiful Southeast Asians, with their perfect mix of Indian and Malay blood. She had killed before—not violently, but with an Apsara's wrath she had gossiped girls to utter ruin, then drank herself into their boyfriends' eager arms. She herself was immune to gossip; no one dared talk shit about a refugee. On her first date in high school she carved a heart into a tree, not to be romantic but to show him that she had a knife, and knew how to use it.

Why did she ever change? When had she become so soft? She was a powerhouse in high school, until senior year, when Mrs. Baker assigned a book on Cambodia for the whole class to read. The book spoke of a homeland so unlike her parents memories—a place stuck in the middle ages, where crime and corruption had been engrained deep into the culture, and where violence was an eternal pathology. Unable to help themselves, the Cambodian people needed help from outside. Her schoolmates nagged her negligence—why hadn't she gone back? Why hadn't she given something? Every flimsy job she got after high school was a waste of her good will, a disgrace to the Apsara. But like the book said, Cambodia was also full of outsiders willing to help unmoor its people out of their own cursed history. Maybe, all she had to do was travel there, and she could help set the hopes of renewal ablaze.

She recognized the mound of garbage in the dark alley, the trash wrapped in broken plastic bags exuding a slimy stench from days of decaying in the sun. She was alone, but not quite alone. An ambulance siren howled in the distance. Part of her knew she was insane, that madness had imprinted itself on her. She knew that with every smile she received from a Cambodian she would not be looking at their mouths, but at their grabby hands, at their eyes scanning her belongings. That was it, the curse.

She passed the same beggars on the street whose legs were lost to land mines. She dangled the fake Louis Vuitton purse at her side as she passed a pair of young locals hand-in-hand, followed by a group of four boys in collared shirts and tight jeans. More of the youth crowded the streets, many smoking cigarettes, none so much as glancing at her. She could barely recognize the street from the night before. Was this where it happened? She was fairly certain. Here was the small child. Here the soft rumble of a motorbike.

She heard the music of an outdoor dance club drawing a crowd of local teeny boppers. They danced on gravel to music spun by a DJ with oversized headphones, who mixed Cambodian 60s rock music with hip hop and club. The boys jumped to the beat, fists in the air, while the girls twisted in white dresses. Several of the girls looked skeletal, though they lifted large bottles of Angkor beer with ease. Sophea drew in, leaning on a thin table that held a bucket of tubed ice. In the two months she had lived in Phnom Penh, she had never seen locals let loose like this. A man in a denim shirt disco danced on stage; a woman in a red dress cut into the DJ booth to take photos of herself; a group of schoolgirls, still in uniform, took turns donning large hats and sunglasses; uncaring cool kids leaned on the wall in sly cynicism. The men were dressed in black V necks and shirts that fit their bodies like the skin of an apple. When she saw one of the women get slapped, Sophea's defenses turned on—she thought of acid attacks, bag-snatchers, predators. The woman was a kteuy whose wig had fallen off. Delirious with laughter, the unmasked queen chased her assailant across the gravel dance floor.

Ribaldry, she thought, trying to find the right word for it, so that when she described it later to her workmates, she could do the event some justice. She put her weight on her right leg and felt herself slip. Pain shot from the cut on her calf and she yanked her hand onto the table to steady herself. The rusted grenade pin made a high pitched clink against the beer bottle. Her stomach sucked down, then up to her arms, lifting the bag. *Holy fuck*, she thought. Her eyes darted for an empty space: the line of women at the public toilet, the outdoor dancers, the curbside bar, where a young bartender stood. Without realizing it, the purse was out of her hands, over the bartender's head. It landed in a crate of Angkor beer bottles. In the shouts of the crowd no one seemed to notice. She turned to run and was blinded by a sudden spark that could have just been the flashing LED light from the DJ booth. She felt her eardrums rumble, the floor seem to pound, the screaming of young people that could have just been the bass from the speakers and the cheers of the crowd. She knelt onto the gravel, arms covering eyes.

"Sister? Sister?"

A group of girls gazed at her. They seemed angelic, with cloud-white necklaces and gold earrings. She felt their slender fingers on her shoulder, their hair drifting into her nostrils. One of them held her purse, the cheap fake leather hanging like molded fruit. Sophea's body tossed back, her feet scraping broken gravel.

She ran. The music went on as the words "Sister! Sister! Your purse!" echoed at her from the bright alley.

Saturday 5:30

The sun rose through the airport windows, waking Sophea from beneath the elephant-printed scarf she had draped over her eyes. It took a moment to recall where she was, that she was running, even if she wasn't officially on the run. With every memory, her eyes welted tears. Here she was, stuck inside this body, this failure of a refugee daughter who had retreated right to the privileged space made for her, the airport.

She had come hours before with only her NGO backpack and stood in line for the only open airline. When she heard two men say they were going to Thailand, she made a mental note and asked for the same flight to Bangkok. Bangkok, where the sleaziest wastes of life went to die under a bottle. So why not her too?

The sun crept over the airfield, the long grassy plains, those silent fields. She tried to erase what she had done from her mind—the lives she had nearly disappeared from existence. She walked through the airport jewelry store, then the booths of novelty magnets. She stopped at a postcard showing an Apsara carved into the rocks of Angkor Wat, smiling for the tourists' camera. But it wasn't any smile. The Apsara was a guardian armed not with a knife or a gun, but with a smile that could crush any wayward intention, could unveil any weapon, no matter its camouflage.

Sophea's leg ached, her breath heaved. What had given her the right to save anyone? She, who had come half-way around the earth just to test fate? And what if the explosive had gone off? The question pressed her, forced tears. No, she couldn't bear to think of it. The screams. The body parts. The burst of smoke. The avalanche of debris. She could not, would not think of it. All she knew was that if it had happened, she could never forgive herself. No, she could never forgive herself. She could never, ever forgive.

An announcement came on the intercom in Khmer, and the passengers slowly assembled at the gate. She rubbed away tears and thought of Yunho. Even in his thoughtless capitalist development schemes, he was still too good for her. The first man to make her love the delirium of love, to lose her body in him, who made her furiously happy without ever asking for a smile.

She stood in a line of white tourists wearing tight shorts and tank tops. A man with an Eddie Vedder haircut snapped open the money belt attached to his REI backpack. She passed a trash bin jammed with aluminum beer cans. Nearby, a group of backpackers gulped down Angkor beer, their passports peeking from their back pockets. Somehow she no longer felt like crying. For once she didn't mind being among these white tourists and their gratuitous grins, their excitement to visit a new place, to get high, to get sexed up, to get *theirs*. Perhaps this was the best she could do. Perhaps she was helping her homeland grow by not trying to be a part of it, but by simply spending her money in a foreign country, then getting out.

Pain pounded from her right leg. She kneeled to hold her calf. The small cut had opened again, and blood throbbed out in small drops, following the rhythm of her heartbeat with small quakes of pain. Eventually, she'd have to properly bandage the wound.

ThinkTravel! Blogbook

Post Date: 2007 MAY 14

User: SkyFaralan

Near the central market you watch Phnom Penh's urban poor gather beneath the shade of an agarwood tree. One of them, a woman cradling an infant, sics the children on you. They ask for American dollars while rubbing their stomachs and sobbing. You are surprised at your own hand as it slaps at a large mosquito on your arm—an astonishingly quick reflex. You wipe mosquito onto a dollar bill.

You buy an Angkor beer from a convenience store, sit on a bench in a public park where the hungry will not approach. A light brown monkey looks you up and down in your disheveled state. You offer him your beer and he takes fizzy gulps, holding the bottle with his arms and legs like an infant with a milk bottle. Some white bearded tourist comes and takes a picture of you both.

In the backpacker district, your hotel overlooks a misty lake where children in rowboats offer circling rides for a dollar. The kids are industrial, following you everywhere, helping you pick out the cheapest things, showing you how to get soused on rice-wine. They guide you past banners of NGO campaigns against child sex abuse. Highway signs show foreigners going to jail, strapped in handcuffs, upside down on a grimy floor alongside dead bugs and food that looks like grass clippings.

Words read: "Happy Ending = Sad Ending"

At a bar overlooking the lake, a girl hands you a brochure with numbers to call when you see a sex criminal. You give the girl some money, unsure why.

A woman hands money to the girl as she works her way down. The woman wears a long plaid shirt and flip-flops, and it takes you a moment to realize she's also a traveler. Like you she's hard to place, could be Hispanic, Eurasian, Polynesian, a Filipino fake.

"How's it going?" you ask.

She seems startled. "American?" she says, putting down a book covered with skulls. Neither of you asks what type of American you are.

She introduces herself as "Sophea, with a hard 'p'." You ask what she's reading, and she tells you about all the terrible things that have happened in Cambodia. She explains the man named Pol Pot who decided to go to France. Then she tells you about all the American bombings, how the U.S. supported one of the worst genocides in recorded history. Then about the intellectuals, the NGOs, the embassies, the whole sordid lot.

"Tragic, isn't it?" she says, fanning herself with the anti-prostitution brochure.

"Tragic, yes," you say, though what's really tragic is that you never knew about any of this until now.

"They call this a rough spot for travelers," her mouth moves fast, driven by your ability to understand her accent. "But it's not all poppy and crunk for locals either. Been here two weeks and I've seen gangs beat up old people with clubs and knives. There are still machine guns on the streets. Here, take a look at this." She hands you another brochure from her back pocket:

The arms trade is booming in Cambodia. The rule of law is weak, and the rich prey on the poor with impunity. How does this happen? With deadly force and illegal arms! We, the State Violence Monitors of Cambodia, are a national human rights organization at the forefront of this war. Volunteer now at svm.org!

"I've been working for SVM since I arrived," Sophea says. "You know how small they are? They're working from the library of a broken down mansion. Our entire military complex blew this place apart, and who is left to put it all back together? Just—volunteers on vacation, that's who."

A waiter brings her a plate of vanilla ice cream. You share your plate of curry, sitting and talking. In the afternoon you hear the Cambodian youth retreat into the air conditioned PC room next door. You sit and talk, sipping mixed drinks to the sounds of gunfire coming from the PC room. A breeze ripples across the lake and a foul smell wafts by. You make no notice, but keep sitting, keep talking. After sundown the restaurant transforms into a club. You sit and talk among a Cambodian dance party, where teenagers practice traditional dancing, their hands in waves to a song that goes "SHE HIT THE FLOOR—NEXT THING YOU KNOW".

You're still sitting and talking, now overlooking the lake while the touts come in from the street to offer you women and cocaine. When you and Sophea head back to the hostel, you're caught off-guard by people popping from the alley like carnies: "You want a girl?" "You want marijuana?" "How about coke?"

You wake up the hostel clerk who takes the wooden boards off the doorway. Sleepily, the man asks: "You want girl?" He lowers the price to $10, about as much as a ticket to see the new Batman movie. "How about a boy?" he inquires. You and Sophea look at each other, measuring each other's reaction to that.

In a room of empty bunkbeds you keep talking. Sophea asks if you've ever bought a prostitute. "No," you answer. "That'd be like paying for a helicopter to take you to the top of Mount Everest."

"That's an old excuse," she says.

Even half asleep, you talk and talk, finding more in common than just your accents.

The sun rises and Sophea says that she never wants to return to the United States. "Most travelers can be separated into three groups," she tells you. "Sexpats, drugpats, and ecopats. Then there's a fourth group. The people who were rejected from their country, and everywhere they go too. They can't stop moving, rejecting every city before it can reject them. You and I, we know where we fall."

It feels like the first time you've ever really understood the power of that word, "we."

After five months of traveling around Southeast Asia he felt like a skeleton. Skyler Faralan, feverishly ambulant, arrived in Singapore with all muscle and tissue melted off. He'd nearly starved himself unrecognizable. He no longer moved for excitement, but as if racing a ticking clock.

Singapore reminded Skyler too much of Las Vegas where he went to university. All shiny and grandiose with casinos and slots and malls. He checked out the casinos and hated them. He saw the beach and it reminded him of Hawai'i, where he was born and raised. He hated that too. He checked his money at an ATM and hated himself.

While unpacking his backpacker's backpack Skyler noticed that the SIM card in his screen-cracked cell phone was somehow connected to a network.

A text from his ex, Kiera Agsalud:

July 13 2007

I kept myself from talking to you for this long but I still miss you. Last week when moving into my dorm room I stumbled across that CD you burned for me during our first year together. "Sky and Kiera Mix 2002." Remember all those poppy punk love songs? Wow. That brought me back.

A week later, she wrote:

You've been gone five months already, who goes on vacation for five months?

Then:

Please come back. I decided I would forgive you for whatever you've done while traveling. We can work. You've seen the world, now come home.

Skyler wrote back:

Hi

The network accepted, the text went through. He waited for her response in his hostel bunkbed, scrunching up that pair of white and blue-lined panties he stole from her years ago.

Skyler. I can't believe I'm talking to you. It's been so long! When will you be back?

He wrote:

When I come around.

That night on the second story patio of his Chinatown hostel, Skyler, drunk on San Miguel, overheard two tourists on the floor below him. His dilated eyes found a blur of two blonde American girls chatting about their trip to Indonesia.

"Indonesians are so nice and sincere and sweet!"

"To you!" Skyler intervened in that punky slur of his, projecting words at them from his patio. "Nice like the hired help is nice! Oh, you think they're-a as nice and sweet to each other as they are to you? Thanks the gods they are so sweet and nice! How much tourism would they get if they weren't all so sweet and nice!"

The girls pestered off only after the less-blonde one defended Indonesian people as "the nicest in the world" and Skyler had nothing to say to that.

Babe. Where are you going?
Do you need money? I've
been talking to your parents.

I'm going to Jakarta.

Where is that?

Indonesia. In Southeast Asia
still.

Why? Why not home?
Please just buy a SIM card
this time. I can't sleep not
knowing if you got hit by a

83

truck or something.

Kiera. We broke up.

We can always get back together.

So what the fuck did I come here for?

Skyler deplaned in Jakarta, headphones equipped. He stood in the no-lines for the Visa and then the no-lines for the foreigner passport check. All tourists made quick for their transfer flights to Bali.

The smog threw a veil over the city. Chaotic streets didn't even move to a beat. There were no bus stops and no stop buttons on the bus, just a tin roof to clank against. When the bus reached a traffic jam, passengers jumped overboard to journey on foot, searching for another mode of transport. Skyler just hailed a taxi. As soon as the driver saw a foreigner, on came a techno version of Sinatra's New York, New York.

New—*bow-wow* New—*bow-wow* New—*bow-wow*

"You speak English?" the driver asked. He pointed to a small four-wheeled vehicle on the roadside. "How you call that?"

"I have no idea," Skyler said. "Looks like something jocks and white men ride."

"Where you from?"

"I'm American, obviously."

"American! No problem! But you no look American."

"Half Indonesian."

The taxi driver touched Skyler's leg. "You know the Indonesian man, the senator, in America?"

Skyler slapped the orange air freshener hanging from the vent. "Fuck off with that bullshit. There ain't no Indonesian senators in America."

"No?"

"No."

That ended the conversation, and Skyler fell asleep. After hours of being stuck in gridlock, he observed the sun setting over the beach like a yellow piss stain.

"Boss, we arrived."

The three-hour taxi ride only cost four US dollars. Skyler fell comfortably back into his seat. "Good, I saw the beach. Now take me downtown."

Dropped off in the Kota red-light district, Skyler found a notice on a club door: "Closed due to cop death." At another club, another notice: "Closed due to foreigner death."

He walked, cars beeping at him, barely scathing him along the sidewalkless roadside. And he couldn't get his mind off his ex. He remembered firing shotguns in Las Vegas, that BOOM vibrating sound when the bullets zoomed across the desert. His friends wouldn't let him touch the guns after he went crazy trying to play Russian Roulette with a semi-automatic.

He walked through not-his-space, his suicidal tendencies reaching a peak as honks summoned him into the afterlife. Disentangling headphones at the roadside, he thought of Sophea's sexual freedom, her delicate madness, her unexplained disappearance out of his life. He understood that need to escape, but did not expect this restless abandon; how travel can drive you, how it takes the wheel, propels you forward until the wind slaps off skin, drying organs like old leaves, cornering the spirit into the herded pressure of a heart promising to explode.

He felt a woman push against him through a layer of white tarp. Another car whooshed by and he could have died. Yes, perhaps it could have ended as easily as the single sweep of a broom.

He sat at a convenience store patio imbibing his third San Miguel, a last meal before running back into traffic.

So punk in drublic, he thought in slurs.

Back in the streets, he veered past a white sedan, dipped down to evade a trucker's rear-view mirror. A car's blinders hammered on and he gasped a last gasp. The car turned away.

Another convenience store, another mirror reflection of himself.

Could I be southeast asian? Is that even a thing?

He knew he was in foreigner-bar-land when he crossed small wagons lining the streets selling Viagra, Cialis, and Nangen. He tossed into a pub of wilted expats, their eyes squinting onto a rugby match. He strutted around with that humorous sense of not being white, pretending those whiteys were just untitled sculptures waiting for the pussy to smash itself.

It didn't take long for the bar to turn into a meat club. A Mamasan brought Skyler a young girl, Pajar. "Guess my age!" the girl said, grabbing his ass as he stiffened up. The mama massaged him back calm. On stage, prepubescent go-go girls in hot pants waddled on a beer-stained carpet.

Am I the only one appalled at how terribly these girls dance?

Not completely inured to sexpat life, Skyler chatted with a pony-tailed server clothed in a little red riding hood outfit. "You know, in the states, I have your job," he told her. "I basically have your life."

"Oh really? You think so?"

"Oye!" Skyler made his best pretty femme face. "Yeah and here I got American privilege melting outta my ass, so we're all getting fucked, right?"

Back on the street, pop music reverberated from every street stall as Skyler dove into a bowl of Bakso soup. A rat scuttled about his shoes. Two transgender warias marched into the tented stall with a boom box. They danced as terrible as the go-go girls. Customers averted their eyes.

Only Skyler put money in their cashbox.

He stumbled about in the middle of a dark street, letting motorbikes swerve around him. He felt their bumps on his arms when they inched past, but he refused to move.

I'm standing here on a one way road.

Headlights blared into his eyes.

No other direction for this to go.

He walked into a pothole, slipped, a taxi swerved by. The smell of burnt rubber.

and we fall down, and we fall down.

Around midnight, Skyler aimed his machine body into a late night fashion market and ordered a three-dollar haircut.

He heard scurrying on the tin rooftop. Wincing away, eyes struck with fear, he heard a voice say, "Don't tell me you're afraid of rats!"

The voice came from a tall waria with wavy blonde hair, her yellow dress patterned like a butterfly's wings, her yellow trucker hat made of thick wool. Her skin, darker than Skyler's, was marked by purple makeup—lipstick, mascara, blush—dark and bold like an imperial gown recovered after centuries of weathering.

"Yes," Skyler said. "I mind rats when they're fallin' out of the sky."

"Oh just get over it, haha!" She pinched his cheek, hard, as if trying to wake a dead body. The fakeness in her laugh enticed him. The yellow bow on her wrists strummed his heart strings. The full eternal lips of her mouth plucked him into the sublime of outer space. Her name, he learned, was Dawn.

When the barber finished, Skyler saw a knockout in his reflection.

"Oh look who is coming out now!" Dawn said, displaying her perfect white teeth. "Damn girl, your real beauty comes out in Indo, of course! Of course? Of course!"

The other chairs were occupied by young women getting made-up for the clubs. The hair curlers, the lipstick and eyeliner. It was all just too tempting.

"I see you eyeing those cans like you want a piece," Dawn chimed, gesturing to the smatterings of crimson in her own wig. "I see that desire pinned up in your eyes. Girl you better do it now. Do you, and let your real beauty come out."

Skyler thought of Mrs. Doubtfire and The Birdcage. He remembered wearing bracelets and rings, wearing goth gear because he liked the feeling of lace. His father telling him to take off a bracelet because it looked gay. People are gonna think weird things about you if you do that, if you act like this.

"I have no ass," Skyler said. "My belly too fat. I don't want to scare anyone."

"See!" Dawn chuckled, throwing up her yellow shaded nails. "You're already thinking like a woman! And you're a hot mess, look at you! Just give in already!"

Skyler paused. Who would ever know? "All right, let's do it, why not?"

Then the laughter and claps. Then the smooth strokes on his canvas-face. Then the patting of light powder, the sudden sneeze after inhaling a cloud. Then the lashes. Then the eye liner, the scary thick pencil aimed right into his eye. The girl's steady hand marked cool lead. It all felt like a deep massage, and afterwards he moved his cheeks, feeling, for the first time, his own skin.

Dawn brought the dress, dark purple like her make up. Perfectly fitted, even the cups.

At first Skyler could only look at himself in fragments—dark eyes, dark red lips, black curly wig.

"So," Skyler cooed, the curly hair of the black wig atop. "You want to go to a hotel together, make a true woman out of me?"

"Wow, you are frank!" Dawn said, smiling so large her eyes squinted tight.

Finally, in a thirty-dollar hotel room made for sleaze, Skyler was able to fuck again. Upon brown canvasses their lips met each other's joysticks. Dawn tasted taut skin, Skyler mouthed loose foreskin. In control, they both became avatars of the other's pulsing heart.

Pulling Dawn in, putting fingers between her perfect teeth. "Perfect biters."

"Oh I know I love my perfect teeth. It's what makes me unique. Ha!"

"We usually say that about small flaws. Like a mole."

"Well, baby, everything unique about me is beautiful, even my moles."

The way this diarrhea-giver fucks makes me want to believe in god again.

He held her lip in his mouth and squeezed his dick into the flab of her thigh, scrotum, and ass. He felt her grow on his stomach, pushing unto his belly button.

Even better when I feel him harden inside me.

"Five months you've been traveling? Aren't you ever going to go home, Skyler Faralan?"

"My home is inside you."

"That's vile. But my home is inside you. So how can this work?"

"Where there's a will, there's a way."

"Anything is possible."

"If god wills it."

I want to be spread so thin I don't know who I am.

Objects: purple bow in her hair. Action: stroking himself feeling her inside. Tension: her bushy pubes.

Jesus was a carpenter, cuz real men handle wood.

"Oh I hate when the sun comes up."

"That's not the only thing coming up."

"Girl, I gotta get to work."

"No. What? No. Skip work. I'll pay your wage, whatever it is. Stay with me, please. Look at me. This wasn't just a one night stand."

Dawn gave that look that said a taxi ride was the only thing cheaper than ass.

Alone, Skyler woke to Kiera Agsalud's texts.

Babe, I've been in touch with your mom and sister. You haven't contacted them either! They want to video phone with you at their Sunday barbecue. Don't be an asshole and pick up the phone.

Nude beneath the covers in his empty hostel room, Skyler saw his mother on his laptop screen chewing a piece of charred pork, her hair up in a heart shape, bound by a long ponytail. The white buildings of Honolulu peeked out through the patio windows. Kiera, her wafer-thin body leaning over a crucifix, spoke for her. "Your mother was just telling me that she knows what you are going through."

"I quit school and ran away too!" Mother Faralan said. "Or did he forget? But are we the same? No. I still called my mother to let her know I was alive! I still called my mother!"

"She still called grandma."

Then on came Skyler's uncle Elmo. "Skyler, we will always love and pray for you. Hope you're keeping safe, ok?"

"Yes," Mother Faralan said. "Tell him we pray that God helps him get through whatever phase he's in."

Then came Kanoa, one of his tattooed cousins, the one who surfed and wanted to join the Marines. "So what, you think America sucks now?"

"He doesn't understand what his great grandfather went through to come to Hawai'i," Mother Faralan sighed.

"So what are you doing *anyways?*" Kiera asked, her bangs covering her wet round eyes. "Just tell me what you did yesterday. As an example. I'm trying to figure out what's so great about Asia that you won't come back home."

"He won't ever finish University now," Mother Faralan said with a choke.

"I went to my local watering hole," Skyler said. "About two *kilometers* down the street, and watched football—sorry, *soccer*—and I cheered for Brazil."

His family subsided into silence—a rare and frightening thing in the islands. Kiera's large brown eyes penetrated him through the computer screen.

"What are you really doing there, Sky?"

His eyes wandered to the white bedding where Dawn held him beneath the covers. He felt her still inside of him, a small beat of pain, deep, grinding further into his stomach, his lungs, his chest. He grabbed his own dick, imagined it was hers. Perhaps he always had two.

The Skype interrogation combined with his little tryst skyrocketed Skyler's libido into deep space. His sexual energy remained onerous, oppressive even, as he walked the broken sidewalks of downtown Jakarta, his dick humming like an auto-tuned chorus, increasing in volume whenever a little brown minx pinged his passions. He ended up in a night club awash in flashing lights. Nestling himself between a group of white expats and a row of unveiled Indo women, he ordered a beer to put off the hunger pangs and chewed on some peanuts so the salt would stymie the diarrhea, spitting crumbs into napkins before they slid down his throat.

He pulled his wallet to pay and dropped the photo of his great grandfather who migrated to Hawai'i, worked on sugar plantations and fought in the Civil War. In the photo the Faralan patriarch stood with a pistol in one hand, the other firmly on his uniform belt. Goddamn sexy.

"Kuta Beach in Bali has the best nosh in all of Indonesia," one of the drunk Aussies said from a nearby table. All three of them wore short shorts and tank tops.

"Cheers to the nosh!" one said. "Hey you, cheers to the nosh, right?"

Skyler lifted his glass. "To the nosh."

"No, Java's got decent nosh too," the bearded one said. "The trick is to not think of the girls as Muslims. Especially the ones without veils. It's like a down-to-fuck flag, not wearing a veil."

"Fill them up with unholy mixed race babies," Skyler quipped. "Show those fag Asian men up."

They all looked his way, taken aback, perhaps, by his mastery of the English language.

"My friend likes you," a woman said, leaving him with a local dame, unveiled (DTF style), with her hair in two buns. She smoked a cigarette from the pack he left on the table.

"You look like my ex," she said.

"Foreigner?"

"He was Indonesian. What are you?"

"Branded. Maladjusted. Introverted. Loner. Deviant."

"Ok then," she said, hazel eyes. "Why come to Jakarta?"

"I love Jakarta!"

"Really? Travelers hate it here. Call it the big durian."

"Well, I hate travelers, and I hate travel, so that's ok."

"But why come here?"

He couldn't answer. "There's never just one thing to retreat from."

A bell went off.

"Last call," she said, hinting.

"Already? It's not even midnight."

"All clubs close early." She tugged him to the overly-lit dance floor. "Because some foreigner was killed."

They danced dirty and Skyler bit her neck slightly; she dug her nails into his shoulder; he pulled her hair; she pulled his back.

But the wig felt more natural.

The lights blared on and Skyler kept running his hands over her and her conservative little white dress and her undone frizzy hair. Another mouth kissed Skyler's neck, two masculine arms reached from behind.

"Every time you kiss her you have to kiss me," a voice stroked his ears. "Ok? Every time you kiss her you have to kiss me. Now kiss her. Ok, now me—"

Skyler lapped them both up. The whole thing reminded him of thrashing around in circle pits at punk rock shows, buoyed by sweaty men until he hit the floor and a million hands came reaching to lift him up. How he always woke up the morning after with bruises and pain and aches.

How he asked his friends to hit him with drumsticks to break blood.

Skyler thrashed in the club's yellow houselights. He tried to form a mosh pit but it was only him ska-dancing in a loop.

"The state looks down on sodomy!" he sang.

He hit a trashcan and when it didn't topple over he hurled it into the glossy bar, shattering beer bottles and heart-shaped glasses.

"As if I give a fuck!"

Two security guards grabbed at him. He thrashed against them like wall trampolines. He wanted to chant "don't call me white," but it wouldn't make sense.

Bam! Face, meet concrete.

"Come on what are you waiting for? Hit a tourist, now's your chance!"

Men toppled him.

"All hands on the bad one!"

The guards moved him into the elevator. He couldn't budge free.

"Help! My dick is jammed!"

Fingers squeezed his neck.

Dawn? Dawn are you there?

Yo girl. Why you buggin' me?

Told you I was busy tonight.

Come to my hotel. No one
here tonight.

It's always been there, tickling my ear, rumbling under my feet.

Sorry girl, I'm just about to
leave for Bali. To see family.

Bali. The island? Can I join
you? I will explore Bali then
explore you.

*Please. If something doesn't change I will die. I have to address
this or I will die.*

Girl, you're so sexy, you
should be in a veil!

Oh, I can do veil. Meet me in
Bali, I can do that.

Bali is Hindu.

Either I do something about this or I will kill myself.

I'm not strong enough
without you. I can't do it by
myself. When I was born my
mother wanted to name me
Kawika. She decided not
to because it sounds too

feminine. She was afraid I
would be made fun of.

It's going to take some time,
Skyler.

Can you not call me that?

Ok Kawika. But it's going to
take some time.

Skyler woke up in the late afternoon weak from hunger. He hailed a taxi to Jakarta's old town and stumbled through Dutch colonial-era architecture, making himself up.

At a spice market older than the United States, Skyler stood on his tip toes as if wearing heels. He practiced balancing and sticking his ass out as he walked past a cover band singing Let It Be. The audience of Indos sang the chorus, women in veils mouthing along: "Mother Mary comes to me ..." The music mixed with prayers coming from a nearby mosque like the wail of an electric guitar, a distorted yawp.

At the hotel he found himself stuck video-phoning with his family again. This time his white half: father, uncle, grandfather, interneting from his father's suburban house in Las Vegas. They all sported beards and glasses.

"Skyler!" his father said, parting his brown hair. "God is blessing us so that we can finally talk to you." Looking at him through new eyes, Skyler thought his father would be quite a catch to anyone who didn't mind his height.

"Be careful in a Muslim country, you hear?" Uncle Frank said, moving the laptop camera toward him.

"Are you preaching over there at all?" His grandfather roared in the background. His deep voice shook through his vanilla swirl beard. "Spreading the Good News and acknowledging our salvation gives us peace in times of need."

"Which church over there are you attending?" Skyler's father asked, turning the camera toward him, center-frame. "You used to love church, remember?"

Skyler tried to think of something other than strippers. That was the last time he saw his father, the bearded man's cock bulging at the Platinum strip club, enticing the darkest skinned dancer to gyrate her nude ass into his face. "This is my son," his father said then, embracing Skyler, using affection to negate the stripper's understandable doubts, or perhaps, using Skyler's brown skin to verify that he really did like dark-skinned women.

That wasn't quite the last time he had talked to his father. It was an hour or two later, in the club's parking lot, as Skyler tried to argue his way to be designated driver, and failing that, struggled the keys from his father's sweaty palms.

"I'm sorry. I'm so so sorry," his father said, as submissive as he was in prayer.

"Sorry for what?" rattling the keys in the car door.

"Just, if I had known, that by marrying an Asian woman. My son would be—you know. I had great genes. You could have been—"

"Dad."

"—a real ladies man."

A cab drive, a plane ticket, and five months later, now here was Skyler, forced to watch his father lead the charge, as if his presence would suddenly inveigle his son out his determination for self-ruin.

It must have been hard, Skyler thought, to have a son that looked nothing like you. Who even changed his last name to stop being associated with you. It hurt, but still not enough.

"Do you remember?" his father said in that downward looking preacher-voice. "How happy you were at church? Being accepted and loved for who you are, is always amazing."

"Well what are you doing over there?" Uncle Frank interrupted, shifting the laptop camera back to him. "Your girl, Kiera, is trying to convince everyone to help buy you a ticket home."

"We're gonna use an internet program," his father said. "All your friends, family, loved ones, are pitching in a little bit to get you home, where you belong."

"Call me Kawika," Skyler said, and immediately regretted it. Slipping off the tongue, the name was so knick-knacky exotic.

It was getting late in the dankest little expat bar in Jakarta when Skyler realized with satisfaction that he had not eaten in two days. Anorexic, one might say, but they'd be wrong. Sometimes food just didn't work out.

A squad of three trans ladies sat across a plane of mirrors.

They appeared to be the only interesting, sexy people in the entire city. The entire world.

Dawn, I miss you

> Kawika, I miss you too much.
> Way way too much.

A homeless man came in begging for money, keeping a stash of bills rolled up in a Pringles jar.

Do you think it's love?

> Ha! So what. My family will never bless us.

I'm not asking for that.

A black out later, Skyler's watch read three in the morning. He lurched over the balcony of a two story 7-11, his chin in a puddle of anorexia vomit—the worst smelling kind, just stomach acid and booze. He couldn't remember much. The yelling, the wandering alone, the nearly getting effaced by a truck.

Please Dawn. I'll die without
you I know I will

> Girl, I'm in Bali right now.

Just come. Meet me in a
hotel.

I'm getting married, that's
why I'm here

I'll pay. I got no cash left, but
I'll max out my credit card.
Buy you anything you want.

Girl are you deaf?

Are you?

Skyler arrived in tourist trap Bali using an already maxed-out credit card. Overdraft fees sank his every step as he marched up a marble stairway to the sandalwood door of Dawn's Presidential Suite. He appeared in a white tank top, flip flops. "Hello, Kawika. Can I call you Kawi? My little Kawi?"

"Doesn't this hotel room make you feel like a colonial?"

"I'm pretty sure colonials didn't get assfucked in a grass skirt."

"Hey! I grew up in Hawai'i, remember? I can rock a grass skirt."

"Yeah Hawaii Hawaii Hawaii, so why come here anyway?" Those perfect teeth, that thin body and that skin.

"Why don't you get in drag?" sitting on the bed. "I brought sets of lingerie for both of us."

"Girl, I don't see no difference when you're behind me!" He fell back onto the bed, Skyler's arm beneath his shirt.

"But I spent all day doing my makeup all by myself. Come on, I came all the way to your country ..."

"What do you want," pulling Skyler to him. "A hand job for having an American passport?"

"Does there need to be a reason?" grabbing those tight white boxers.

"Well, it's Bali, sweetheart. God ain't watching."

That evening they strolled through the "authentic" "ethnic" "art" and "culture" "village," Ubud, a tourist city perfectly arranged to appear unarranged. They watched a Kecak fire dance in one of the dozens of ancient Hindu temples. Skyler turned Kawika was out with fake pigtails and a long black skirt.

Kiera Agsalud buzzed.

Are you still alive, Skyler?
What are you doing now?

Dawn noticed the distraction. He felt cock beneath the skirt.

Watching a fire dance about
saving the princess.

You can lie to your family
with that bullshit but not
to me. What are you really
doing over there?

Dawn took the cock out, folding the skirt down.

Now I am watching two
young Virgin girls get
possessed by a ghost.

He used both hands to sculpt man out of clay.

We have all the money ready
for you, all you have to do is
get on that plane. After five
years, you owe me.

When the crowd stood to cheer for the dancers, Dawn's
fist squeezed the pecker until a tear came out of its slit.

For dinner they swayed into a Rastafarian themed joint,
where every light in the room brightened a larger-than-life
statue of Bob Marley.

"This band is terrible," Dawn said, his arm on bare leg.
"Haha!" That enticingly fake laugh.

"Tourism only begets money," Skyler said, back in drunk-
en-rant mode. "Not education. Local becomes another
word for servants. It was the same in Vegas and Hawai'i."

Dawn chowed down on some fried rice. They drank rum
straight, head spinning.

"Kawika, just eat, girl! Eat *something*, skinny bitch."

"Why is it wherever I go it's always brown people serving white people and not the other way around? Las Vegas. Hawai'i. California."

"Baby. Eat something."

"Thailand. Laos. Vietnam. Cambodia. Singapore."

"Look, I know you're new to performing femme, but not all women are anorexic, damn!"

"Why is it wherever I go it's always brown people serving white people and not the other way around?"

"Ugh!" clanking down his silverware.

"Let's go I can't stay here," getting up, feeling naked in the thin blouse, walking along, rubbing tears.

How long could he go before it all collapsed on itself?

Skyler passed a local woman on the street, her fingers in the mouth of her light-skinned baby. Next to her three tourists dressed fashionably dirty and ragged.

"Why am I putting up with you? Skyler, come on!"

"And what do they get for all this tourism? Do you see a great university around here? Have you met a Balinese scientist, or even a transfer student? What do they get out of it?"

Skyler leaned on a wooden banister and stared at more tourists, each cloaked with that sheik pedophile style.

"Fuck your European shit-fucking heritage," Skyler spouted in a strange accent: part Thai part Cambodian part Vietnamese part Laos and all the other places he'd picked up. "You fucking faggots."

A moment of still silence. A camera flash blinded him. Laughter like screeching tires.

He clenched his fists. He grabbed a bottle of San Miguel. Tomorrow's headlines: Another Bar Closed Due to Tourist Death.

Dawn's voice came. "Kawika. Kawika. Kawika. Look at me. Kawika. Come on. Don't be such a sass. Come on, little girl, let's go home."

Breath came faster than words.

"Kawika. You really want to live without teeth? Kawika. Save your bite! Kawika. Come on. Girl, there are all sorts of ways of destroying yourself, you know!"

The bottle dropped and tears streamed down. The name was oxygen, but it wasn't enough.

Back at the hotel, Dawn consoled Skyler on the bedside. Skyler waited for him to leave in the morning for his new wife. Once Dawn left, he'd decided to end it. Dawn could never know. It would be too hard to make him think he failed. But the man was wasting his breath.

"Kawika ... Kawika ... Skyler ... Skyler ..."

He stared at that mascara-ridden face in the mirror. Blurry vision saw nothing wrong. He saw himself, still, his mother's offspring.

"Ok," Dawn stood up. "The sun is up and I'm out. You be strong. Eat something, sista. Let me know how you're doing."

"Go marry your Muslim girl," Skyler said.

"Kawika," he said. "I'm not marrying a girl."

"What? What do you mean?"

"I mean—will you ever see me? When I live in America?"

With the indignation of a million betrayed souls on his face, Skyler stared Dawn out of his own hotel room.

Skyler walked Bali's Kuta Beach at sunset, languid, dizzy from low blood sugar. He listened to a middle-aged man in sunglasses and unkempt hair explain that this beach wasn't discovered until the 70s. "Before that," the American said with certainty, "there was nothing here."

On the road Skyler passed Hawai'i/Bali restaurants selling musubi and goreng. He passed souvenir shops selling tortoise carvings and stickers that said "aloha," "hang loose," and "what happens in Bali stays in Bali."

He passed groups of large Aussie men casually dressed in the latest genocide of Polynesian tattoos and tank tops that carried a large red map of Australia with the words "Fuck off, we're full."

He passed a group of drunk Aussies wearing stickers that said "I love pussy" and "cock is for fags." He passed giant wooden carved penises.

He walked until nightfall, reaching a part of town where taxis whizzed by like cannon balls and beggars crowded the street edges. Skyler walked into the middle of the road. A dark car without lights shot by. In an alternative reality, he just became roadkill.

His pace quickened, unpredictable. He knocked over boxes of peace offerings. He kicked over oil, oranges, incense.

"Sir, massage?" "Boss, young girls?" "Just come have a look."

All these places make a straight line, a shot of seeds, from the anxious world onto the desert stomach of Las Vegas, then onto the untouched tits and bursting nips of Hawai'i, then onto the thick-lipped guzzling face of Bali. Just Blesh! I'm done.

He paced through a dark tunnel the width of a single car. A motorbike jetted by. Blinding flashes of light, then the rush of wind. Skipping over a pothole in the street, he neared a blind turn. In the middle of a street overlooking the beach, he squatted down, closed his eyes, and tried with every blood vessel not to cower.

but there's so many ways but there are just so many ways.

Babe, it's been two days and we are still waiting for you. Did you get the ticket? Where are you? You're not answering your phone.

Babe, I tried to call that hotel in Bali but they haven't seen you. After five years!

Skyler, your parents are freaking out. All the money we put in that account for you has been withdrawn. We all

put money in, but no ticket.
Where is the money?!?!

> To everyone:
> Thanks for the cash, but I
> won't forgive you that easily.
> Also fuck you all.
> -Your punk

She landed in Macau like the new snow, nattily attired in a black dress (black because of mourning) that encircled her frame like barbed wire, all eye-fucking the cute boys and girls as they tilted her way. She folded her umbrella to let them gaze upon her short sleeve bodice. When she smiled, they smiled.

She waltzed around the shore in front of the MGM munching on Portuguese butter buns and yilan dumplings. She prayed to the Gold Lion who shined his light on her.

She pulled her passport out of her bra and entered the casino. "Yes, mam," said the large security guard. She whisked her black hair, couldn't wait for it to get long, so long it reached her hips.

She paced about the fashion stores, humming along to a song in her earbuds, doing her thing in the mall and going into the woman's restroom daring anyone to stop her. Inside a stall, she pulled down Kiera's blue and white panties.

She passed tourist booths proclaiming Macau and Hong Kong "The Gateway to China." She perused tourist magazines looking for a trail to follow.

She passed rows of spinning slots. She felt the hearts of mermaid-themed machines. It was her first time playing, and she didn't start low.

ThinkTravel! Blogbook

Post Date: 2007 AUG 28

User: SkyFaralan

A man with a pig carcass slung over his shoulder stomps on an upside-down cockroach, mashing it into a slimy paste. You find this beautiful because you're in Hong Kong, where every streetlight thrusts you into the ineffable sensuality of a Wong Kar-Wai picture. You imagine seeing a demure Faye Wong fixing up Tony Leung's empty apartment near the high-speed travelator. Hong Kong cinema makes everything sexy: build- ings, stray cats, cigarettes, gum-stained concrete, and of course, Asians themselves. And you among them. You, the Fil-Am Eur-Asian Hapa-Haole, are one hot piece of Mango meat.

Coffee shops stand like wardens at every street corner. You stop in for a café au lait, sifting through a free newspaper protest- ing low-wages, wealth inequality, and living spaces the size of coffins. Between articles you admire how the sauna-like tem- perature creates sweat that shines from every gorgeous pedes- trian body. During lunch the streets are carpeted with them, the Miss Universe: Powersuit Editions from every country in Asia and Europe, jostling about the sidewalk like a runway. Each bit of eye-candy jolts you into a sex high so extraordi- nary you wonder if it's possible to overload and inflict perma- nent self-injury.

You're giving that meeoow look to a faux-hawked waiter on a cigarette break. His stare back flattens you into your morbid body. The women here are so sexy, you couldn't possibly mea- sure up. Fine, you say, hating the game, since it's better than hating yourself. The man's cigarette flicks your way; you are the ashtray.

Headphones blaring pop punk to bring up your spirits, you wonder about this whole gender binary transsex nonsense. Could you keep going? What the fuck else could you become? And what happens when you run out of ammo? Above you, a rusted air conditioner blows spores of black mold. You read somewhere that fungi have over 20,000 sexes, each one a mystery until the act occurrs, and a gender is invented.

You feel a world inside of you, raging against barbed wire.

You're batting eyes at a dark-skinned truck driver when you get a text from Sophea:

> Do you think travelers can be
> more than lone wanderers?

You respond:

How else could we stay
afloat?

She writes that she's in Thailand. Doesn't feel the need to apologize for disappearing, for being presumed dead. You beckon her to Hong Kong.

Very welcoming, lots of hot
Asian cock.

> Don't be gross. But that's an
> idea.

That afternoon, as you're taking the tram to Victoria peak, Sophea calls you.

"Just so we're clear," she says, "I'm not in a good place. And, I'm not into cries for help. Try any of that travel-inspires-you-to-find-yourself bullshit and I will toss you over whatever boat we're on."

"Agreed."

"So, now that's settled, how strict was Hong Kong airport? On a scale from one to five? I mean 'five' if they're guaranteed to rift through my baggage. 'One' if I could bring in a stick of dynamite and it wouldn't turn heads. 'Three' if you think a garbage bag full of pills could slip in no problem."

The clanking tram full of Chinese families comes to a halt. A sour taste drips onto the back of your tongue.

"They don't check shit," you tell her.

On a bus through the Pearl River Delta, Skyler Faralan persisted, spitting out residue from the factory smog. He hadn't time these days to contemplate his gender, too busy hawking spit into a green convenience store bag made of impossibly strong plastic. It was hard to focus on transitions of the body when the city outside never stopped moving—buildings and parks and towers and buildings again, a time loop of grime, smog, and cyclists in white masks. He hadn't lasted a week before that itch again drove him to travel cumulus-like around Asia, and his gender dysphoria merely added to the usual teenybopper bloomings of twenty-something backpackers. Suffice it to say he remained lost, the kind of lost that he had no interest in curing—for being lost now felt like floating in an untethered air balloon, traversing the modern Orient with one buoyant thrill after another. He felt it even on that bus. Sparks of joy from the foreignness before him pounded into the meat of his heart, mustering mouth-breathing delights, urging him to wake the fuck up.

Shot down on Guangzhou's main road, our lone wanderer passed parks where elderly practiced tai qi and hip hop breaking. Skyler was nearly pummeled by a muddy yellow burlap sack slung by workers from a truck as he made his escape from the hot chaos into an overcrowded library where students read on the floor like soldiers in a trench, sitting back to back, pinching each other's fingers to keep from falling asleep.

In the hostel, Skyler met Adam from Australia doing push-ups on the black tiled floor. Adam worked in outsourcing. The Brazilian man Gaupo also worked in outsourcing, managing a factory that assembled Brazilian leather into shoes and seat covers. There was another: Sophea, Skyler's travel buddy, a reformed NGO vanity tourist who once sought to save her homeland from god knows what. It didn't matter what because she was done with all that noise. Outsourcing, she said, is where the future's at.

These conversations occurred at four in the morning, when Sophea and Skyler were drunk on the hostel couch. Skyler with that black dress whose rounded neckline hung over his chest like it was left out to dry; Sophea with her hotel-concierge black shirt tucked into torn-up gray jeans. Like barons holding court, they called young travelers to impress them, their feet up over Guangzhou tourist maps and stacks of Lonely Planet books. Perhaps it was their American accents that tethered them together, but probably not. Or perhaps it was the cotton underwear that peaked from Sophea's oversized plaid shirt that made her look convincingly like the brown goddess of sluts, and Skyler, both giving and seeking approval, responded with that carnal urge to steal her ruffled panties.

Adam popped from his sit-ups and tried to squeeze himself into the couch between Skyler and Sophea. They unwedged him, heaved him to the floor like the white tourist scum he was.

"What say you, then?" they spoke with conspiratorial tones.

The man kept his head to the carpet, hoping perhaps to settle the spinning room. "Yangshuo," he said.

Skyler pinned the map with a plastic butter knife. "That fabled city. Only a six hour bus ride north."

The man faced skyward, his glasses fogged up from the humidity. "I tell you, it is the most beautiful place on earth."

Sophea groaned. "This man has been infected."

"Yes," Skyler said, lured by the prospect of a new city to disenchant. "It is the blight, and it must be stopped."

The sun peeked through the green construction tarp of Guangzhou's downtown towers as Sophea and Skyler brolike took turns following each other from one incompetent travel agent to another.

After filling their stomachs at a Halal noodle house, they lined up at a station kiosk to purchase a bus ticket to Yangshuo, determined to vanquish the ideological supremacy that masked the tourist playground as the supposed beesknees of stuff to look at. In line, Sophea taught Skyler how to cut a pocket in her bag to slip in contraband. But Skyler didn't listen, enraptured as he was by the female teller with the star hat. He clearly had a thing for Red China. Something about commie women. Something about their tendency to humiliate, to purge, to discharge the capitalist right out.

"Two tickets to Yangshuo," Skyler said when he arrived at the teller. Despite the woman's refusal to communicate in English, Skyler kept asking: "Yangshuo?" "How much?" "Yang-*shuo*."

A Buddhist monk wearing a pollution mask offered to help, bought a ticket, and walked off, having successfully cut our travelers. No matter—watching the monk converse with the commie gave Skyler a full erection. See that grin, like a man in the back of a strip club, gin in hand, bar stool at a cool thirty degree angle, all the possible combinations of Communist-attired pollution-mask kinks rattling in his head.

Sophea, on the other hand, lost her shit. "That head-shaved bitch bought her own ticket!" She turned toward some old guy squatting in the street, picking his nose. Screamed: "What's wrong with you?!"

They left the line an hour later, tickets in hand.

"That was an adventure," Skyler said. "Part of travel."

"Our first quest," Sophea nodded. "And we smashed it."

Skyler the Summoner

Shat out of the bus station in Yangshuo, Sophea and Skyler wandered around West Street, the main drag, puncturing tourists out of their dizzying imperial fantasies with people-of-color sneers of disgust. They pursued a blonde shirtless American man unashamed of the Chinese calligraphy tattoos on his backside, dreaming in an iron bubble.

"We must break the demon's spell," Skyler whispered.

Sophea glided into the wretch at a convenience store corner. She chanted at him, holding a rolled up tourist map to his temple: "Forshame!"

"Hey there," The man-child said mid-chew. "Get a hold of

this petrified egg." He lifted a chestnut-brown egg as an offering. "Just bite into it. They soak this thing in *tea*!"

"Rang yi rang!" shouted another man accompanying this stoned tourist. This one: seemingly American, seemingly black. "Bu yao!" he shouted, shooing away an old hawker.

"You can speak Chinese?" Skyler said through his afternoon stubble.

Skyler and Sophea stared at the pair, suspicious of their own kind. Arthur, golden haired, tall, chin like ass-cheeks, a Chinese dragon tattooed on his cushiony arms. Winston, mixed race black of some sort, his hair a modest afro, his clothing smattered in Southeast Asian cultures: Thai elephants, Philippine flowers, Vietnamese-toned words. More Americans. It was like a homecoming. But also, noticing how easily Winston spoke Mandarin, our royal pair thought: No more of these Chinese lines.

So Sophea and Skyler recruited these other Americans, putting up with Arthur's morbidly exploitative senses-capes in exchange for Winston's old-China-hand expertise, his tongue going "click" for every word he did not know. Winston, for his part, was morbidly lonely, and he let them follow like lost calves.

Winston the mulatto expat, Sophea the artful smuggler, Arthur the hyper-real blonde, and Skyler the confused summoner of nothing in particular; together the four Americans took a six pm cowboy chap stroll through the fruit stalls around West Street. Winston's mouth ran in the ecstasy of meandarin, resolutely trilling the Beijing-accented "hard r" in every conversation as he copped a free "bonus" from a young female masseuse. Intrigued by "curiosity," the four travelers entered a small uninsulated house that perversely trapped heat like an oven. Attempting to forget the canopy of spider webs above, Skyler asked Winston where he was from.

"Lived in Singapore for a long time," he responded. "Lived in Thailand for over a year, and loved it, but the child prostitution killed it for me. One day I attacked a child molester on Soi Cowboy, beat him pretty bad, woke up in Thai jail and was told never to return. I can speak Thai near-fluently."

"We meant your race," Sophea clarified.

"A quarter Ghanaian, West Coast Africa by way of slave ships and rape-happy slave masters, another quarter Brazilian black by way of Spanish colonial rapists, then a fourth Japanese by way of forced occupation and systematic rape of local women—that was my grandmother, a Filipina comfort woman."

"I'm just white, by the way," Arthur snorted. "Plain boring vanilla bitch-ass white."

After the massage, our young gang strode up a stairway to Monkey Janes, a snazzy rooftop bar where foreigners and Chinese sat separately, casually insulting each other in their own language. Our four Anglophones settled in like band-mates on an album cover.

"I'm not gonna order anything," Arthur said, pulling a one dollar bottle of rice wine from his front pocket.

"American so cheap," a young woman uttered from a nearby couch.

Skyler folded his legs toward her and opened his arm in her direction, as if to spoon her. "I guess it was that micro-finance course I took at Oxford. I guess I'm just not used to being rich yet. My name is Richard, by the way."

"Yeah and my name is Scooby-Doo," Sophea said.

The woman burst into laughter, "why you wear a dress?"

"It fits into my backpack easier."

"Not normal in China. Why you travel here?" She didn't bother to explain why she was there.

"I have less privilege in China than in other Asian countries," Skyler said with a smirk. "Few people care about me. No special attention."

"I came to sit down," Sophea added.

"I'm here to find my ghost," Arthur said with a grave nod, capping his empty bottle of rice wine. "In Nanjing a ghost appeared to me. She was of some minority group here. She said the Han Chinese fucked her people up. Bad. Wanted me to go as far West as I could, to find her, and tell the world."

A silence breezed by.

"I came to hang out," Winston said.

"What is this about ghosts?" the woman asked. "You are searching for a ghost?"

Arthur continued his slow, gravitas-infused head nod.

"Wow." She shook a cigarette from its case. "I hate ghosts. You Americans must be brave." She landed the phrase with a drag.

"Hah!" Skyler sneered. "American men are *not* brave. They sit at computers and press buttons to send bombs and sit in front of TVs and say Mexicans do no work and sit in front of spouses and say oh me dick no working tonight. Fuck America, and fuck Americans!"

The third gendered summoner sipped from his gin and tonic, while the nearby Aussies, Europeans, and Chinese, waited for the other Americans to mount a defense. They didn't. In the after-pause, Skyler took his dress off, exposing swimming shorts and a tight white bra purchased from a convenience store. It wasn't an invitation—it was just that hot, even at night.

The lights flickered off and a red guard lookalike appeared in the bar's entrance, a woman impeccably coiffed with a straight pin on her tie and a curved hat poised at her ears. The officer cleared her throat as the other foreigners vacated to their hotel rooms. But not our fresh-faced Americans. She approached their immobile bodies, stone-faced to Skyler's gawking eyes, his bra, his unsolicited package. She asked in Mandarin where they came from. Winston responded that they were American students. She shook their hands—Skyler beholding her sexy black baton slung from her leather belt—before she smiled and left. The lights went back on.

Our four heroes felt un-intimidated. It suddenly occurred to them that, even in this totalitarian society, they could do anything they wanted.

In the mid-afternoon our four Americans rented bikes and rode out to Moon Hill, a small mountain with epic views of the Karst mountain peaks. The tribe trudged for an hour up the mountain staircase. At the peak Skyler stood in shock, staring at the sunlit countryside of stone hills like he was knifed. He took no pictures, just gaped in surrender at the daunting landscape.

"This isn't fair," he said to no one in particular. "These tourists did nothing to *earn* this. This is it. Right here. And none of us deserve it."

A Chinese tourist stared at him, befuddled. Winston translated Skyler's words best he could, and a woman laughed so hard she slapped her husband's arm bright red.

Winston the Pure

The next afternoon, Sophea, Skyler, and Arthur found Winston slowly stirring a cup of congee in one of the hostel's oval wooden lobby chairs.

"While you were all sleeping I fell in love," he said, eyes to the shiny wooden table. "Beautiful Chinese girl. Traveler from Shanghai. Crazy in love. We talked all afternoon. But—nothing. She wanted nothing to do with me. I think she just wanted to practice her English."

The three travelers huddled in a litter around Winston. "It's all right," one of them said, "we'll stick by you." "You're one of us." "You're heading to Kunming next, right?" "We're going that way too."

The three travelers smiled with the innocence of a tetherball strung around Winston's neck.

Breathe, Winston thought. *This is your travel karma.*

Winston shepherded our wayfaring heroes to Kunming where they stopped at a rooftop hot pot restaurant, "a traveler's institution," Winston explained. He asked the Indian waiter to throw in whatever he recommended. The waiter, dark skinned, loaded'em up with Halal goat—all except for Arthur the goddamn cheapskate, who was content chewing on a fifty-cent oatmeal bar and thieving an occasional munch from the family plates.

Winston practiced Mandarin with a woman seated near their table, her dark hair blazed with two green streaks, and her shirt decked in silver studs that made a skull. They fed each other questions about national beauty when she hit him with that familiar question: "ni de mama cong nali lai? Zhongguo ren ma?" (Where is your mom from? Is she Chinese?)

Winston smiled and didn't ask why the Asian in his genes had to be from his mother.

"Can I touch your hair?" the woman asked. Winston let her. *Plus travel karma.*

"So, you are all Americans?" The lady asked, moving her hand from Winston's hair to a disinfecting wipe to her mutton sandwich. "Why you all come here?" (never mind why she was there).

"I am a level three gender-bender," Skyler said, buffing his fingernails. "I'm trying to level up to four."

"Yeah, and I'm a level five necromancer," Arthur stated.

"Level twenty drug smuggler," said Sophea.

"I'm a level fifty flaneur," Winston said.

"What the shit is a flaneur?" Arthur asked just before stabbing a piece of goat meat with his chopstick.

"It's French," Winston brightened, finally on a somewhat intelligent subject. "It means travelers who *think*, who go through shops just to observe, who pierce through the social ignorance of our glorious empire."

The travelers looked at each other, crass smiles.

"Flaneur?" the woman said. "Sounds like rich man with too much time doing nothing."

After dinner our travelers stumbled upon a trendy night district encased in an aura of inebriation wrought by alcohol, cell-phone accessories, whatever-the-fuck-chemical-was-in-the-smog, and the stench of sewage seeping from an open manhole. See our posse frozen mid-stride, Winston whistling, Sophea dodging a bamboo pole, Arthur kicking water from a mud puddle, Skyler overlooking the sacred pose of a Chinese mother in a tight dress. Tipsy with the pithy presumptuousness of the traveling American, Winston waxed Arcades Project: "To be a flaneur means not making immediate judgments. You observe, try first to understand, and if you feel enough outside of yourself, then you start to empathize. Think beyond good and evil."

"Let's try it," Skyler suggested. "Let's be flaneurs."

They saw a small boy follow his mother with his hands under her skirt, his fingers latched onto her ass-cheeks.

"That is a child," Skyler said.

They saw a woman in a royal blue dress decorated in silver spherical ornaments spit sunflower seeds on the sidewalk.

She crunched slowly, snapping shells with a loud "CRAK."

"That is a seed," Sophea remarked.

They scuttled into a swampy fly-ridden market of pig heads and vegetable mountains. The stench made Arthur dry heave until he coughed out the remnants of his yogurt muesli. Winston said the sign in Chinese above the stall read "dog soup."

"That is not food," Arthur coughed. "That is shit."

"You are not being very *flaneur*," Winston scolded. "Wait, you never had dog?"

"Gawd no."

"Should we get it?" Skyler asked.

"No." Winston scoffed. "Dog is a *winter* delicacy."

Skyler nodded. "I get it now. The flaneur does not eat dog."

"Yes," Winston nodded. "Because it is not winter."

They paced silently through the night market, where Chinese folk turned toward Winston like proximity mines, trying to guess his race, their hands hovering above his thick hair. A young girl in all pink stared at him as she walked down a stairway, her eyes mesmerized at his sight. He smiled at her, showing geometrical white teeth, and she fell in a faint, her back slamming on a stone rail with a frighteningly loud snapping sound. As her family rushed to help her up, Winston squeezed the smooth wooden armrest of a park bench.

I made a little girl fall onto a stone rail. He felt his travel karma plummet.

Sophea the Sot

On the train to Dali, the ancient city of Chinese minorities, Sophea connected with her Chinese buyers: a man with a hat sporting the Apple logo, and a woman with long hair and a wavy dress. They sat together on a wide berth passing a round of baijiu, the get-drunk-off-your-ass-in-twenty-seconds-flat rice wine.

"You no Chinese, they no check," the woman told Sophea, her glasses nearly fallen from her nose. "We Chinese, they think—we go to Thailand, of course, must have drugs."

"So I've brought Thailand to you," Sophea said with a smile, handing the woman a black garbage bag of travel-sized pill cases.

"So where's the money?" Winston butt in, his legs cramped to his jaw in the small train seat. "I know how this goes down, ok fellas? We're no smuggling expat amateurs. I lived in Thailand too. Reaping the benefits of my blue passport. Teaching English for five times what a local would get, smuggling anti-depressants and painkillers into Singapore. And I lived *well*." He took a swig and passed the baijiu to Skyler.

"They paid by internet," Sophea said, baijiu still swishing.

"Rookie mistake!" Winston beat against his chest. "That's evidence."

"We run a hostel up north," the man said. He had at least ten years on the others, though he dressed the poorest, with a white polo and faded jeans. "We would love to host you tonight. My name is William, and this is Audrey. We appreciate the opportunity to use English with you." Before Winston could say no, Arthur threw a coughing fit.

"It's just allergies!" Arthur claimed, totally a lie. "Wow, you Chinese are really scared of sick people here, huh?" He scratched his growing beard, whispered, "so how do I tell them I probably have the flu?"

"Or that those pills are mostly aspirin?" Sophea whispered.

Images of Time Magazine covers announcing China's latest humanitarian atrocity flashed before our heroes' minds.

"We accept," Skyler announced, going all-in on the theory that when you die your clearest memories will be your deepest regrets.

The hostel owners spirited our heroes from the train station to an old Daoist temple bordering Erhai, an ear-shaped lake. Jasmine flowers adorned the pillars overlooking the water. Our heroes paced up the temple's five-storied pagoda, every step croaking beneath them. Expecting a police raid, or a triad-style ambush complete with gung-fu pistol whipping, our sojourners instead discovered hordes of gigantic spiders staring at them with their militant eight-eyes. They walked carefully with hands held behind their backs, ducking beneath thick taught webs and biting their tongues from pointing out the absurd Oh-faces on the angry god statues. At the temple's shrine, William's legs stuck out in the sunlight like two fat logs.

Audrey chuckled. "William, he prays for a son."

"See," Winston gave a loud whisper, arms akimbo to the Dao gods. "It's always like this with Chinese. Long life, health, reproduction."

"You are trying for a child?" Sophea asked Audrey.

"No!" she spurted, fiddling with a toothpick in her mouth. "William is my brother! And he has no girlfriend. Chinese girls don't like him. Too short."

"Girls like strong guys?" Sophea asked.

"Ew, no," she stuck her tongue out in disgust. "We like skinny, tall, white skin. White skin is most important. It makes up for the other two."

"All over the world." Sophea stepped over the wooden banister into the temple and kneeled next to William to pray.

"Ugh, another religious kook," Winston commented, keeping his cynical flaneur-distance.

Though there was a million things on her mind, Sophea couldn't think of a thing to pray for. She plopped onto the weathered wood, her feet facing the angry god. Her eyes followed the broken planks to the blue lake. Near the shore, a duck fluttered within the reeds, struggling to swallow a large fish. A fisherman's iron ring tightened the creature's neck, bracing its throat.

Arthur, Witch Slayer

The next day the Chinese buyers traipsed our heroes off to Lijiang, that backpacker's paradise full of consumable ethnicities. Along the way, Arthur, whose ill enervation had caused his body to take on the form of white pus, spent the entire bus ride coughing out phlegm and hawking loogies into a plastic bag. As soon as the van arrived at Lijiang's north gate, the new Chinese friends, an assured distance from our heroes, waved a "this-is-forever" kind of goodbye.

Our Americans ventured out into the old rainy city, inventing new words to cope with the slippery streets: "sliptastic," "slippage," "slipgasim." And since Arthur had infected the gang with his flu, they trudged through Lijiang's ancient city like old men, their heads bent over in stupidly nauseous gasps. Trundling along the city's hazardous stone steps, they collapsed at a karaoke bar. A pair of waiters fetched cold brew and our heroes rehashed their progress.

"This is my third time here," Winston said. "Gets worse and worse. Ten years it'll be the next Bangkok."

"We gotta get a move on," Arthur sputtered with the haste of a day-trip tourist. "I'm running low on cash."

"Are we in pursuit, or in flight?" Winston asked. "What's the game here?"

"In Laos I was runnin' low on cash too," Skyler slurred, holding a pillow to his stomach. "So I just prostituted myself."

"You must have elevation sickness," Winston finagled some aspirin and anti-histamine from his bag. "It's common given Lijiang's 2,400 meter elevation."

"And this is what can happen with elevation sickness?" Sophea asked. "Spontaneous honesty?"

Skyler consumed the pills rapidly and slurped some "over-the-bridge" noodles.

"The ghost spirit who called me here was a prostitute," Arthur said gravely, also infected with the blight of elevation.

"Made so by the Han Chinese who killed her. I fucking hate these Han Chinese. Look at how they parade their minorities around. It's in-humanity-arian!" His eyelids squeezed tight as he endured a screaming headache.

Skyler appeared on stage, his black dress patched in brown dust, a silk black tie somehow roped around his neck in a perfect Prince Albert knot. He sang: "I wanna feel the heat with some-bo-dy!"

"I am not enjoying China," Sophea said, catching herself imagining Skyler singing just for her. "I have a half dozen bottles left. I say we find a buyer and skedaddle."

"And what in fuck's kingdom are we selling?" Arthur asked.

"Let me guess," said Winston. "opioid painkillers. Codeine, or maybe something harder, if you're suicidal."

"I am. We are."

"I hate Asia!" Arthur sobbed. "I'm so much more comfortable with Caucasian people. What the fuck am I doing here? I just want to find her." His sniveling took on the strangely primordial sound of an amphibious dinosaur chewing on its young. Before Winston could call him a racist idiot, Arthur lurched back, coughed hard into his arm, and hawked a loogie onto the ground. His body lunged to the stage as his hand shot up for karaoke. He ordered a familiar American song to twist the words:

America,

I gave my heart and soul to you, girl

Didn't I give it baby ... Didn't I give it bay—aby!

Did everything I was supposed to do girl,

Didn't I do it baby ... Didn't I love you bay-aby!

I've pledged every day to you and that's no lie

It seems to make you laugh each time I cry

Didn't I blow your mind this time, didn't I? Oh!

Didn't I leave your ass this time, didn't I?

Oh! Oh! Oh! I got to live, baby! Oh! Oh! Oh!

With that, Arthur performed an exile's mic drop, juggling the cord like a yo-yo before nunchuck-whipping it into a half-full jug of beer.

To the West

After three days of incubation in their hostel bunk-beds, our heroes returned to daylight to find that their clothes, left to dry, had molded after being left in the rain. They abandoned their attire to catch a tourist bus.

"Where we want to go?" Winston asked in the tourist line.

Arthur pointed at the sky, at an airplane scudding over a horizon of wedged peaks. "That direction."

Hours later, our pilgrims gazed at the rural scenery outside a bus hugging the Yunnan mountainside.

"Shit!" Sophea shouted, stunned by the view of a waterfall bursting through a mountain, an abscess spilling into a river valley. The bus careered above the village, hills, and rivers below. Arthur's camera went "click-click-click" in a typewriter's rapid tat-tat-tat.

A tunnel's darkness blanketed our pilgrims. They burst back into the sunlight at full speed, the mountains staring them down, propelling them through different moments in history. Then a dark tunnel. Darkness fogged the air. Then back out, gunning it through mist hovering over lakes, past tall bare mountains silhouetted like abandoned ghosts pleading.

Then into a tunnel.

The bus of tourists stared at the scenery for hours, mesmerized by it: the fleeting, infinite beauty of it. Temples to unvanquished gods flew by like polygon jets. Arthur, equipped only with his Canon digital camera, could not shoot them all. He pushed his camera lens onto the window to focus on the foliage and not the glass stains. He wrapped his hands around the camera's edges to keep out the glare. When they entered another tunnel he cycled through old pictures, freeing up space to make room for the next barrage of beauty.

When dusk approached, golden sunlight revealed a waterfall below them, its thick cascade pouring like tea from a kettle into a vertigo-inducing drop. Passengers screamed "oh!" as if they had just gotten a glimpse of the afterlife. But Arthur's camera missed it.

"God damn it!" Arthur screamed. "It's that god damn glare. Winston!"

Comfortable in his VIP reclined chair, Winston adjusted his reading light.

The full moon kept the mountains alive and contemplative. Our heroes stared back, safe in their rumbling beast.

The moonlight shimmered off the river below like the Milky Way; streams above and rivers below. And the beauty. It never stopped. The boundless beauty. Is this what if felt like to be a river? they wondered. Molecules jetting among the fish and algae. Just moving along, soaked in an endless splendor.

"I've run out of room for pictures," Arthur said, eyes tired but still staring.

"What the hell are we doing here?" Sophea asked, wiping beads of sweat. "What is this?"

"We're flaneurs," Skyler said.

"You can't just make up a word and say it's *us,*" Sophea snapped. "Dumb shithead."

"Are you *reading*?!" Arthur shouted at Winston. The man remained supine in his bunk, his window covered with a mesh curtain. "Have you looked outside *once*?"

"Don't get me started," Winston flipped to the next page of *Beyond Good and Evil.* "A waterfall is just a big faucet. You've seen one, you've seen'em all."

Filled with the unfocused energy of China's countryside splendor, Arthur slapped the book from Winston's hands, opened his curtain and pointed toward the river far below, sparkling in the glimmer of a white moon. "Confront the beauty, Winston! You may never see it again!"

"I've seen it all!" Winston shouted, his voice cracking as he drew the curtain closed. "Where have you traveled, Arthur? You travel just to find some ghost whose language you can't even understand. What about your son, huh?! What about your wife? It's all about this ghost until you get drunk, then it's all about your wife who abandoned you. Don't tell me what to do. I'm just your translator, remember? So go do what you do, let me do what I do."

The bus drifted along, the engine barely noticeable on a downward slope. A blanket-covered woman wrestled in her chair, half-asleep.

"I don't care!" Arthur screeched, standing. "You must see this!" He lifted Winston out of the bunk with the strength of ancestral spirits seeking their due reverence. "You going to sue me?" The half-awake passengers watched silently as Arthur dragged Winston off his bed and into the aisle, toward the front of the bus.

"Bad monkey!" Winston shouted, then in Chinese: "Huai huozi! Huai huozi!"

"Help our master, friends!" Arthur yawped, hailing the other disciples, Skyler the porcine pervert and Sophea the pugnacious Naga. Together they hauled Winston into the front passenger seat near the sedated bus driver and pressed his face against the windshield. "You can hate us," Arthur screeched, simian teeth bared, "but you are going to look at this—*look at this*!"

Face smashed against the cold window, Winston felt the engine's chugging vibration as the bus rolled uphill. He resisted at first, but his eyes couldn't help meet the dark fogged valley, flushed with the luminosity of a full moon. A flood slowly filled him. The river below infused him with a bold energy, but the disciples kept his body paralyzed in place. He was floating in space, watching the world, the cosmos, in that river. The flaneurs saw it too: the sinking, the gasping, the drowning. The loneliness of the stark moonlight and the terror of the mountain and the crusading water, thinking: there's just too much there's just too much there's just too much.

And went into a tunnel.

Kawika the Princess

Once landed in Chengdu, our heroes headed straight to "Bar Street," where women feigned crying to lure customers inside. Adorned with beer logo stickers, the workers balled into their hands dramatically, pleading for an intoxicated savior. Each bar catered to only one type of beer. All Budweiser bars, all Coors bars. Different levels of hell. Arthur relented and ordered a warm Coors.

The flaneurs followed Bar Street as it stretched along a riverside arcade of boutique shops. They took long carefree strides across the boardwalk. Sophea sweat; Winston whistled; Arthur picture snapped; Skyler mused, hands behind his back. Gallantly they protected the purity of their wallets from the touts, until Skyler disappeared into a boutique and emerged in transformed attire: a daring red brocade cheongsam imprinted with scaly gold dragons.

"Needs makeup," Arthur said.

"And tits," Winston commented.

"Hot," Sophea sweated.

"Can flaneurs be princesses too?" Kawika said. She spun in place, hovering upon red floral heels, the nothing-in-particular summoned forth to play.

An endearing musical-number-like joy rang when our heroes found a bar selling an array of international beers: Beerlao (dark and light!), Taiwan Beer, and Japanese brown ales. Caught in the euphoria of inter-Asian taste, they smiled at the expat customers giving them those "you-American-idiots-invading-Iraq" glares. Hero Arthur felt swayed by the pool sticks held by two blithe Chinese women dressed in see-through red dresses. "Hey, little cuties," he said. "Who's winning?"

They smiled at him, long habituated to sex-tourist speak. He leaned into them, eyes a-shimmering.

"China would be wonderful it if weren't for all the Chinese people," a voice said. "Rude, intolerant people can ruin a travel experience." This gentlemanly voice came from a table of four men playing cards. Threadbare sports jackets. Boyish conceit. Slovenly tilted barstools at an uncool forty-degree angle. Crapulous railings of first world conceit.

"I know them," Kawika said in her light femme voice. "The blight of flaneurs everywhere."

The men had found new uses for their shoes: beer-mugs. The game they played was simple—whoever had the lowest numbered card had to drink from their shoe.

"I know them too," Winston said. "The only thing worse than a racist expat."

"A *drunk* racist expat," Arthur said.

"D-R-Es!" Kawika added with amusement, adjusting her Mandarin collar.

"They're all over Cambodia and Thailand too," Sophea sneered. "They do anything they want. They call themselves minorities."

Our heroes gravitated to the bar, giving light conversation to the pigtailed barkeep who homed in on mosquitos with an electric fly swatter. But our heroes' dandified modesty—as well as Kawika's skin-tight qipao—gave them away in an instant.

"Americans," one of the DREs grumbled before slapping down another card and sipping Carlsberg from his white Nike.

Protected by their flaneur coolness, our heroes chatted among bottles of Tsingtao beer, all the while listening to the DREs who sat only two tables away:

"Where do you think his balls went?"

"Little faggot."

"Don't let him cough on you, you'll get his AIDS."

Flaneur observation: Things are escalating.

"That's why the Muslims are dominating the world!" One of the DREs shouted, mop of red hair, sports-team polo shirt. "Fags too busy playing dress-up to go all the way. That's why they failed in Vietnam. Too light-hearted. No *pride* in your Empire!"

Our heroes, steadfast to let the DRE world sluice by without comment, could not help but listen and remain, knowing they should have left for their air conditioned bunk-beds. But such was the flaneur. Unwilling to will something anew; too curious to leave it alone.

"Forshame!!!"

The mop-headed DRE stood up just as Hero Sophea, worked into a righteous fury, popped him across the face with the electric fly swatter. Sparks ignited the man's fuzzy boy beard.

"Down goes Kangaroo Jack!" Arthur cheered.

A chair rocketed into the bar. It ricocheted off Arthur's leg. Our hero fell, mad with laughter.

"Forshaaame!" Sophea flipped the blighted DRE table, spilling shoe-sized amounts of beer onto the floor. Kawika closed her hand-sized mirror and scurried off. Winston grabbed one of the DREs mid-punch and tossed him in a cartwheel right into the bar's edge. A rack of decorative beer bottles crashed to the ground in lightning cracks.

"Stop! Bie luan!" a voice yelled—a cute commie security guard with a bludgeon.

Our heroes made a hasty retreat, following Kawika through the kitchen and up to the bar's second floor, a maze of small massage rooms. They bolted from room-to-room, bounding over scantily-clad women chewing betel nuts. Arthur laughed, hopping on one leg with Winston supporting him, and fell giggling onto the white sheets of a dank laundry room.

"I left my backpack down there," Sophea said. She left, then re-entered moments later. "Yup, whoops."

Arthur: "Come again?"

And Sophea: "They got it. The stash."

Silence.

"This might not be good."

"Huh?"

"I mean we could be in trouble."

"Right."

"I mean, shit, there's, like, a shit ton of illegal drugs down there."

"Ok."

"The cops will be here, I guess."

"Ah."

Unable to register panic in a land of unchecked impunity, our heroes looked to Winston with that hey-you-know-something-about-China look.

"I—I've never been here before," Winston stammered. "What do we do?"

"Run?" Kawika suggested. After a pause, she clanged her silver rings against the washing machine. "I said run, you fucking cucks! *Run!*"

A Kingdom Restored

Serried lines of clouds hovered outside Chengdu airport's massive windows. Cumulus clouds, like a white army holding off our heroes' escape. Skyler paced about the airport windows, smoothing the dirt off his black dress. He turned to the flaneurs loafing on cushy airport massage chairs, each with Starbucks drinks in their hands.

"My friend Melanie said there was *one* job opening at the English school," Winston said, his legs splayed out from his shiny seat. "No guarantee any of you will find work."

An announcement reminded them that their flight to Manila would begin boarding in fifteen minutes.

"Come on," Sophea said, "I've known the worst fuck-ups ever who still got jobs teaching English in Asia. And made pretty well doin' it too. It ain't hard. No degree? Use photoshop."

"And besides my credit cards, I'm flat broke," Arthur said. "Your parents got a condo, right? Just sittin' there, unused, while the unwashed masses gawk in disgust."

An airplane circled in, nearly diving into one of the surrounding hillsides. Skyler could hear the hungry slurping of the passengers onboard.

"One week," Winston said, bright-eyed. "But I'll take you all around Manila. My city. The nightlife especially. Man, party every night. They all speak English, and watch American cinema. Easiest country in the world for an American."

Skyler turned to his friends, freeze-framing them in his mind. Sophea arched sideways in her chair, eyes on the ceiling, the bones of a spicy chicken foot degrading in her mouth, her legs folded over Winston's lap, her shins supporting his laptop; Winston's fingers tapping on her ankle, unable to sit still until he was well out of Chinese airspace; Arthur pouring over a newspaper, driven perhaps by a clue to the whereabouts of his ghost, or his wife, or some new unmarked territory. Without discussion, they stayed together. Were they a family? A traveling cadre? Executors for each other's last will and testament? When Skyler was older, having breezed in and out of so many places, would he still remember their names? Or would they, in their aging years, high on their own supply, gather around a hearth at some beachside resort, and recall this moment: "Remember guys, that first time we met?" "I'm still trying to forget." "Wow, all that mayhem we left in Yunnan." "Ha! We were such irresponsible assholes, weren't we?"

Two uncrushable men, thick and stone-faced with McDonald's bags in their hands, took their seats behind the flaneurs. American soldiers, going to their military bases.

Skyler turned to the window again. A red-striped jet brought another megalomaniac. Another airplane. Another bus. Skyler found himself short of breath, agony leaching onto his throat. He sensed something back there hiding, calculating. In the sky, the airplanes were vultures circling an injured beast, descending upon it one by one, ruthlessly snipping at its meaty arms and thighs, never going for the jugular, because to end its suffering would mean losing out on an exotic feast.

Skyler fell to his knees, arms heavy on the stiff carpet. There was no border strong enough to hold them. No screams of death loud enough to keep them at bay. They just sat and snacked, dipping bunches of french fries in sweet ketchup, saying "chink" like they were in Nam, arguing for the lowest price for the highest girl, loving Asia because you didn't have to tip, learn the language, or give a flying fuck. Like demigods they rode roughshod over Asia, ransacking cities, claiming the colonial inheritance left to them and their mixed race offspring.

Our heroes gathered around him. Skyler's face resembled the horror he felt; his eyes tilted into his head like a sleeping alligator; his lips sagged. A man slowly drowned, a woman awake to the terror.

"We are leaving, aren't we?"

"Right Skyler. We're going right now."

"We're leaving here."

"And going there."

"But what if—what if there is just the here-to-be?"

TWO

Ressentiment

ThinkTravel! Blogbook

Post Date: 2007 SEPT 12

User: SkyFaralan

For nightlife in Manila, the Guidebook insists upon "going to streets parallel to P. Burgos Street," but says nothing of the street itself. It then suggests bars "for anyone needing to escape the debauchery of nearby P. Burgos Street," and advises the traveler "not have too many drinks or you may do something you regret in nearby P. Burgos street."

Nothing seems more tempting now than P. Burgos Street. You seek it out in a crowded jeepney as you nervously hand change to the other passengers to hand up to the driver, who is accompanied by a Filipina knockout.

You disembark the jeepney and male sex workers rush you, all speaking English. One of them has muscles that make his tank top look like a thong. They ruthlessly follow you through bars, clubs, and cafes.

"Don't say queer or gay," the one with a mole on his upper lip says. "We are homos!" the man then spends fifteen minutes ranting about the HIV signs posted around the bars and clubs, which describe the disease as something you can inhale. He is Patrick, a bioethicist who was invited to attend Columbia University, but refused to live in the very country that colonized his people. He tells you about his work with Cambodian sex workers, how they have become experimental bodies for medical corporations, and that these corporations refuse to even acknowledge the side-effects of their drugs when these anonymous bodies begin to decay. Then, keeping up with your

*long striding walk, Patrick asks why America is so homopho-
bic.*

"They're not."

"Look at you, so American!"

*After a week in Manila you have done nothing but read books
at stations and coffee shops. Bored, you start photographing
the boredom: the Embassy clerk who delayed you another day,
the malfunctioning ATM machine, the pay phone where you
spent hours attempting to catch a flight, the woman asking for
change while holding a very cute light-skinned baby.*

*Meanwhile, the mall nearby your hostel gets bombed. Another
irritation, more delayed flights.*

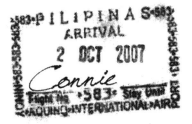

Connie saw her people emerge from gate C14. Four college-age women wearing full survival gear: khaki shorts, hats with webbed mosquito nets that bunched from the hairline, and tan jackets that announced their nationality in a red, punctuated English: KOREAN. Connie had waited two hours for their arrival from Cebu City to the Manila airport, yet the group walked right past her, not recognizing her in her black T-shirt and black jeans, her darker skin and curly hair, with no sign proclaiming her nationality. Perhaps they forgot she was one of them.

Unsure how to announce her presence, Connie followed the group past the Chinese mascots of the dim sum carts to the passport check line. She approached them and whispered "hey fellas," then lurched back to prepare for the oncoming hugs and laughter. It wasn't pleasant. For the past two weeks, the group had all been to the other half, to a land of mosquitos, charred pork, stomach flus and cold showers. And all of that seemed present when Connie felt their embrace, but only for a moment, before they went back to the line and she was again that awkward Korean American English teacher dressed in all black. She held her friend Chun Hye's hand, eyeing those legs that shot down from her hot-pants like Grecian pillars. Chun Hye's skill with an umbrella was remarkable. Two weeks in the Philippine summer and not a hint of sun on her body.

"Look what I found in the duty-free shop," Chun Hye said in Korean, pointing her chin at a sparkling pink striped skin on her phone.

"Changmal Jamie issoyo"—*Way interesting*—Connie said.

Outside, the tropical heat reminded them they were still in the third world. The four girls latched onto Connie through the English-speaking maze and into a yellow taxi. After three years of traveling in Asia, she was the natural choice to lead the group's three-day expedition into Manila. For her, the smell of gasoline, the sweltering heat, and the sound of car horns, did not rouse the same fears of an unknown world ridden with poverty and brown bodies.

She squeezed next to Chun Hye in a taxi's back seat, feeling her celadon green blouse rubbing against her arm. Chun Hye smiled like a model, though she must have also heard the constant wail of car horns, must have also seen the same underwear hanging on clotheslines, the same black puddles on the street that children played in, the same cartoonish Virgin Marys on passing jeepneys. Connie nudged closer into Chun Hye's warmth, though her face seemed cold. She moved her hand to grope Chun Hye's gorgeous ass, an ass that never went appreciated by her Korean boyfriend, an ass Chun Hye herself never acknowledged until Connie commented on it, then took her into the Philippine coffee fields to bite it, lick it, and henceforth take every opportunity to squeeze it. But now, away from the fields, Chun Hye was unresponsive, as if she had landed into a different body.

"Is that a Louis Vuitton!?" Chun Hye exclaimed, tossing her right leg over Connie's left, anchoring herself to peer out the window. She whispered something to the other girls, something fashion related, which Connie, in her black jeans and tank top, apparently didn't need to hear.

Dropped off in Ermita, Connie maneuvered the four girls through the sizzling-hot streets, between groups of tourist men crowding every outdoor bar. The hostel she had reserved for them, the Malate Pensionne, was an old wooden building that had no air conditioning, but did have a Starbucks melded next to its front door like a prosthetic appendage. When the group gave frightened faces, she only tried to talk Chun Hye into staying. Using their smartphones, the young women reserved a room at the nearby Pan Pacific hotel, a $200-a-night tower of cosmopolitan chic.

As the only one among them without parental funding, Connie spent the night bunking next to two Korean men in a humid room full of hanging wet clothes, which would never dry in the dank urban tropic. She couldn't help but cry, alone, covered in sweat, inhaling the mildew-thick air, her wrist itching from the blue, red, and white beads that made a bracelet. The leathery strings were made by hand by Rowena, a village girl in Negros. It was supposed to remind Connie of the Taekwondo, ESL, and painting classes Connie had taught the village children, as well as those authentic Filipino meals, her hosts the de Asis, the summer camp sites, the horror of mosquitos. And the wristband was at least one material object to show for the $1,500 USD that it cost to volunteer. Plus, the band was knotted so well that Connie hadn't been able to take it off. It didn't matter. She had told Rowena that she would wear the bracelet forever, so it might as well last another week.

Robinson's Place

Even at ten in the morning, the streets were scorching hot. Connie walked north through the balmy sunlight to join her group's tour of Rizal Park and Intramuros, the old Spanish garrison. After only two blocks, she ditched the whole tour idea, seduced by an eddy of air conditioning coming from the Robinson's Place Mall. She had enough culture for a lifetime, she thought, and enough heat in the villages. But AC was here, and it was now.

The female security guard checked inside Connie's small black backpack and then examined her crotch and chest with the same unflinching curiosity, going way beyond a simple pat-down. Connie felt a spur of embarrassment as those plastic gloves groped her body, putting her on exhibition for the awaiting crowd. The guard even gave her a "that was good for me too" backslap as she stumbled through the entrance doorway. Perhaps the woman has a thing for young Korean girls, Connie thought, as she restrapped her bag. Or a thing for Korean Americans who looked Filipino.

She slid past hand-in-hand shoppers, through the serpentine hallways, with no goal in mind other than to stay near air conditioning. In Korea she avoided malls at all costs, easily overwhelmed by the noise, the ads, the untampered cloning process. And this mall was even more confusing, layered in five floors of added-on extensions like an underwater reef emitting a light-yellow haze that left Connie so disoriented she found herself circling time and again to the same female guard who had molested her.

She found herself in a Jollibee, the most American of the Filipino fast food stands.

"I receive two-hundred pesos" the cashier said, ending the word 'pesos' with an upward slant that soon divulged into a grinding sound, like a tuba wavering to hit an erring note. Compared to the mush of gigantic peppers and pork she had eaten every day in Negros, the Jollibee hamburger tasted magical.

With no goal but to stay near air con, Connie followed the blue stripes on the floor and paced through the mall's tug of smells: the shaobao carts, the sprayed shoe stands, the ground coffee beans. Her legs moved mechanically, letting the stripes pull her like a shoe on a conveyor belt. She felt the shape-shifting of every advertisement turning her body into fragments lacking accessories, each unringed finger now empty of life and value. She felt advertisements tempting her, calling her toward the manikins wearing bright pink heels, the ice cream carts barnacled with young people. She let the ads of sexy mestizo models and over-joyous middle-class families tweak her mind, beckoning her to shift and shape each undesirable piece of her body into some recognizable form. The cosmopolitan mall spat her through the cosmopolitan world: worldly films, worldly books, worldly music, worldly cuisines. The stores carried the same myths in Robinson's as they did everywhere. For the first time, she did not mind all this adjusting. In fact, after two weeks in an unforgivably materialless island, she thought it rapturous.

At the end of the blue line, she found herself in a circular courtyard and short of breath. She walked clumsily, as if she had just gotten face, until she got a clear view of an enormous banner that spanned all five stories. Like a gigantic flag the banner flapped in the mall's air conditioning, advertising some skin lightening cream with actors eyeballing each other like in a daytime opera. The Filipino models looked nothing like the villagers of Negros. Their combed hair, their pristine light skin, their jubilant expressions. Nothing about them seemed Filipino.

A young hipsterish mestiza woman passed, around the same age as Connie, attired in a short form-fitting red dress and shiny red heels. She was trailed by her maid, a whole head shorter than her and several shades darker, loaded down with shopping bags. In the reflection of a store window Connie saw her own wafer-thin figure that men liked to call petite, her sinewy legs, her flip-flops. Her prom was the only time she had ever worn heels, and she had the concussion to prove it.

At some point Connie sat down, exhausted, slurping up a mixed fruit smoothie. Its colors matched the beads on her wristband. Blue, red, and white.

"Oh god dammit," Connie said to herself, realizing that the colors on her wrist matched a certain flag's. "*That's* embarrassing." Hopefully, she thought, that wasn't intentional.

In sugar-high bliss, Connie breathed in the air conditioning, which spat directly on her with a loud whirring sound, freezing the heat off. Heat: the swampy soil of Negroes, the dark tan that, back in Korea, would stir ridicule. She longed to get rid of it, the wretched heat of that long grass field where she taught English to children who sat with their legs pointed out at her. There had sat Chun Hye, holding Rowena in her arms like she was their daughter, looking so motherly under her yellow parasol. And Rowena, with her short unwashed hair, her loose hanging blue tank top that kept falling off.

"Happy anniversary," Connie had said, slowly so the Negros children could pick up her American accent.

"An-e-vur-sir-i," Chun Hye repeated, sitting on her folded legs, just like Connie had taught her.

Connie liked teaching English, and saw it as a promising career option, though she often felt like a low-paid babysitter. Language was a powerful gift. Speaking Korean, too, had a useful distancing to it; she could mean something entirely different than her words. When she and Chun Hye prepared for bed in the village dorm room, she would tell her, "hand me a comb," in Korean, "gae bijoosae." For Connie, *run away with me.* "Let me use your lotion," she would tell Chun Hye, "lotion saung," meaning, *Please, please leave your pissant boyfriend already.*

Connie paused and found herself, for the first time, in a Victoria's Secret. She felt the shop clerk's eyes assess her. Certainly, she was a fake. Fashion stores were museums to her. She fidgeted with a bra and sniffed its material like it was an artifact. She checked a lingerie tag not for its size, but for the place it was manufactured. "What are you looking for?" the store clerk asked. *What business do you have in this place? This space where everyone and no one is welcome.* The store clerk could see it instantly, in Connie's muddled hair, her black clothes and colorless face. She was looking for nothing.

Outside, the setting sun cast blocked shadows from the tall hotels that made sharp bars across a massive five-lane highway. Hundreds of dwellers sat watching advertisements streak across the block-wide, five-story mall. Walking toward her hostel, jeepneys and panhandlers pushed her further into the road's gutters, then drove her into an outdoor bar populated with white tattooed men and their Filipinas.

The girls were not much to look at, all got up in sparkling skirts and aqua eye shadow. Connie thought that if she too was male, white, and wealthy, she could do much better. At the sight of a cantankerous old vet, she dove into a seat next to a younger, 20-something crowd of expats.

"Mind if I join you?" she asked.

"Coma esta po kayo?" said one, a young black man with sunglasses, his thick hair blown up in shotgun-riding glitz.

"This idiot speaks English," said another traveler, a young woman with blonde hair woven around her head like a straw basket.

"He's just a fake Filipino, not like me," said a dark rail-thin kid wearing a black garment—Connie had to lean in to see it was a dress, reaching just below the boy's knees.

"You're a fake *everything*, Skyler," said the girl at the table's end, surrounded by empty bottles.

Just Connie's luck—American travelers. Or worse, expatriates. For the past three years, Connie had gone to telling lengths to avoid their kind in Seoul. Whenever she did catch up with an English-speaker, they turned her into the trusted Korean representative, invited only to translate pickup lines and sing Korean karaoke ballads while they slam-dunked tequila.

"I'm Skyler," the dress-wearing boy said. "The nice one is Melanie, the crabby one is Winston, and the worst one is Sophea. Let me guess, you're Fil-Am, am I right?" He pointed at her with a beer bottle, meaning Filipino American.

Connie nodded. Why not? Let's see how far this all went.

"Ah, a homeland returnee," Winston said, jamming a fork into his chicken sisig. "I did all that when I was your age." He fidgeted, wiping condensation from a beer bottle. "I bet you wouldn't believe I'm half Japanese." He went on with the same expat story that Connie had heard in her travels around Thailand and Burma. All American expats, it seemed, were bitter, bent on escape, and had come to agree with the rest of the world that their countrymen were simple-minded, and that's why they always preferred war over peace.

"What the fuck are you jabbering about?" said another traveler, a white guy in a marijuana-leaf tank top who appeared just behind Connie. "Wait, let me guess. These two dickheads are spouting some nonsense about being a tight-knit traveling commune of American flaneurs, coercing this poor Filipina with promises of things to come."

"No," Connie said, moving her chair back to keep her eyes on his hands. "I was promised cookies."

"Huh," the man said. "You mean nookie. That's the real reason anyone comes here."

"Don't be a perv Arthur!" Melanie said, slapping his arm with her jeweled fingers.

"You know where I just came from?" Arthur said, plopping down in a plastic chair. "I followed those Christmas-light cords on the next street, and guess what I discovered? Bunches of whores, decorating the sidewalk like tinsel. I walked along, expecting the usual call-outs, and guess what? We Americans are the lowest priority. *Lowest*, that's how far the West has fallen. Prozzies were all wooing people from the street, first with 'summemassang!' for the Japanese clients. Then 'Annyong Hasseyo!' for the

Koreans. Then 'Ni how ma!' for the Hong Kong and Tai-wanese. Only after these failed did they even look my way and revert to that old-fashioned language, English: 'Hello, how are you! Come here beautiful boy!'"

"It must be really weird for you," Sophea said bluntly. "Not being the only imperial asshole."

The group burst into peals of laughter, and Connie with them, infected with their gleeful immaturity. After a moment of beer sips and noshes of pork kebab, Skyler, unprompted, explained how they came to travel together: "Sophea here left the States to be an NGO do-gooder. Melanie just loves the food, what can I say. This guy Arthur saw a ghost, and he's been Eat-Pray-Loving his way to find her. Ok, then piece-of-shit, Winston, grew up on army bases so he's the traveling native. And me, well, I was in a religious family. Fucking insanely religious. Like, gay-people-invented-all-diseases type of religious. No need to say why I came out all mixed up."

Connie noticed Skyler spoke with a slight lilt, femme but still boyish. She felt tempted to ask him what he thought he was. But being asked was probably exactly what he wanted, a trap he let out just to see who would trip it. She went for a safer question: "So what do you all do now?"

"Not a damn thing," Sophea said, her applied purple hair streak crossing her right eye.

"*I* do something," Winston said. "I own a pearl business, I make a great deal of money. I own a goddamn condo in Makati. I'm supporting these assholes until they move on."

"He's basically our pimp," Skyler added.

The subject of money turned the air static, and Connie saw that it was her turn to explain herself. She tried to remember why she left Kansas City, but she couldn't even begin to describe the bitterness. Was it her first love that made her leave? A girl who drew Yaoi comics with her, who loved but wasn't in love with Connie, and who, out of the blue, announced she was dating a man with bulging muscles? Or was it good old fashioned racism? The kind she discovered when she started banging on drum sets, making noise from the break up rage, a Korean adoptee now permitted to hit stuff, only to find that the rage she felt went way beyond her ex—it was in her face, her hair, her entire projection. One day, it just occurred to her that getting out of Kansas City wasn't enough. Not the city, not the state, but that entire forsaken continent.

"It was all the whiteys," Connie said, hoping that would be enough. Like good travelers, the others knew not to inquire further. Instead they watched a Filipino singer rap an Outkast song.

"That guy sounds ridiculously black," Arthur commented, open-mouthed. "Like, way fucking blacker than you, Winston."

"It is a tad unnerving," Winston said.

"Eminem is very good," Melanie said with a sigh, "but I just don't get hip hop."

Legs shifted in discomfort.

"Ok Why?" Winston asked.

"I don't know," Melanie shrugged. "It just ain't real music, you know?"

This set off a grand inquisition. Suddenly the group, Connie included, wanted to know all of her prejudices. The blonde girl from the American South was a fascination, the most American of them all, a reminder of why they left.

"I ain't a racist!" Melanie cried out, finally catching on.

"It's just their culture, right?" Sophea said accusingly.

Connie thought of the villagers on Negros. Dark skinned, darker than most black people back home. And those villages—only foreigners called them villages. They were small decrepit towns of farmers and decayed work houses, just like the towns she grew up in. All those economic reasons for migration. The years of bouncing around shitty small towns to even shittier small towns, holding her backpack in the back of her father's beat-up sedan, with its check engine light that had been on for years. She was born itinerant, meandering among towns that looked like they had been ripped from depression-era photographs. Just like the village.

Negros? she thought. What a strange name for an island of sugar pickers and dark-skinned debt slaves. Had life overseas made her that blind?

Someone nudged her shoulder. "Too many whiteys in the Philippines, am I right?" Arthur said, shaking his head.

The Mall of Asia

The next day Connie skipped breakfast, her throat retching from the dank air of the hostel room and the oozy Jollibee mayonnaise. She rode a tour bus with her volunteer group, letting Chun Hye sit two rows ahead, squeezed in with the other three even though the bus was only half full. When the bus arrived at the Cultural Center Museum, Connie told the young boy sitting next to her that this was the place where Imelda Marcos allowed dozens of Filipino workers to be crushed and suffocated by concrete.

The boy took a picture of the gray building with his disposable yellow camera.

Outside the bus, the four women formed a small circle, consoling one of the girls squatting on the roadside, crying into a pink dotted handkerchief. Connie approached carefully, knowing this could just be some over-dramatic episode. It wasn't far from the truth. One of them, Cho-Un, was in tears from seeing a dead cat in the road.

"She must really love animals," the British boy said, his polo-shirted family nodding along, taking each other's hands, perhaps to pray for her. Connie knew better: Cho-Un hated animals, especially cats. It was the dead, smelly carcass that brought tears. Not tears of sadness, but of disgust.

Connie used the distraction to sneak away. She hailed a cab with a "Jesus is my co-pilot" bumper sticker "to the nearest mall," she said, which happened to be the Mall of Asia, the largest mall in the world. A digital rotating globe met her cab's approach.

At the mall's entrance, a Pinay security guard's hands groped Connie's legs, thighs, and ribs. Connie had never really been touched like this before. Even her father had seemed embarrassed holding her. The palms patting her body felt like small yanks, like she was a spirit being pulled back into the real world. A firm pat on her ass and a shove into the mall, and she was back in the universe of air con.

She crossed an outdoor sky bridge and followed a marquee declaring 'Hypermarket' into an adjoining building. Inside she found a refuge of comfort: a large warehouse store, similar to the Wal-Marts she had grown up with, where she had chosen her signature black outfit, one of a small variety available in K-Marts and Targets that were implanted into every small mid-western city. She sat on a red couch with cushions like bulbs, absorbing the whispering air con and clear aisles. She recognized the sofa. The same brand as the one she sat on in a hotel lobby near Oklahoma City, where a hotel manager—just as bulbous—inspected her, not believing that she was her father's adopted daughter. "Is he really your father?" the woman asked. "Where is your mother? How did you get to the United States? Can you speak any English?" Her strong-armed father begged Connie to "just tell them, hey, tell them you're adopted. Tell them we're a family." And the hotel manager with her pitying eyes fixed on Connie's Korean cheeks and brown skin, a girl waiting to be rescued. At the time Connie couldn't comprehend the situation, didn't know that a young Asian girl hand-in-hand with an older white man could mean so many things. She couldn't know that she merely needed to stop playing with the sofa's broken springs and speak with her plain mid-west accent, and all would be cleared up.

So the 'largest mall of Asia' was a lie. The complex was, in fact, a combination of a large superstore, a cinema, an arcade, and a large department store, all thrown into the same block and called a mall. The only mall-like section happened to be in the middle, a transit point between the other buildings connected by sky bridges and small verandas bordered by butch security personnel ready to feel her up. Despite the mall's disappointment, it was full to the brink with groups of young locals watching the skating rink and loitering near coffee shops.

On a sea-side patio overlooking Manila harbor, polo-shirt-ed Korean tourists lined the walkways, their skin far fair-er than their underdeveloped brethren. So many bridges, monuments, and museums had the imprint of Korean de-velopment, with melded-in plaques in Korean characters announcing their goodwill. Connie joined the Western tourists crowded at another Manila Bay viewpoint, most of them taking pictures of the small peninsula in the bay. When she peered over the bridge for a better view, a tour-ist motioned her away from his children. A blonde girl in a flower dress gave her a puerile grimace.

"Excuse me, excuse me!" The father yelled at her, his tri-pod pointed toward the children at Connie's side.

"She doesn't understand English Dad," the girl said, tap-ping her foot in annoyance.

Connie stood, leaning on the rail, taking a small glimpse of the bay, until the father gave up and took the picture anyway, with the dark-skinned Korean adoptee staring contemptuously back.

In five years, Connie thought. I'll still be in your family picture, gae-sag-ee. You'll see my ass in these black jeans, shi-bal byung-shin. Right in your children's faces, boh-jee.

She walked without purpose from the deck and found her-self in a clothing store. She felt the eyes of the staff upon her, their smiles hiding their reservations. There she was, like a cartoon character, always dressed in the same black T-shirt and matching jeans, the clothes her mother select-ed for her because they matched her Asian hair, face, and dark skin tone. Black was easy. Her mother was satisfied with anything cheap, quick, and, like her adopted daughter, something made in Asia. That's why they didn't adopt Russian. Like cheap bulbous motel couches, Connie was an easy sell, a commodity imbued with the precocity of a math whizz in her brain, and the frame of a lotus flower in her cheeks. Would they still have chosen her if they knew that she would become a musician, and worse, a lesbian? A girl too dark for her homeland and too bitter to return home.

She rifled through racks of clothing, her fingers rubbing material though she couldn't tell the difference between linen and silk. It seemed obvious to anyone that she had spent her life in a fashion enigma. Afraid of confusing those around her, she had felt a duty to reflect the same image every day. But in Korea her friends had difficulty accepting her fashion taste, of all things. No matter the amount of kimchi she ate, or how sharp her Korean became, it was her lack of clothing that had kept her from a true homecoming. Now she felt the same suspecting eyes watching her sift through expensive outfits, knowing that she was a phony, that to her these fashion symbols were merely well-organized pieces of fabric. She took a loud yellow blouse from a rack, then a floral ankle-length skirt, whatever looked awkward, absurd, or unconventional. It all came with her into the dressing room.

First she tried on a large white leather purse with silver shoes, a yellow leopard hairband and a dress that hung like white drapes. In the mirror, she looked just like a Mexican dancer. The transformation was incredible. More.

Next came a short dress with blue, pink, and red flames on a black background that made her look unmistakably

Japanese. Then she tried on an 80's style pink shirt and the Japanese woman in the mirror transformed into a middle-aged Korean. Next, she donned a white and black striped dress with a thick silver belt, and the Korean woman turned American. She then slipped into a black dress that left one shoulder completely exposed. Her appearance seemed to be a Filipina girl, perhaps, holding the hand of a white man, older and in some unearned bliss. She felt like putting on make-up, changing her hair, everything.

Then it happened: the small red shirt, accessorized with a white top, complemented with a small red circle streaking across her stomach. Red the color of moving body parts, activated in crimson. Red the color of commie China and red the color of lamps and small envelopes full of yuan and red the color of gambling under-garments and red the color of motel couches and mestiza heels. But then came the pièce de résistance, a red plaid skirt with belt-straps sewn down the left side and fake opened zippers on the right. A British style that had morphed into a Japanese costume that had alchemized into a fearless Korean pop ensemble. Connie's image in the mirror quieted her breath. The perfect symmetry of lines and colors punctured her deep within. The outfit was a mash of different brands, British, American, Japanese, Filipino, all from factories in Bangladesh, Indonesia, India, China, the Philippines. And the girl in the mirror seemed frightfully enigmatic, a symphony of colors and shapes, and even better because it was not a painting or a sculpture or an advertisement: it was her. To think, all along, *red* was her color.

Then what to do about that? Connie thought, staring at the beads on her wristband, which stuck out like a bruise. She gave a quick tug at it, but the thread held strong. She pulled again, and the thread imprinted a bright red circle on her skin.

When darkness fell, Connie took a cab back to that sleazy outdoor bar, where the group of American expats sat with heads on tables, in hands, and held back over their chairs, as if trying to stymie a nosebleed.

"You left too early last night," Skyler said, looking up from the same black dress, its neckline now stained dark with beer. "We got rip-roaringly drunk," he said proudly. "I got my ears pierced."

"Shaved my head," said Arthur, glancing up only for a moment to point out his head, now fully bald. Next to him, Winston sat hidden beneath a yellow elephant-printed scarf. "Yup him too," Arthur said, patting Winston on the back.

"These cuckholds," said Sophea, hardly visible beneath a dozen empty beer bottles. "They all pussed out before the party barely got started. I just threw up and kept right on drinking."

"Holy bananas," Connie muttered to herself, taking the same empty seat from the night before. "You all never went home?"

"It was supposed to be a pint or two," Arthur said, eyes on her. "Then came an hour of free drinks in honor of some dead guy. Now my head looks like Skyler's pummeled ass cheek."

"Don't talk," Winston mumbled from beneath the scarf. It was translucent in places, and Connie could see his scalp resembled the spotty, ailing baldness of a cancer patient.

"You look good," Arthur said to Connie, sticking a cigarette into that fatuous American smile. "I mean you're looking *good*."

"I went to the Mall of Asia today," Connie said, landing the statement with a sip of beer.

"The Fil-Am homecoming," Skyler clapped his hands in a single stride. "Did you find your true self in the adobo and cornsilog? Did it whisk you home, my lovely?"

"'Largest Mall of Asia' my ass," she said. As she described the mall, she felt Arthur's cold palm on her right thigh, not quite still but not quite grabbing her either. Her words became stilted, awkward, and she saw the others grinning, nodding, even as her tongue stuttered and her story became filled with awkward tics: "um" "right?" She looked to Winston, whose eyes rotated to Arthur's hand in anticipation. The hand reached into her, through that gap of skin once shielded by her black jeans. She saw that it wasn't only his hand, but the eyes around her. They all moved over her like oil, feeling her torso, toward the red circle near her stomach.

"Did you find the rhythm of the Filipina's *tsismis*?" Arthur said, his eyes finally settling on her forehead.

Connie smiled, teeth grit. She had played drums for years. She knew how to hit things into submission, to beat them back to her own beat. She could take a beer bottle as a drumstick and beat new sounds out of Arthur's smiling corpse.

"Hey ya'll, I just learned this new word." It was the white girl, Melanie. She stood behind Connie carrying a small shopping bag and wearing a dark red summer dress. "Ya'll are a bunch of LBHs ... know what that means? LOSERS

BACK HOME!" She laughed in a geyser and pumped her fist, "Whoop whoop! Nailed it."

Connie felt the hand gone and quickly rose to her feet.

"Red!" Melanie burst, taking Connie by the arm. "Look we're twins today!"

"I've always wanted to try twins," Arthur said, gas passing from his mouth.

"You're such an LBH, Arthur," Melanie shouted at him. "I'm not gonna lie."

Connie left—just left. She maneuvered past the servers and tables, securing her black backpack tightly like a packed parachute. She took wide strides to her hostel batting away tears, trying to forget the feeling of that hand creeping up her thigh. Who the fuck just takes a piece like that? Any person she had ever dated, man or woman, had slinked away before a week was out, their dignity worn to a frazzle. Goddamn bastard, she thought. He never said anything. We speak the same language and he never said anything. And then the woman, Melanie, grabbing her arm. Like Connie was one of them, like she needed their touch.

"I've had it with this chintzy shit," Connie said, tugging at the bracelet on her wrist. The fabric tore but wouldn't break. It looked like yellow hair growing out of her skin. "Fuck," she blurted. She knelt on the sidewalk as a colorful Mother Mary jeepney zoomed past. Her eyes stung with salt.

The way he looked at me. Like I was a manikin. Like I was skin with no biography. Like I was a pineapple drink on a hot day.

Greenbelt

The next day Connie turned her phone off to ignore whatever cultural excursion the Korean volunteer group had planned for the day. She sat at an outdoor café near-by her hostel, until the sun chased her into a cab heading for the four-building long Greenbelt Mall in Malate, Manila's business district. Once out the taxi she felt sunlight toast her chest, the exposed skin that her black T-shirt had always kept hidden. Entering the mall, she used her left hand to hide the wristband and felt the sudden up-draft from the air conditioning, billowing up her skirt.

"Connie!" A voice came from behind her—that white girl, Melanie. "I thought that was your sexy ass in front of me!" She laughed and made to hug her, but Connie pulled back, blocking her chest with her backpack.

"I'm scary I know," Melanie joked, her voice growing timid. Something Connie did seemed to pummel the girl's smile. They both wore the same outfits from the day before—red and red, all the fashion they could afford.

Connie felt the impulse to help her, and when she opened her mouth the words snuck out: "Your friends are dickheads."

"I'm sorry," Melanie said. "I'm really sorry, but you know how it goes, you're just stuck with your people, right? I love living in Asia. I love Asian people. But the isolation gets to you, ya know? But they' like my kids. Someone's gotta watch over'em."

Connie wondered if Melanie had ever taken a gender studies class. The domesticated home-keeper, the angel of the house, the southern belle. Would knowing what she was make it any better?

"Going shopping again?" Melanie said, her voice shrill. "As you can see—I need to pick up some casual wear."

"I just wanna walk around," Connie said.

"Right on, I can do that too," Melanie said. "I don't really have money to spend anyways."

Inside, the mall was a blank hue of milky white. Lights came from chandeliers shaped in sharp icicles. No music played; the only sound was water running between small stones and window panes. As they strolled through, never was the sight and sound of water ever out of their vicinity: water running lightly down glass, scentless, transparent, clean, whisking away the smallest bits of dirt, blurring the white lights into distant stars, slowly disintegrating the people passing by.

"I' been meaning to return some items, actually," Melanie chattered behind her. "But I'm afraid they won't understand my accent. Maybe you can speak Tagalog to 'em?"

"I'm not Filipina," Connie said, squeezing the rail toward the second floor. "I'm Korean. I teach English in Korea."

"Oh? I used to live there too."

"Teaching English?"

"Yeah. Typical, right? Hey, does your school have any openings? We're lookin' for work, as you can tell. What're you doing here anyway, if you ain't Filipina? You part o' them Korean tour groups? Did ya go visit a village? Is that where ya got that bracelet? Don't villagers make those for tourists?"

Seeking to get rid of her, Connie led the way into a small high-end art shop.

"Cool, I love art!"

Connie skipped the exhibition plaques and paced into a hallway of paintings. A moment passed before she realized what the abstract dark figures were supposed to be: the village children in Negros. Dark skin, curled hair, loose and earth-stained shirts, tattered hemp trousers. The images were blurred, as if a hand had purposefully blotched them into obscurity.

"Does this remind you of your trip to the village?" Melanie asked. "Sounds downright inspiring to be around children like these. I remember, when I was teaching in Kuala Lumpur, my students inspired me ..."

Connie tried to block the white woman out, believing she could bring herself to vomit if it came to that. She thought of when she was very young, and her mother rented a Korean movie, just so Connie could see the Korean actresses. Her mother told her, "You're gonna look like that when you're big." Connie was punched speechless. All her life she'd been positive that she was going to become white, like mommy, and that her Koreanness was only a condition of her childhood. Something to grow out of, like her teeth. That was the first time it hit her: She would never, ever, grow up to be a white woman.

From the gallery window Connie spotted the four Korean women from the volunteer group, standing in the mall's outdoor garden like ivory statues beneath the colorful parasols protecting their skin. They carried shopping bags and talked in that high-pitched, cute voice that Connie herself always mocked, calling it *wanchun gweeum*, "perfect cuteness." Their shopping bags were full to the brim of bright folded fabrics. Soft pinks, loud oranges, and turquoise, the flavorful colors of Korean chintz. And Chun Hye was with them.

With Melanie distracted by manga pop-art, Connie slipped quietly down the gallery stairwell and into the garden. The girls walked right by her, perhaps, not noticing her in anything but black. They sat on a park bench while Connie listened from behind a row of bushes, absorbing Chun Hye's perfume, watching the small of Chun Hye's back from behind the bench, that valley of light skin. The girls sat there for what seemed like an hour, with Connie shifting her sitting position every minute, marking up her now-exposed legs with small cuts.

The surrounding shade grew. A hazy radiance refracted sunlight. Wind came fast, blowing the bani trees eastward. Rain pattered on asphalt, then built up like popcorn. Then a torrent of rainfall. Thin screams rang from the girls as the wind tossed their umbrellas inside out, while Connie retreated with them into the mall, her red shirt drenched into maroon.

The storm brought dozens of shoppers inside: foreigners with their putas, the Filipino elite with their suitcases above their heads, those packs of East Asian tourists covering themselves with brochures. Everyone shared in ironic laughter, each one shivering from the huffs of air conditioning, their hair splashing acidic liquid about the white walls. The Korean girls wrung out the blouses and skirts that their shopping bags had failed to protect.

"Connie!" a voice shrieked. Melanie's tall figure waved from outside, floundering in the storm. Two workers waved her toward the doorway and she fumbled her way inside. She didn't bother drying herself off, but approached Connie, clasping that red, white, and blue bracelet in her hand. "I," she panted, "saw you. The rain must have loosened it." Her voice was shushed by the buzzing air con.

Connie plucked the wet bracelet from Melanie's palm. Behind her, the girls giggled to each other. She felt Chun Hye's eyes, those eyes that spoke in stabs of ice.

Connie took Melanie's hand unsure what she would do. Her skin was gentle, permissive, obliging. She wrapped the bracelet slowly around Melanie's wrist, feeling her veins tense, tickling her palm as she wove the thread into a knot, squeezed tight.

"For me?" Melanie said with a shudder, letting Connie's fingers linger upon her own. "I love it," she sucked back tears. "I'll wear this bracelet forever, I swear it."

"Goddamn it," Connie moaned. "Dude. You really are a Grade A USDA certified blonde, aren't you?"

Melanie shrieked with wild laughter and grabbed Connie, hugging her so tight Connie thought she could vomit if it came down to that.

The Flaneurs Spacechat

Chat log/February 16th 2008

Sky4Flaneur: announcement: Melanie and I are still planning on cleaning up Yeonji park tonight, after some people, (i.e. the majority of people in this chat) mucked it up and tossed shit everywhere. Thats 10pm.

Sky4Flaneur: there will be booze and cigarettes of course

Sky4Flaneur: so come

Sky4Flaneur: you know everyone talks about the rise of Asia but no one cares about the rise in my pants

Sky4Flaneur: thats a joke Im just at half-staff

Sky4Flaneur: cuz Im teaching children

Sky4Flaneur: everyone got my invite to this chat right?

Sky4Flaneur: new tech learn to use it

Sky4Flaneur: asia is the future

Sophea_S: Yes we got your fucking chatroom invite.

Sophea_S: Are you getting this? This chatroom is always open?

Sky4Flaneur: yeah if youre using on your computer you have to keep an eye out. Im using it on this smartphone

Sophea_S: The future and its mother-humping nonsense.

Sky4Flaneur: shouldnt you be teaching little bastards?

Sophea_S: I am. They're taking a test. Thursday mornings are quiet days for teacher. They sit and take quizzes while I down M-150 energy drinks.

Sophea_S: Well, Monday and Friday mornings too. Those are teacher's quiet days.

Sky4Flaneur: so youre hung over every day pretty much

코니: skyler I just saw your drag on a gay dating website

Sky4Flaneur: thanks Connie yeah its an ego-massage thang

코니: you gotta work on your make up. you want to look like a drag queen fine but a woman?

Sky4Flaneur: since youre revealing everything about me how about you tell us the story of how you became a true cock-hating lesbian

코니: its called 10,000 Sexual Episodes without an Orgasm by Connie Ho

Sky4Flaneur: don't you mean Cunny THE Ho?

코니: chode

Sophea_S: My crass immaturity has infected Skyler. Not sexually. Well, not sexually this time.

KingArthur: FUCK THIS CHAT

KingArthur: ITS MY BIIIRTHDAY FUCK

Sophea_S: I'd jump for joy but I've got six six year olds in front of me.

KingArthur: SEX six year olds?

Sophea_S: Don't want to spoil them.

Sky4Flaneur: on my birthday my students gave me whitening cream and I threw it back in their faces

코니: youre not supposed to deny gifts in Korea

Sophea_S: You might've offended them.

Sky4Flaneur: where are you now arthur? Bali?

KingArthur: yes indeedgot rid of whole passport page w/ sexy indo visa.

코니: whoop de fuuuuucking fuck

KingArthur: JELLY

Sky4Flaneur: what?

KingArthur: me jacking off to delicious stamp-porn

Sky4Flaneur: please PLEASE go on

KingArthur: heres china im stroking to it now

코니: yikes

Sky4Flaneur: I need to hear this

KingArthur: so fucking hawt so fucking red

Sophea_S: Class is over, gonna get wasted now.

Sky4Flaneur: comin to the bar to join

KingArthur: FUCK HER PUSSY SKYLER

Sky4Flaneur:	only because you said so
Sophea_S:	I suck with monogamy, not the mushy type.
KingArthur:	be prepared ta cry during sex
코니:	you'd know
Sky4Flaneur:	yay! Sophea is here with me!
Sky4Flaneur:	we got certain chemicals in us and we're happy
KingArthur:	heeey ist it wierd?
KingArthur:	you and i?
KingArthur:	never hooked up?
Sky4Flaneur:	honky tonk who the fuck are you talking to?
코니:	its sad watching you expats try to build some kind of community
Sky4Flaneur:	calm down ho
Sky4Flaneur:	come drink with us
KingArthur:	aall i want is just a hammock
KingArthur:	aaaand a river to shit in
KingArthur:	aaaaaand a wife
KingArthur:	this time one who speaks no english
Sky4Flaneur:	sophea just puked all over the bar
Sky4Flaneur:	smells sexy

KingArthur: try it as lube and report back ASAP

코니: weren't you all supposed to be cleaning the park?

This was Skyler's second stay in Khao San, Bangkok's backpacker mecca of the world. After only a year since he first came, the district already felt kitschy and gentrified. He wove through the vendors selling loose summer clothing and bootlegged DVDs. He shouldered past the newly arrived backpackers who walked at a glacial pace. He jeered through the steam of pad thai carts. The street touts put all the tourists on constant guard, an exhilarating "this is fun" anxiety. "Madness!" screamed one bearded tourist, falling backward on his friends, as if to give himself fully to the void. Skyler felt none of this desire to be wowed. Winded by travel, his eyes remained unfocused: another steel edifice, another pig carcass, another herd of smiling children. Muscle memory alone guided him. He knew to turn left after the Lizzy Bar stairwell; he knew to avoid the stomach-piercing pole of a makeshift jewelry vendor; he knew where to widen his gait over puddles of urine; he knew which alleyways to take to the British-owned café, where he went in the afternoon to read beneath quiet ceiling fans.

For five afternoons he had sat there, savoring every moment of peace before he would have to return to South Korea and resume teaching English to middle schoolers. Only a year ago, he had traveled to Thailand to escape his old scraggy skin and begin anew. Now it was a different kind of escape, the saddest kind of escape.

When Cherry, the Thai waitress, stopped at his table, he didn't need to invite her to sit next to him. She wore a red shirt with a white collar, two sizes too tight, and a spotted Minnie Mouse bow.

"What's in the news today?" he asked her as she applied lotion to her calves.

"Who cares?" she waved at a tourist to come in, but the man did not notice her. "Yellow shirt, now red shirt. Bullshit all again. You care?"

"If I'm ever hoping to retire, I care. I'm still on a piece-of-shit contract." He spat a piece of coconut shell at the foreign flags lined in a trellis around the café windows. "And my private school ain't payin' for this."

"I don't care. Just don't leave Khao San today." She stole a sip of his shake. "Many police everywhere, they beat you."

"Why? What's going on today?"

"Just don't leave Khao San. Go, you get beat. Who cares?" She folded her barbecue-brown legs onto her chair and bummed a cigarette, in the mood to vent. "Oh, you won't believe what happened to me! Customer came to me, tell me I'm beautiful—*beautiful*, right? Asshole. Can't be honest. I'm no beauty. Obvious to everyone. Asshole. I mean, to call *me* beautiful, I know what I look like. Look at this face. No make-up today, no Victoria's Secret. Only ate McDonalds. Look at this stomach. Fatass. Stupid asshole, come to Thailand, thinks he can pick up the plain girl, plain girl must be easy. Can you believe it? Hold on." She stood to help a customer.

Skyler toyed with the mint leaves in his coconut shake, watching the street where a dreadlocked girl on Cloud 9 reeled from tourist to tourist, anointing foreheads with coconut oil. Once in a while, when a customer came in, Cherry made her rounds, and he read Michel Houelle-becq's *Platform*, until she returned and her venting continued. For the past five days, since he first sat at the humble outdoor café surrounded by multicolored umbrellas, she clung to him in this manner, disclosing the day's events to him, while he nodded along. Perhaps she saw through his disguise, and knew that despite the "I ♥ Bangkok" t-shirt he wore and the blonde dye in his hair, he was not quite like the other tourists. He also knew her, the smile-wearing server in a society filled with sculpted eye-candy. Skyler too had accepted early on that he would merely subsist on the wages of service work, where he belonged with the other mulattos. In Las Vegas he had worked jobs for $5.50 an hour where he cleaned, smiled, and absorbed all the stored-up resentment from every customer. In the year since he started traveling, he found that no matter how you spun it, being served was always better than doing the serving. In that café of rotating fans and cigarettes, he was safe in his skin. He could sit for hours watching the pedestrian street, as he might watch a sitcom, silent, letting the laugh-track do all the work.

Cherry landed beside him, hands reaching up to tuck stray wisps of hair behind her ear. "So I scream at him. And my uncle, he kicks me out. Sleeping on the floor anyway. Can you believe that? I tell him I work late, must come home late, he thinks I'm dirty and kicks me out. Very dirty, he calls me. What an asshole."

Skyler glanced at his watch, hoping to hit his daily dose of air conditioning at a movie theater. "That sucks," he said.

"Yeah. So I need a place to sleep. Can share with you? You staying at the Happy Visit Hotel? I know them, they let me stay with you. No problem."

Skyler couldn't help but continue nodding his head. "Ok."

"Ok. They let me in, no problem. You tell them, they let me in." She ashed her cigarette and went to seat a trio of customers sporting aviator sunglasses.

Skyler maneuvered through Khao San during the early evening's lapse, when the tellers were packing up and the clubs had yet to open. He heard a protest march behind the buildings that walled Khao San, a screaming mass of firecrackers, cackling plastic and chants of "Ahw Bai!" The white faces of Khao San looked up from their foot massages and beer buckets to listen to the chants and police bullhorns, nervous perhaps that the demonstration would come too close to be mere landscape.

As the protestors' screams turned to hymnal singing, Skyler popped into a PC room full of young Thai women wearing headsets, many of them smiling and smooching into webcams. He sat at the PC closest to the door, next to one of the girls. From his periphery, he could see a shirtless white man on the screen next to him who looked like an American soldier. He imagined sucking the guy off, wrapping a belt around his waist to keep his balls at his lips.

"Honeeey," a girl said to the on-screen soldier. "Don't mind your Captain. Captain like fathers. And all fathers mean best."

Skyler wondered if the soldier was in Iraq. He wondered what unit the man was serving in, if he was at one of those bases frequently attacked by mortars and IEDs, if he knew Skyler's cousin Kale, also serving in Iraq. He clicked through Kale's Facebook photos of broken buildings, the fires and the dust of the sandpit that came in a chaotic hail of snapping images. He came across a new status update: "Kale has been injured during a routine operation. No information for classified reasons. Please pray for him," followed by a torrent of comments from Skyler's family: "Prayers for Kale," his niece wrote. "God bless Kale," his mother wrote, "and God bless America."

Skyler shut off the screen. Kale, his cousin. The huge, muscular pidgin speaking Hawaiian/Filipino mixture—it would take a missile to injure that meathead. Skyler saw his own frail fingers; Kale saw his scabbed stump. Skyler heard the taps on each keyboard; Kale heard live rounds in the far off distance, coming from every window and alley where the enemy had camped. And here Skyler could hide from the politics, the police, as easily as hiding from the heat.

The last time Skyler saw him, at his uncle's barbecue in Waipio, Kale was about to leave for his third tour. They had run indoors during the afternoon storms and were eating Kalua pig on thin paper plates. There Kale described his last firefight, recalling a mess of synaptic activity: firing death blossoms in all directions, then chucking a grenade toward the nearest house, where the gunshots were perhaps coming from, then being thrust by a tremendous force off a stone bridge, into a dark canal full of used plastic bottles. Twenty minutes later Kale was found at a shallow part of the river, drifting. Just like a good Hawaiian local, even near death he could still float.

That ended Kale's story then, but at night, when just the cousins went out to Honolulu's strip clubs, Kale divulged the rest. Nothing ended so easily in war, he told Skyler. His squad's response was vengeful and quick. They searched the homes nearby, arresting every male they found who wasn't decrepit or still in diapers. They threatened to execute mother's sons if the family didn't give up what they knew. They went full on Rambo, blasting into the same house that Kale's grenade would have pulverized, if only he were a better aim. "I've been bullied before," Kale said, tossing the rest of his one dollar bills near the stripper pole. "Kids used to pinch my cheeks walking in the halls." Kale was always like this after so many rounds. Out in the sunlight he was the perfect son, serving and protecting those he loved. In the bars he only spoke of the teenagers they killed, and the LBFMs (little brown fucking machines) that his fellow soldiers passed around like blunts on their last burn.

Now here Skyler was, in Bangkok, in a room full of LBFMs, the scent of danger so palpable that even naïve backpackers were retreating to their windowless hostel rooms to avoid it. And the constant images of war on his screen would never give him the peace that came easy with a coconut shake.

He retreated, back into the Khao San street.

"Skyler! Skyler!" a voice hailed him, a voice he couldn't recognize through the massive chants of the non-visible crowd. "Yo Sky, my negro! What is up!"

He found a familiar face sitting under a large Guinness sign: Arthur, dressed full douchebag in backpacker elephant patterns. He sprung from his seat and shook Skyler's hand in spastic shakes. "I knew it!" Arthur said. "You got stuck in Khao San too, right?" He pushed his sunglasses back. "I had a full day planned, I was gonna hit Nana, to flush out my balls asap! But my concierge was all, 'you leave Khao San, you die.' Whatever though—thank the yellow shirts! Whatever political cause they represent, I'm all for it. Any movement that gives me an excuse to sit right here from morning to night has my vote."

Skyler sat next to him at another outdoor bar surrounded with multicolored umbrellas and plastic tables. Arthur ordered a beer for Skyler and two for himself, so he could offer one to any scandalously dressed girl walking by. "Hey, join us!" Arthur called to the girls on the street in an off-kilter Irish accent. "Aye, I got a cold one right here for ya lil' lassies! Go democracy!"

The English teachers in Korea loathed Arthur, and always felt nervous around him, especially when he was drinking. There was an anxious hyperactivity to the man that made vulgarities spew from his lips. But Skyler had encountered far worse in the many hostels around Asia, and had learned to categorize Arthur's inhibitions as slapstick entertainment. So, weeks before, when Arthur found a weekend job in Bangkok where they simply had to play the part of foreign businessmen, listen to speeches, and shake the hands of Chinese entrepreneurs, Skyler didn't turn it down. For him, a single plane ride with Arthur wouldn't keep him from an easy thousand bucks.

"Listen, I want you to meet someone," Arthur said, and then slammed his fist on a nearby table where an older man with an eggplant-shaped head sat staring at a menu. "Hey Pension! Pension, you still with us here?" Arthur snapped his fingers back and forth, trying to assess the old man's mental state. "Skyler, this is Pension. Pension, Skyler."

Some time passed before Pension turned his head, giving Skyler a crass smile, gasping oxygen in and out of his large torso. A stream of drool spilled from his large lower lip.

"That's fucking disgusting Pension," Arthur said, wiping the drool with a floral-patterned napkin. "Look at yourself, Pension, you're barely alive."

"Why do you call him Pension?" Skyler asked.

"Because he is a pension, that's all he is anymore!" Arthur tucked the napkin into Pension's pocket. "You want to tell him, Pension? Can you tell your story?"

Pension looked at his watch, then took two white pills from his pen-pocket. He shoved them into his mouth and drowned them with Thai iced tea.

"Aw, he'll never be able to tell it now," Arthur said, shaking his head. "This here is death for you. This man right here. Stare into his eyes, those beautiful blue ageless gates, you'll find a cavern on the other side. You're a pension now, right, Pension?"

"Those pills looked like Vicodin," Skyler muttered.

"Ah! We have a winner! Pension came here, what, five years ago, was that it, Pension? He's an army vet, made it pretty high. Captain, or Lieutenant, or somethin'. Came to Thailand, fell in love with a beautiful Thai girl, as we all tend to do now and again. But this girl was different. She's got the pills man, she's got Satan's ball-sack juice, and now she has his balls. Now Pension just wanders Khao San, a zombie, giving her his pension every month. Right, Pension? He'll tell you all about it if he ever comes down."

Pension nodded his head, his stomach visible beneath his polo shirt, expanding in and out of long breaths. The buttons on his shirt nearly snapped from the pressure. "He seems happy," Skyler said. "I mean, it's an exchange, right? The drugs? And, you know, if he really loves her."

"Really loves her," Arthur echoed with a sneer. "Could there be a better drug? Well how about it, you happy, Pension? You're a happy dude, right? Look, this mofo killed a bunch of bitches in Iraq, smashed a desert full of sand pussy, but look at him now! You could smack him in the face, he would still stare at you like you were a coked-out sister of a drug lord. All that love for your country, and this is where it all gets you. Hey Pension, tell us about your girl. He'll tell you. She avoids him. And her brother? Guess what he is? A police officer. And a Thai boxing instructor. You don't mess with that shi-it. And his passport? They took that too! He can't leave, so here the man sits. Happy, as you say."

"What branch did he serve in?" Perhaps he was a Marine. Perhaps he had known Kale.

"What branch? Does it fucking matter? They all end the same."

Skyler ordered a round for them and Pension. The waitress laughed at the very thought of the stoned man drinking. "He'll enjoy one, I think," Skyler said.

"Man," Arthur mused. "Pension don't enjoy nothin.'"

The waitress brought three Heinekens and stayed to watch the farce, leaning over the table in suspense. Skyler placed an opened bottle into Pension's hand, then attempted to clink the bottles together in a "cheers."

"To you, soldier." Unsure what the usual toast was, Skyler added, "Semper Fi." He lifted Pension's arm and the beer spilled all over the man's drool-ridden chin.

Both Arthur and the waitress clapped in excitement. "Good goin', my friend!" Arthur said, coughing out laughs. "Point proven, sir, point proven!"

"I get more napkins," the waitress said, and disappeared behind a curtain of red beads quivering with laughter. When she returned, Arthur and Skyler silently watched her scrub the tables in her tight black skirt, still chuckling to herself.

"So, according to the news, the night might start early," Arthur said, checking his Korean smartphone. "Cops just moved in on the yellow shirts. Beatings, yada yada, but the point is it ended early. So, in honor of democracy and freedom, I say we hit the worst of the worst—Soi Cowboy."

Skyler listened to Khao San. The chants and tunes from the demonstration were long gone, fizzled out by something unseen. He just heard the backpacker chatter and the yawps that came from the insect cart selling dried scorpions.

"It's over already?"

"Come on, we know how this goes. March, scream, get your good deed in for the day, and then—oops! Utter violence everywhere. They went out with a bang, my friend." He took a sip of beer. "I thought you were smart, Skyler."

Skyler shared in the sip. "Not when it comes to fighting."

"So in that case, you'll come with me to Soi Cowboy? Celebrate the end of the world? It's gonna be *sveeet*."

A groan came from across the table. Pension seemed half-awake, staring at Skyler, then at Arthur.

"Tonight's for you, Pension," Arthur toasted, beer in the air. "Tonight's for you."

$

Six days before, on a full flight from Seoul to Bangkok, Skyler and Arthur practiced becoming businessmen. They practiced the Windsor knot, shaking hands while handing over ivory business cards, and gesturing their fingers in small circles as they spoke. Their black suit jackets with matching ties and lapels would allow them to pass as quality-control experts for a company run by Chinese entrepreneurs. To get a thousand bucks for two day's work, all they had to do was smile, make toasts, shake hands, and strut around in fifty-dollar business suits, looking as natural and important as their American accents.

Two of the Chinese company men met them at the airport, shaking hands vigorously with Arthur, then pausing to look over Skyler's long hair and brown eyes. The balding businessmen discussed something in Mandarin, pointing at Skyler. His hair, his eyes, his skin, things that a suit could not hide. One of them took his hand and pointed to the back of Skyler's palm. Skyler looked at it himself. In Seoul's winter, his skin had become a pale beige.

"Um, do you understand what's happening?" Arthur asked, his voice rasping through his tight white collar.

"I know what this is," Skyler said. "I totally know what this is."

The businessmen took them to a hair salon near the business district. They were to get full makeovers. And for Skyler, that meant transforming his long femme hair into short blonde uniformity. Skyler said nothing as the girls wrapped his hair in foil and lathered his face in whitening cream. In the U.S. he could never do this without feeling like he had betrayed every part of himself. He would never be able to look his family in the eye. But here, in Bangkok, he felt excited. He was going to be white, he thought. A white man in a business suit handing out cards. Holy Malcolm, I'm going to be white.

When they arrived at the hotel gala, none of the Chinese questioned Skyler's white American authenticity. The main ballroom looked campier than a high school prom, but instead of balloons there were firecrackers and Thai-Chinese women dressed in dragon-printed cheongsams, the same kind Skyler would have snuggled into were he not now on the other end of the spectrum. Hands were shaken, cards passed, smiles given, nods exchanged. The company's image—an image of connection, progress and venture cosmopolitanism—was secured by Skyler's and Arthur's fair complexions. Only after the first day of working the room did Skyler discover that the company he represented was a mining firm, interested in North Thailand deposits. In fact, their product was on the business card he had been handing out.

Skyler Humphrey. Selling the Very Best in White Gold.

B

On the bus to Soi Cowboy, Skyler and Arthur wore their business suits, though their faces wore the awaiting grins that preceeded an all-night sexcapade. Unhinged by his rich-man persona, Arthur struck up a conversation with two tight-skirt college girls about the state of American business. Back at home they would be bums. Here they were young entrepreneurs, buying and selling identities in an endless race from the bottom.

Skyler fiddled with his suit's polka-dot pocket square, the only place that gave him freedom to add some pizazz. Otherwise the suit made him feel trapped in its many layers. What if he needed to run, or fight off a mugger? Dresses were so much better for the traveler. Easier to pack, flexible, wind-resistant.

"Put a dimple in your tie," Arthur said, fixing-up Skyler' collar. "Hoes love dimpled ties."

Released into Soi Cowboy, they followed a crowd of expats blowing streamers and stadium trumpets, chanting "DEMOCRACY, BITCHES!" Except for the elephants, Soi Cowboy looked like 1950s Las Vegas. Go-go girls danced below cowboy-shaped neon lights wearing genuine-looking smiles, many of them in white leather boots and black cowboy hats.

"That's where the sex be my nigger," Arthur said, pointing at a smiling Thai dancer with Japanese-style make-up and a pink fur bikini. "That's where it be. Right up there."

Two girls in pink pumps dragged them into club Déjà Vu, past a garish pink dance floor and into a black booth made of fake leather. Both girls looked in their late teens, though Thai age could be deceptive. "How you doing honey?" the short-haired one said. LBFMs, Skyler thought, and the thought clouded his mind. Before Skyler could send them away, Arthur spread his arms on the couch, inviting the girls to snuggle next to him. "We're doing fine with you fine ladies. This is our last night in Bangkok!"

The girls cuddled in, letting Arthur squeeze his arm around them. "You know why this is our last night?" he said. "We got the client. All packaged up and signed. A done deal, we call it. This is a celebration, bitches!"

The drinks arrived, colors awash in bisexual lighting.

"Cheers!" Arthur said, toasting his Mojito. "To our last night in Bangkok!"

"To our last night," Skyler nodded. He and Arthur clinked glasses. They took slight sips, hoping to make their ten-dollar drinks last.

"You buy us a drink too?" one of the girls said.

"I would, but I barely know you!" Arthur responded, his face sinking into their arms.

Another girl plopped into the booth next to Skyler. She leaned her head back and kicked her leather white cowboy boots onto a fuzzy ottoman. A pink cowboy hat hid her face and she seemed not to notice Skyler there as she stretched her arms and ordered herself a drink.

"Hello," Skyler called to her. "And your name is?"

"Kh!" She laughed in a lilting voice. "Kee. You think you

can remember that, huh?" By her voice Skyler guessed she was Kathoey, what tourists called a ladyboy. He eyed her broad shoulders, wanting to hold them. He looked at her thighs, wanting to taste what she had between them. She gave him a single eye, peeking from beneath the cowboy hat. Azure brown, eyes like floating Autumn leaves. He couldn't figure out if he wanted to be her, or to be inside her. Perhaps they were one and the same, an erotic hand up the puppet's backside. Did it go both ways? Did she also want to be him—male, traveler, American jet-setter of first class life worthy of ego-tripping despondency? Was sex his hand up the puppet's rear, or her sharp, manicured fingers, pulling his strings?

That leafy eye rolled back as she took a sip of her drink, watching the dance floor of older men with their after-dinner specials. Her skin was light, lighter than Skyler's own, and her hair a sharp blonde. She too, was in business.

"Kee, what's going on tonight?" Skyler leaned into her.

"Looking for a girl to fuck me," she said, saying 'fuck' like a moan. "Girls pay me a lot. You surprised? All girls are perverts you know." She walked off, the bar's sallow light gleaming from her long blonde wig. Skyler was baffled; her rejection was off-putting, but just terse enough to be slightly teasing. It was a magnetizing performance—and hopefully he would not need to pay for an encore.

"Hit that shit!" Arthur said from beneath go-go girl giggles.

Just as Skyler stood to pursue her, she returned stirring a gin and tonic. "Where you going, business man?" Kee said, sitting next to him, her long fingernail tracing his outer thigh. "What business you in?"

An involuntary spasm quivered through him. Her long fingers swelled his erection like fanning a fire. "I'm not a businessman," Skyler said. "This is all fake."

"Mmm!" Arthur squealed from his straw. "True dat! This nigga' here just got out of the American Army. I'm the businessman, but he be a *soldier*, dis one."

"You're an American soldier!" Kee taunted. "And still so nervous? The protest is miles away, you know. No bomb coming here. No guns. Only boobs. And pussies. And other things."

"I'm not nervous," Skyler said, wondering if they could see through it all: the dye, the whitening cream. "It's just this suit."

"Well you take it off then!" Kee cheered, motioning for him to stand up. The other girls joined in. "Take it off! Take it off!"

They stripped him, yanking off his jacket and tie, unveiling his skin. Seeing him pared down to his hairless, light brown torso, the girls became silent.

"Is he really an American soldier?" one of the girls said.

"Wait right there." Kee searched for something behind the bar. Her high heels clacked as she returned with a bright yellow T-shirt that read *Bangkok* in Comic Sans. "Put this on!"

Skyler struggled to fit into the Asian-sized shirt. Kee clapped and collapsed giggling into the booth. "Yellow shirt! No American soldier! You're a yellow shirt now!"

"Yellow shirt!" The girls cheered.

"Democracy!" Skyler joined in, a fist in the air. He saw Arthur's lanky figure on top of one of the go-go girls, straining, as if trying to jam a suitcase shut.

"You all right?" Skyler asked.

"I'm happy!" Arthur shouted. "Just getting my happy on makes me happy!"

Kee took Skyler to a love hotel just behind Soi Cowboy, where each room was held for only one-hour increments, and every floor contained free pornographic DVDs and large booklets full of escort cards. In a dark red velvet room, she tossed him on the bed and gave him sharp kisses.

"Wait, you clean?" she asked. He said yes. "But we still need a condom."

"I get tested once every three months," Skyler said.

She laughed, picking up his yellow shirt to throw at him. "*I'm* the top, soldier. Condoms in the bathroom. Hurry."

She had no implants beneath her bikini top, but finally he could see her without the kitsch cowboy hat. Neither of them went to turn off the lights. The first touch of her skin made him shiver. Her eyes seemed to grind against him as her body did the same, her fingers pinching at his flat chest. He undid her belt and pulled the skin from her dick, massaging her balls and shaft. She worked very matter-of-factly on lubing up his asshole while he avoided her eyes, fearful his heart would surrender to her beauty. He sucked her nipples, her penis, her pleats of skin. Her reddish estrogen-infused tits gleamed with sweat as she fucked him. He turned on the AC and drew himself into her as goosebumps dotted her backside.

After his orgasm, she didn't bother finishing herself or resting next to him, but began strapping on her pink bra and white boots. Still in that post-coital faint, Skyler could barely respond to her when she asked for ninety-nine dollars, USD. He didn't even have twenty.

"Come on, you businessman, you soldier," she said. "This not funny. I need it."

"But," staggering up, finding his balance, remembering the tension he had nearly escaped. "I never promised you anything."

"Honey, this is my job," she said. "You have to pay. I like you, come on. Just pretend it's for the taxi home, and my home is very far away. You gonna leave me without a taxi fare, soldier boy?"

He sat for a moment, pretending to look through his wallet, as if the money would materialize in front of him. He could barely believe it when she began to cry.

"Why is it so hard for you?" she sniveled, turning away from him, toward the window that faced the alley's immense darkness, thick as black paint.

"I'm sorry, but I never paid for it before," he said. "I'll get you the money."

She paced the room and stood in front of the doorway. "It's always like this with you types. Soldiers, businessmen, tourists, all looking for LBFM. But no pay. You're an evil man. Your whole country. Evil!"

"I'll get to an ATM," he pleaded, pulling on his yellow T-shirt. "Trust me, give me five minutes, I'll come back."

She took out her cellphone and called someone, speaking to him in Thai. She started screaming into the phone, looking vilely at Skyler as she did so. He leapt into his pants then scrambled for the door, her eyes bulging at him.

"Sorry!" he shouted, sprinting down the hall.

A voice screamed toward him as he flew down the stairway. Then into the pink and purple streets of Soi Cowboy. He heard the patter of someone chasing him. Her pimp? Her brother (who probably knew Muay Thai)? He had left his glasses at the hotel, and when he looked back he could make out a bald figure in black jeans, just a few seconds behind him, running at him with his arm outstretched, as if he merely wanted to talk. Skyler continued charging down the broken concrete. He leapt over plastic tables, maneuvered between cartons of caged chickens, skipped over caked mud. He passed large families, incredibly large, as large as the families in the sandpit, who would wait anxiously while the American soldiers searched their homes. He imagined sprinting through gunfire, leaping over mines, edging past firefights, dipping and veering from one home to another. Reality hit when Skyler flung himself into traffic and a taxicab swerved from mowing him down.

He kept running even when he could no longer hear the man behind him. His footsteps sent stray cats scurrying across gravel. Soon it wasn't tables and bikes he was dodging, but bon fires, police tape, and barbed wire. He wasn't sure which direction he was headed, but he prayed it was Khao San, the old city where Bangkok's tourist police could protect him.

He wandered in the dark, thinking of Kale. Skyler heard girls wave at him, saying "Honeeey;" Kale heard the whistle of an incoming rocket. At least Kale would have paid for it. He would have called her LBFM. He would have blocked his eyes from her big dick. He would have told his friends later about that time he was so drunk he tried a ladyboy. But he also would have paid.

A spotlight blinded Skyler, sending pulses of alarm to his brain. Then another. Then two more arched from nearby rooftops, splitting his brain. He heard shouts in a foreign tongue. He felt himself on the frontlines, with the maddening fear that at any moment some garbage can or left behind bag could be his end. A megaphone shouted at him in Thai.

The yellow shirt! Skyler thought. He pulled up on the tight cloth, turning the shirt inside-out over his head. He heard the clamping of military boots as he struggled to pull off the yellow target. He remembered what Cherry had told him: rumors of snipers, of calls to shoot on sight anyone wearing a yellow shirt. He pulled as hard as he could, but his strength only made the clothing stick from his head like a cone. From the funnel he had created, Skyler saw flashes of dead bodies, charred and blown apart by an insurgent's explosive. He fell onto the street after someone kicked his ribs, then another man pushed him down, a boot at his throat, shouting at him in Thai. Skyler felt the boot on his neck, the dirt and grime on his belly. "I'm not Thai!" he screamed, crawling his head out of his shirt. "Look! Blonde hair! White skin!"

At four in the morning, Khao San road was silent and empty. No music came from the underground clubs; no Kathoeys were out picking off the tourists who had drifted from the herd. Even the McDonald's, where Thai students went to practice English, was padlocked closed. Skyler stomped over discarded yellow leaflets from the days' protests and nodded past the old woman at his hotel, whose head remained in a deep sleep on the counter, yet somehow still nodded back to him. She didn't seem to notice the encrusted dried blood on his face, or that his arms were swathed in bandages. From the elevators, he swayed into his seventh-floor room and found Cherry buried beneath blankets on his small bed. There was no window or air conditioning in the room, so the fan needed to be on its highest setting. Its unstable gyration and rotating sounds diminished the sound of the door closing.

He felt the dull pain of his broken skin as he took off his shoes and crowded into bed next to Cherry's hoagie-like shape.

Skyler fell in bed with a Thai waitress, his body covered in concrete scathes; Kale slept in an army hospital, arms swollen and rheumy, neck burning from a sun rash, tongue livid with sores from biting it in pain.

He felt something trace up his shoulder, a single finger. "Skyler? Cannot sleep?" Cherry whispered.

"I'm ok," he said.

"You sure?"

He nodded and heard her head rest. He pulled off his yellow shirt, the bruises on his side hurting with every breath. The wind from the ceiling fan cooled his sweaty skin. Somehow he had survived, all intact. When the military men saw his blonde hair and pale arms, they merely seemed annoyed. He wasn't a yellow shirt, surely, and he probably was not the first foreigner to wander directly into the line of fire. White, he was just some dumb tourist, no threat to anyone. Brown, he could only wonder.

He stared at the dark ceiling, thinking of the many things he had seen since he had started traveling. All the people, the tours, the drinking, the drunken wisdom. At the end, everything was supposed to lead to a moment, to some spark of genius, some gestalt, some enlightened wisdom. Yet at the edge, there was nothing but the caverns in his eyes and a local woman to keep him sated. He might as well have gone to the sandpit to fight alongside Kale. Afterwards, he could spend the rest of his days knocking back Vicodin and waiting for his pension to run dry.

"Can't sleep?" Cherry said again.

He sighed.

"Did you masturbate?"

"What?"

"Masturbate. Am I saying it right?"

"Yes. I mean, no I didn't. Not really."

"Ok. Let me help." Her hand searched in the dark for his boxers and then cradled him. Skyler felt tears come to his eyes. Was this the Thai way, or was it just her? Was it his blonde hair, his light skin? Never mind that, he thought, his mouth gaping in a frisson of pleasure.

"And more? Help you sleep?" she said plainly.

"Alright then," Skyler whispered. His mouth fell open as she climbed on top of him. Her hips felt painful on his bruises, like a rough back massage. She ground into him, and when he protested she slapped his hands away, grabbing onto his chest. He murmured for her to stop, tears blurring his eyes, but she ignored him, or perhaps didn't trust him, as his hands continued to grip her breasts. He felt a moment of release and she tumbled off, leaving him alone with a helpless stare and his eyes drying out from the ceiling fan blowing empty gusts.

The Flaneurs Spacechat

Chat log/May 30th 2008

KingArthur:	got two bimbos ordering for me
KingArthur:	i thumped her and her friend
Sky4Flaneur:	how'd you swing that?
KingArthur:	put out an ad for a language exchange partner
KingArthur:	requirement: female under 120 pounds
KingArthur:	i hadnt met a virgin in over a year and spring came early
코니:	youre still in Thailand I presume
KingArthur:	anywhere is better than Korea
KingArthur:	btw last night I was talking to this chink
KingArthur:	just testing you you sensitive fucks
Sky4Flaneur:	hey connie and sophea—you guys still asking for translators for your radical feminist movement against the forced importation of american beef?
코니:	not sure?
코니:	havent heard from Sophie
2BWinston:	guys ... sophea pulled a runner last night. Got drunk and a bit abusive ... got into a fight with some waegook tourist. Then ... split I guess
코니:	SHE was drunk and abusive?

코니:	youre the one who throws bitch fits all the time
코니:	fucking can't leave without breaking something
@Melz:	mel needs ou explain ... pull a runner???
2BWinston:	said she was going to the airport ... guess she wasn't lying
Sky4Flaneur:	she say why?
KingArthur:	FUCK i was gonna ask her for her bangkok contact
Sky4Flaneur:	to smuggle dope into Korea?
KingArthur:	Im not suicidal
KingArthur:	was thinking shanghai maybe nanjing
코니:	a white man smuggling opiates into china. cant you colonials get a new scheme?
KingArthur:	don't knock our greatest traditions
2BWinston:	yeah connie ... racist
코니:	WiseCRACKERs all o you
KingArthur:	crackers dont have legs as beautiful as sky's in drag
KingArthur:	like a picked cherry
2BWinston:	true sky does have beautiful legs ...
KingArthur:	skyler we only loves you when youse a woman

Sky4Flaneur: Im actually a woman all the time not my
                 fault you only see it when I wear lipstick and
                 a dress

KingArthur: you dress like a dude

Sky4Flaneur: so does connie

KingArthur: your voice sounds like a dudes

Sky4Flaneur: how is a woman supposed to sound?

2BWinston: ENOUGH of this gender-bending shit

코니: if you really wanted to be a woman, you'd
                 have gotten surgery while you were stuck
                 in Thailand. Change your face, give you
                 breasts, take away your useless dick

Sky4Flaneur: now connie my gochujang sister would you
                 be into me if I were a full time woman?

코니: well theres a question

KingArthur: yeah

KingArthur: well

KingArthur: no ladyboys for me

KingArthur: going to red light in about 5ish

KingArthur: gonna bang a REAL whore

KingArthur: btw got ripped last time negotiating prices

KingArthur: any suggestions?

KingArthur: what if its just hj?

2BWinston: depends if the girl is providing her own
                 place

2BWinston:	should be cheaper if she comes to your hotel
KingArthur:	THANKS NEGROMANCER!
KingArthur:	wait one more
KingArthur:	bout viagra
KingArthur:	how long it usually takes to do its thing?
코니:	jesus fucking christ no wonder sophie left
Sky4Flaneur:	did she say where she was going?
2BWinston:	nada
Sky4Flaneur:	did she say *anything*?
2BWinston:	besides the drunken rambling? we were talking about ressentiment ... the need for revenge ... but being too weak to really do anything
Sky4Flaneur:	filter out the grandstanding.
2BWinston:	ressentiment: you want revenge against the blonde beasts but true revenge is impossible so you look for other ways to cope
코니:	that sounds like being around arthur. Or any of you
KingArthur:	yeah but WHO GONNA STOP US HAH???

MUMBAI IMMIGRATION
30 MAY 2008
Sophea
AIRPORT

The train clattered along inner-Mumbai. Women in gold patterned saris followed the tracks with baskets full of pastries held atop their heads. A row of khaki-clad police passed through the cabins, their faces slapped with thick mustaches. "Name, passport," they ordered.

"Sophie Pang," she said, handing over her navy-blue passport. Unlike South Korea, where American military bases shadowed every city, or Cambodia, where US dollars were the necessary currency, here in India she felt like she was finally outside of the American frontier. They had their own evil empires here, their own nasty racial structures, their own sorts of oppressions, accents, bureaucracies, and pop-culture references. And yet, even in the face of all this foreignness, she recognized the faces pitted on every scrutinizing policeman.

The police tossed her passport back and left. She heard Dave snoring in the bottom bunk; his lanky feet jut out into the aisle. The police hadn't bothered to wake the white traveler. After a three-day tryst in New Delhi, this seemed an opportune time to ditch him. She would re-member Dave as the guy who locked his legs around her as she slept. She would remember how easy it was to sleep feeling trapped. On airplanes, on trains, or caught in his grip.

By the time the train pulled into Churchgate Station in Mumbai, Sophea had already slipped away, her backpack hanging loosely behind her.

Sophea plunged into Mumbai's swarming streets of people blended together in the evening's soft golden glow. A group of women squeezed her with their bellies; an undulating stream of piss flowed between her sandals, coming from a small boy facing a brick wall; a cycle rickshaw's wheel smashed a pile of cow shit and a swarm of flies sniffed the fresh aperture; a bull's tusk nearly gut a man riding a motorbike. An old hijra with a red jewel in her nose slapped Sophea's wrist to demand money, holding a sleeping infant in her arms. The woman cackled in Hindi, bringing her hand to her mouth to gesture for food. Sophea stood with her knees at a slight bend, apprehensive, as the woman's begging drew a new crowd. Nearby, some young local man checked her out.

That got her thinking of Skyler—the unbuttoned Skyler in a collared shirt; Skyler in a collar barking; *Skyler his arms around me arms around Skyler with no kiss; Skyler on that day in Phnom Penh after we accidentally flipped a table full of drinks—a useless but encouraging smile—Skyler on my last day in Seoul after I mustered the gall to kiss him—but it was a pity kiss; Skyler kissed with pity.*

Travel was supposed to free them–but that mixed up wannabe flaneur only got nastier with every new city. "Goddamn it," Skyler had told her just before she left. "Why can't you just get over it? You can be anyone you want in Asia, do anything—you're not just some weak minority in America, that's what they want you to think."

She could never understand how easy it was for him to transform himself. Could she stop being Cambodian? Stop being a refugee? Stop the history, the memory of her family, the debts she owed? And yet, as if to prove him right, here she was, going anywhere she wanted. India, a place she had never cared to go.

She tried not to remember much—remembering had to be rationed. Most of life, she found, needed no memories—no thinking about who she was, what her family went through, her upbringing in the States, all those onerous histories. Memory had driven her mad once; every recollection had peeled away the membrane protecting her sanity. Now she intended to keep herself, to keep her head, no matter what. So she let go of memory and gave herself to the feeling of being swallowed by the things around her: Dogs, piss, cows, shit, camels, geckos, touts, urchins, legless beggars, street children, fleas, dirt, exhaust, heat, the sun's inescapable glow.

She shot her right arm to mark a clear path and charged through the street like a tractor, her feet skipping across the red bricks. She could still feel the eyes of the children burning into her back, wondering perhaps *Where does she keep her money?* and *How cheap is the foreigner?*

Outside of the crowd, Sophea dove into a nearby movie theater. She paid three-dollars to watch the Sex and the City movie, and for two sweet hours forgot everything.

She left the theater with the unease of walking into an unknown city's nightlife, that feeble shadowed panic of being blotted into the unknown, without a bed, a partner, or a mind-map capable of growing.

She passed hotels but entered none, her body caught in a frisson of anxiety and daring. Unable to stop her legs from moving, she strolled along the promenade, speckled with packs of foreigners and tourists armed with open-carry bottles of wine and thin needles of hash, their bodies attached to tall British-era residence walls like seaweed wavering to and fro against a stream. The street directed her through hand-in-hand pedestrians, jostling youth, and young women Bollywood dancing for hand-held cameras. A nurse wheeled an old British man who stopped to stare at her, his eyes in a cranky tilt. Sophea bought a lamb kebab, wondering how long the man would stare her up and down, his wrinkled face scrutinizing her clothing, perhaps, trying to assess her nationality. She knew what he was thinking—does she belong here in this tourist area? This ragged brown woman? She wondered the same thing herself. Mercifully, the man flicked his cigarette and the nurse pushed him away.

She sat on a bench overlooking the tourists. She could sit in stillness, but only for a moment. Her body would not let her rest, not if it was to expunge everything.

Streetlights began to fizzle out. Gigantic bats swarmed through Gothic towers, their silhouettes like floating ash in the moonlight.

She kept moving, undaunted by the night.

She walked among the city's concrete towers until she happened upon an old British colonial-era building converted into a nightclub aglow in purple and green lights.

A line of posh youngsters vined through a small night market. Sophea bought a Cuban cigar from a street stall and saw an Indian woman in Bara sandals smoking at the club's backdoor entrance, one foot sticking out the door, the other keeping her balance on the metal pole of a barstool. With the confidence of a local, Sophea brushed past the woman and went inside.

The club was packed with local men dancing close enough to sneak a whiff of body odor. As if to slap Bollywood stereotypes across the face, the women were all dressed in monochrome black dresses, with exposed tan lines on their cleavage and short skirts. None of them danced, but stood chatting and occasionally relocating.

One woman stood out, a beguiling beauty that reminded Sophea of herself as a teenager. Wavy hair tamed into a rippling helix. A sash across her bodice read "Real Indian." A sharp red light leaned on the woman's cheeks, making a fuzzed bright ring from the bottom of her nose to the edge of her ears as more red lights zigzagged across her large breasts and shoulders, transforming her body into a cackling fireplace.

It occurred to Sophea that Indian women looked more like her than Cambodian women did. Her mother had told her once that Cambodians were descended partially from Indian blood. So this was a possible excuse for being here—the homeland's homeland, the seeds of the roots.

A short smiling man with pomaded hair made eye contact. The nimble teen danced on Sophea's right leg, churning between her thighs. The Real Indian beauty scrutinized him, said something in Hindi ("Jaldi Karo!"), and pushed him away. "Check your pockets," she told Sophea.

The boy had a smile so irresistible that, upon reflection, Sophea didn't really mind being mugged, since he had only stolen a hundred rupees anyways.

"Thief!" the woman yelled to the bouncers, who trotted out after the boy. "I apologize, these people are such animals," the woman said in a British accent. "How about I buy you a drink, darling?" The woman looked so much like Sophea, they could've been switched at birth.

"Thanks," Sophea said. "I'm Sophie."

Taken by her accent, the woman asked, "American?"

"Second class American." Sophea noticed a group of men dancing nearby, swooning at them both. "Should we dance with them?" Sophea asked.

"Dear heavens, no," the woman scoffed, her eyes on Sophea's. "They're lower class."

Sophea tucked her blue backpack, noticing the woman's large leather handbag. As dark as the woman was, her face seemed white as a mask.

A group of three khaki-clad policemen appeared at the bar, checking IDs, their hands rested on sub-machine guns. "Name, IDs," they commanded.

"This is rubbish." The Real Indian woman scoffed. "Accompany me to the loo, will you?" She picked up a pink drink and took Sophea up a stairway crammed with nestling couples.

The bathroom did not carry the ornate glow of the rest of the club; it seemed to be the only place that wasn't immaculately clean. Ash was strewn about everywhere from used incense, and cheap stickers of Hindu gods were littered over the mirror next to a statue of a blue boy playing a flute, a god that Sophea recognized as Krishna, the god of karma who assigned one's fate.

"Can you help me darling?" The Real Indian woman unbraided her hair and turned around, expecting Sophea to get to work. But Sophea grew up with brothers, never braided her own hair, let alone a friend's. In the bathroom mirror, she saw her own frayed hair, her red dotted Indian dress. The woman was not her double—she was taller, richer, with fairer skin. And Sophea? Chubby, dark, with an oily face like a maid's.

"Darling?" the woman said. Sophea gave a smile, saw in the mirror how vacuous it was. Here was not the brown beauty, but the girl who hadn't changed since she was ten, maybe eleven, and exchanged her virginity to a man for free weed and booze.

And there was Krishna, flute in hand, counting her karma.

"You all right darling?"

"Excuse me," Sophea said. "Nature calls." She blundered the words as she stepped into a corner stall. She sat on the covered toilet, the cleanest place in the restroom, squeezing her hands together as if she were warming herself at a fire.

"Excuse me?" the Real Indian said to another woman, another victim mistaken for the help. "Darling, can you be a doll and give me a hand?"

Sophea languished in the stall. A window provided a view of the Marine Drive crescent. Large rocks filled the beach, splitting apart the ocean currents, collecting the sea's plastic bottles. A lone orange streetlamp illuminated the blue tarpaulin rooftops of a nearby alleyway. Makeshift houses whisked about in the breeze of an oncoming rainstorm.

"So long, darling!" the Real Indian woman said, but it was unclear who she was addressing.

Gigantic bats flew above her; stray dogs howled around her. The smell of smoked corn from a street stall wafted by as she stood in line for another cigar. Her hand went fumbling into her pocket for bits of change.

How long would she walk? When would her feet give her back the controls?

She followed a stream, not caring where it led. To walk was a requirement, to move was to stay a beat beyond that crushing nothing striving to outpace her. But movement was also a luxury. Merely to go, one foot in front of the other, crossing streets and bridges and demarcations, was extravagant.

Rain fell in a torrent. She kept under awnings, skipping upon loose bricks. A cycle rickshaw blew water onto her waist. The street ahead flooded and she waded into the water, feeling debris pass over her sandals. She held her backpack taut against her palms, her hands checking each zipper to secure her passport, wallet, and the purple "got chai?" hat that she had bought at a hawker stall.

Curious eyes stared her down. This Western brown woman so far from the tourist district. If life was a karma game, it seemed stacked against her. It was unfair that her brothers could cut through a garden park in the middle of the night in Oakland, fully confident, undaunted by the eyes staring about them.

She hadn't planned to walk all night, but her feet showed no sign of stopping. They moved in a rage, possessed by the spirit that hated her lot in life. She hated white people, sometimes. Hated America more often. And all of that hate bewildered her. There was so much logic in it, so much reason, so much justification. So many lies, so many bombs, so much death, so much hypocrisy, that anyone who didn't also hate America must have been living under a rock or in some white power fantasy. There was plenty of hate to make up for, plenty to take on.

She passed a child pleading for coin. She gave ten rupees and the boy scuttled off, into a large tunnel made of cardboard. She followed him into a market slum. Feathers and blood and chicken flesh were splattered around her feet. Bunched together bullfrogs croaked from inside red plastic nets. A giant turtle stuck its head from a blue grocery bag. She wondered how old it was, if it was in this world before her.

She frantically lit the Cuban cigar as she paced through the slum's drenched, soggy soil. Gas and paint fumes exuded from a small warehouse crammed with skeletal-thin workers.

She stepped over bodies sleeping on curbs and passed families under mosquito nets and tarpaulin. A group of shirtless boys followed her through the slum's tangled alleyways. She stopped to catch her breath and the boys merely pushed her aside, revealing a new walkway by teetering along the rim of a long construction pole. Their skin was far darker than the other Indians, their hair as clumped as cotton candy. Dogs passed with loose scraps of skin hanging from their stomachs, then oxen with thick leathered hides.

She found cover beneath a square of tarp as the rain came in a rush, drenching the streets. She watched the shirt-less boys diving into drainage gutters like slip and slides. Roosters leapt across the muddy streets, followed by mangy dogs with sagged breasts. Electric wire coiled fee-bly around the satellite disks atop each abode.

She was trained to only see decay, a place in need of sav-ing. But these too were refugees, minorities, commoners, locals. Their fate, like hers, was said to be writ from the misdeeds of their past lives. The space struck a memory within her, stories her mother told of the refugee camps in Cambodia and Thailand. There the camps were adorned with billboards proclaiming the Red Cross and the UN's many Human Rights organizations; here streets were bor-dered with NGO banners declaring it a developing space. There life was coordinated, governed by rules that cast suspicion on every brown body; here life was cast away, an eye-sore only visible to those who didn't mind the view. But Sophea saw in both places, the camp and the slum, life unruly and willing, full and fertile. The muddy streets made up a basketball court. The broken rooftops housed industrial work, carpentry, business, retail, and residenc-es all in the same space. She passed a bedroom converted into a cockfight pen, another into a shelter for stray cats, and another into a jewelry market. Her cigar smoke dissi-pated into a welder's steam.

When the rain let up, she kept moving.

Out of the slum, Sophea waded through a flooded street, her blue backpack held atop her head. She followed a grainy neon sign in American-diner font reading "Sunlight Cafe." She slid through a wrought-iron gate, opened a heavy door with a loud metal screech, and descended a stairwell into a quiet lounge.

The late night pub exhibited no intimacy. Customers sat on solid white leather couches framed in reflective steel. Several booths were made of large wooden planks, and the walls were decorated with framed photos of German-bred boxers. White belts and black striped ties hung loosely from white armchairs, and tables mimicked Chinese porcelain. The presence of a brown woman hung like a pall in the room. She received stern glances from the room of white and Indian men, half of them bent over newspapers, kettles of English tea at their side.

A young Indian waiter wearing tight cut-off jean-shorts brought her a towel. Her throat parched, she said "water," in a ragged gasp. The waiter nodded and sat her next to a large man with a kippah and a fat bottom-lip.

"I'm Gerald, nice to be meeting you, ah," the man said, mimicking the Indian accent and extending his arm. Sophea shook his large hand, nearly knocking over the small vase of plastic daffodils at the table's center. Gerald's age filled out his face, and wrinkles followed the V-line in his shirt. Sophea thought of movies like A Passage to India, about the colonial experience. These were the British remnants of the Gentlemen's clubs. Play, conversation, tea.

"Tea, mam?" said the waiter, placing a glass of water on the faux porcelain table.

She ordered coffee. Gerald took out a ream of pictures tied together by a rough pink band. "Have you ever seen a real, authentic Jewish wedding?" he asked with a welcoming smile. "This is my daughter's, married last month. That's me in the corner. I assure you, past th' dancing and the glass-breaking, it's just a regular thing, about love between two people, which is not so interesting, right?"

The electricity in the room blipped on and off, and the television in the corner set to the BBC had to be reset. The air conditioning surged stronger than before, causing Sophea to shiver.

A light skinned Indian man emerged from the back room with his hand in the back pocket of a young boy who wore a Yankees baseball cap, ripped jeans, and a purple shirt with the words "delicious" in pink and yellow rhinestones. The man sat next to Sophea, his teeth stained in bruised purple. Gerald introduced him as Kahn. Kahn had the face of a Bollywood star, with Gucci sunglasses, a black striped shirt and suede jeans, and most important, fair skin. But his demeanor was that of a prison guard. He gave her an aloof handshake and debased his driver waiting outside. "A big problem," he called him.

"And your name?" Gerald asked.

"Sophie."

"American?" Kahn asked. Sophea nodded. "But look," assessing her, "you don't look American, yes?"

Sophea was silent at first, noting how plainly Kahn sipped his tea. The waiter approached to refill her coffee. "My family migrated from Cambodia."

"They speak English fluently?" Gerald asked.

Sophea nodded. "They're Catholic." Of course, they had only converted to escape the camp.

"Cambodia," Kahn said. His tongue snipped against his

teeth to make a 'tsk, tsk' sound. He stood up to chat with another group of British men, his hand embracing a new boy next to him, pinching the boy's exposed belly. All the men had their dark-skinned boys. One laughed a burly laugh as his boy's head balanced on his protruding collar bone; one gave a wild accompanying cackle as he felt his boy's hips.

Sophea's eyes drew to a sign above the bar, in barely readable cursive:

The Dharavi Orphanage for Boys

She felt the blow of the air conditioner upon her neck, turning the rain water into an icy trickle down her stomach.

"It was hard for her growing up in the mid-west you know," Gerald said, talking about his daughter. "No one understood her." His voice was as coarse as steel wool.

Another group of older colonials stood up and walked sideways down a small lime-green hallway, hand-in-hand with their boys.

"As I say," Gerald continued. "People will either get what you're doing, or label you something convenient. I was a lawyer for twenty-six years, believe me, I've been labeled all sorts of unfair names."

A boy came out of the lime-green hall wearing only underwear, cleanly white. He joyously leapt onto Gerald's lap, his chest scrawny with dark patches as if he had been sewn together. Gerald held the boy by his stomach.

"Who is she?" the boy asked, trying to decipher her.

"Cambodian American," Gerald said for her.

"Cambodia!" the boy said. "There—bad thing happen, right?"

"That's right!" Gerald laughed with one tooth missing from those flat pink gums, a window shoving the world into his dark mouth. "Something very bad."

All the lines from history books occurred to Sophea though she could not say them. Cambodia, where the US, for eight years, secretly and illegally dropped more bombs than all the bombs in World War II. Cambodia, where America, the same year they passed the Civil Rights bill, killed people by the hundreds of thousands, capturing the sympathy of no one.

"Cambodians just like Indians," Gerald said, flipping through his book of wedding photos. "Made passive by religion and culture. They never fought back. A quarter of their country—a *quarter*," he pointed to Sophea as if striking a needle into fabric, "all killed, with no resistance whatsoever."

"Bad karma," Kahn said, returning with his strapped-up boy in his arm. "They had done something terrible in a past life."

Sophea looked up to a water-stain on the ceiling, the cracking paint; signs of age were everywhere. She could not register what they had said though she had heard it before. In history books. In public lectures. Whispered about on internet forums. By her girlfriends behind her back. But in America no one would ever say it to her face. Was that why she had come all the way to India? To visit a place where she, the refugee, garnered no sympathy, and was expected to show no gratitude? Where she could meet the naked world of men whose confidence reflected a lifetime of getting what they wanted, city by city, slum by slum, child by child?

The men about her had retired into the lime green hallway, their jeers echoing into the lounge, much smaller now than when she arrived.

She stood up. The air conditioning caused her to jitter toward the door.

She did not know which way to walk, so she just followed the nearest light-haze. Her feet moved in a rush, hoping to outpace everywhere she had been. Her hands balled into tense fists; she felt her heart relapse into madness. Anger weighed her body so heavily she could only stare at her sandaled feet as they skimmed through mounds of refuse: twigs, splinters, lopped off flower stems, sloughed off scarves. Lifting her head would risk a frightened glance or expose an onslaught of tears that came as regularly as drizzle from an overcast sky. Whatever it was had caught up to her, and now even in movement she remained submerged, only popping above the surface to catch bits of the world—a beggar, a street sweeper, a dealer. She breathed in quick gasps of oxygen before sinking again.

Still, she kept moving. When there was nothing left, there was always movement. From China to Vietnam to Phnom Penh to the countryside to the camp to the boats to the airplanes to the ghettos to the suburbs. And now here. The migration. She was born moving, made to move.

A hand waved from a second story window. A girl in a red sari, her face made up in matching blush. "Sir!" she called, smiling to a line of cars passing by like a herd of elephants.

Nearby were hundreds of women in brightly colored saris. They coated the street, summoning the passing cars and pedestrians. They cooed from windowsills, from street corners, from alleyways, grabbing at the men's belts as they roamed by. The herd of street cars forced Sophea to walk through lines of girls that never seemed to end, a mile-long wall of prostitutes hobbling to the cars on high heels.

A woman nearly touched her and she jerked away. She marched in the middle lane of a gridlocked street, expecting the wall of clamoring women to end. There were thousands of them. A sea of brown bodies decorated in fake jewelry and red saris.

Finally her legs began to give. Finally, exhaustion began to reach her, as if gravity could aim its forceful pull onto her alone, forcing her to stop. She turned down the nearest alleyway, crawled her arms against stone walls and sat on a plastic chair. She ended up in a square courtyard somewhere within the maze-like complex of windowless rooms. No one bothered her, she just sat staring at her sandals.

To transform herself was a foolish dream. The karma. The rightful place. She understood now why there was so little anger back where she grew up, why it all went into her. There was no beating it. No thinly disguised wire she could cut that would bring the entire imperial apparatus down. No weakness that could explode everything in a single Death Star-crashing victory. If it could not be beaten, what use was there to hate it? The answer was never as radical, never as rebellious as she wanted it. Defeat or be defeated, she knew how to keep moving along an unknown path.

Slices of sunlight cut the enclosure into thirds as dawn began to break. Away from the street corners, the courtyard now seemed a delicate space. A girl passed wearing a blue jumper with white floral patterns that fluffed about in the gust of the alley breeze. A group of women in blue slippers sat eating rice and curry with their claw-like fingernails, their heads flat with tightly woven hair. A pair of women sat beneath a naked yellow bulb picking at a sachet of chai granules, mixing it into their tea cups. Beside them, two teenage girls braided each other's hair, their feet kicking a rain puddle. One of them held a baby feeding from her breast. Blossoms were strewn about them like flames.

An older woman approached Sophea with a pregnant stomach. She wore one of those striped green and yellow pants made of flecked scales, which so many backpackers found fashionable. She gave Sophea's cheek a pinch. "So skinny," she said, and offered her a tray of dal curry and rice, motioning for her to eat. There was no fork, nothing visibly clean. Sophea felt the warm curry with her fingertips. The rice gunked in her nails as she stuck the congealed goop into her mouth. It went down warm. Her stomach rumbled, starving, though she hadn't known it.

"How is it sister?" the woman asked.

Before Sophea could answer, three khaki-clad policemen appeared at the courtyard's only escape route, wearing flat tan hats and AK-47 rifles. The women's chatter subsided into cowed silence. The men checked names and IDs, first in Hindi and then in Marathi. One of the women with chai granules in her fingers spoke neither language. As they took her away, she cried out in her mother tongue.

One of the policemen approached Sophea. He said something in Hindi, then in Marathi.

"I'm sorry?" Sophea said.

"English?" the man said in a rusty voice. "Name, Identification."

The other two police approached the woman in the blue jumper who had remained still as a decoration. She began to sob before the police even questioned her. They took her away into a smoke-filled alley.

"Name, identification!" the policeman stomped his foot, his black boot splashing mud across Sophea's legs and feet.

Sophea lifted her head to see the air brighten as the sun peaked above the cement houses. She watched the red saris and blossoms of the courtyard soften in the daylight as the clouds collapsed into bright silver streaks. The day seemed to renew itself, whether or not she was there to see it.

"Identify yourself!" the man said, kicking the plate of dal curry onto her jeans.

Warm peas coated her, but she would not move. Sophea only stared up, thinking: but when they take me, I will not scream.

The Flaneurs Spacechat

Chat log/June 12ᵗʰ 2008

2BWinston: at the bar ... smells like ass today ... amd cockroach on the floor

Sky4Flaneur: you know after a cockroach touches a human the first thing it does is lick itself clean

2BWinston: i thought you only licked dick skyler

Sky4Flaneur: I fancy women sometimes

Sky4Flaneur: whenever there's no lube around

2BWinston: which one feels better?

Sky4Flaneur: there's only one real difference between pussy and dick

Sky4Flaneur: pussy has better PR

2BWinston: thank you for that ... you coming to the bar tranny boy?

Sky4Flaneur: drinking alone tonight and playing xbox thank you

코니: that was my bar YEARS before it was yours

2BWinston: typical guai-po

2BWinston: so because youre korean blood everything belongs to you?

2BWinston: i can read korean fluently

코니: you cant be korean you barely even drink

Sky4Flaneur: thats because he's hopped up on prozac

코니: really?

2BWinston: my brother was the poster-child for it ...
now I am ... prozac does miracles

코니: your on prozac right now?

2BWinston: happy pills ... and yes ... its better than
losing brain cells—that's what depression
does to you

2BWinston: says Donne: my rags of heart can like, wish,
and adore, but after one such love, can love
no more

Sky4Flaneur: and woe is me

코니: i prefer you on prozac at least you wont
throw any little hissy bitch fits

Sky4Flaneur: are you out Connie?

2BWinston: Wheres Melanie been, anyway? she rarely
comes out anymore

코니: Im out with my koko friends

코니: as for Mel i made her stay at home

2BWinston: lets talk about this word *made* her

코니: she needs to practice. Ive been drumming
since I was 10. she's just started the base.
this band thing is gonna take off soon

2BWinston: white women can do anything ... never

took a class in education in her life yet
here she is making bank teaching english
... meanwhile I had to get a masters AND
provide a police record

Sky4Flaneur: because you grew up in asia?

2BWinston: no because Im black you banana scum

Sky4Flaneur: I prefer twinkie at least theyre sweet and
artificial

코니: dont fuckin minoritize yourself. All you
all are part of the exact shithead expat
negativity that Melanie needs to avoid

2BWinston: I get it lets do everything to protect the
white woman from the lustful negro and ...
whatever skyler is

Sky4Flaneur: twinkie

2BWinston: melanie is a white christian woman from
florida ... she's THE WORST of them

코니: no one is worse than arthur and you know it

KingArthur: I STILL ON THIS CHAT dweebs

2BWinston: where are you crackerjack?

KingArthur: gettin paid to be a pretend businessman in
tokyo.

KingArthur: staying in a 4 star hotel and well the knock
on the door is relentless

KingArthur: inspiring but relentless

코니: didnt know you were the type to say no

KingArthur: only when theyre 200 usd a pop

2BWinston: japanese love me ... never had to pay

KingArthur: WHY DOES YOURS ALWAYS HAVE TO BE BIGGER?

KingArthur: GIVING A CRACKER ANXIETIES OVER HERE

2BWinston: not that ... I just fancy the women-pleasing condoms

KingArthur: do those really work? CONNIE?

코니: how THE FUCK would I know

2BWinston: ask sky

KingArthur: as if that fag would ever use a condom

2BWinston: condoms and real women skyler's worst nightmares

Sky4Flaneur: zing

June 13th 2008

The bouncers were the only fully dressed men at Club Pulse. Besides them, gorgeous men squirmed into an indistinguishable pit of muscles like earthworms wringing in a mesh of flesh and dirt. A local boy reeled Skyler in with a dark blue scarf. He tottered away, toward the disco balls strung upon the smoke-filled ceiling. The bartender flipped the bottles six times before pouring Skyler another one.

"Jackie!" A man yelled. 'Jackie,' the name Skyler used the last time he visited the club, when he wore a shark suit and poked at the crowd with a fake harpoon. Skyler folded up the collar of his jacket to disguise himself and squeezed through the crowd. Unable to resist the sweat of festive floating worlds, he licked his tongue about in a paintbrush on the surface of anonymous pumping bodies as they pushed each other aside to receive his sacrament. He felt the *poke poke poke* of another harpoon at the back of his neck, but nothing would sabotage this purifying ritual.

He felt his smartphone vibrate with a text message and retreated through the back exit. It was Winston, no doubt ready to booze it.

2BWinston: Hey pimp, I'm here to whiskey you away

Skyler sat at a fast food patio table stacked with hamburger wrappers and chicken nugget cartons. Nearby, a young woman in a mini-skirt cleaned her partner's ear, scraping it with her nails and then blowing to whisk the dried wax out. Seoul's international district, Itaewon, was a foreigner's paradise, especially once curfew passed and the American soldiers from the nearby base were forced to leave. Skyler scarfed down leftover nuggets and shuffled between gridlocked taxis, diving into an alley where someone has chalked "Before I die, I want to _____" on a brick wall. Dozens of responses followed: "thank all the soldiers," "visit North Korea," "find love," "read Lord of the Rings," "love everyone," "ask for forgiveness."

Another vibration. Why did Winston even bother anymore? Their tribe of dejected expats once brought on a spike of courage, like a tequila shot to start off a night they'd eventually regret. Now, Skyler felt punch-drunk. Every line of chat, every text message, every invitation to "the bar," brought on a high pitched, headache-inducing ringing in his ears, made him see himself from afar, the self that he could not unsee. He walked on, picking up the pace, trying to stop that image from bleeping in, but there it was: the American not-quite-Asian-and-not-quite-white heathen queer. The butt of all jokes, the end of all cautionary tales.

He brainstormed cheap accommodation, confident that he could find the sauna where he and Sophea slept on drunken nights, when they were the last expats standing. He felt the vibration of more text messages. He refused to check them until he was in a sauna's bunk-bed alongside a hundred other derelict bodies, safe from the night's seductions.

On a railway bridge, his eyes connected with the city's homeless. They dressed in pink, yet their funk was the same as anywhere. His phone vibrated warmly against his thigh. He couldn't help it and cycled through their messages. They began innocent enough,

KingArthur: Who wants to get fuuucked up?!

But the night was already erupting into predictable ire.

2BWinston: Fucking cunt-bitches don't even make eye contact.

He found the trashcan where Sophea dry-heaved toxic breath, singing Journey into the yellow can, laughing at her own echo. Here was where she had turned left.

At the sauna's front desk, a friendly elder handed Skyler a water-proof key and a locker number, which he tied to his wrist with a rubber strap. Even in his dark dress and filled-in bra, Skyler was too nervous to ask for the women's section. With Sophea, he was one of the girls, without her, a pervert hoping to sneak a peek. In the women's sauna, he and Sophea had washed each other with a white shower tube, both nude. He had lathered her hair and slapped soaps on her body while she scrubbed his back with a grated towel. "That fucking sweet Filipina ass," she had said, slapping his rear. "Turn around you. Again. So exotic, little lady. Come on, around around around."

When he first met Sophea in Phnom Penh she asked him why he traveled. He told her he wanted to walk like he was dying. With uppers and juicers for all. And there was something about his brown skin and his American passport that made this method of dying even more epic. They strategized together, drinking Beerlao at a former French hotel, imagining all the places where they could go to disappear. The destitute bakla bars of Manila. The lakesides of Yunnan. The Himalayan foothills, then trek to Varanasi when it got cold. They would just need to work for a couple years, save enough, then boom—with new names, they would disappear. But until then, the sauna was the best place to drift in exile. Instant comforts, ready-made conveniences, immaculate cleansing, purifying fermentation rooms. And no one ever asked your name.

Mangas and self-help books lined the walls of the lounge, where men loafed upon striped brown couches. Skyler followed a forty-something woman until she reached her husband and son. He gave up the chase, venturing into a karaoke room to practice the few songs he learned to get women wet: "Hello," "Your Song." Then the songs to get gentlemen hand-in-pants hard: "Unbreak My Heart," "Killing Me Softly."

Korean Christian music shouted exaltations from the sauna's Samgik restaurant. Skyler sat across a family: the father scolded his youngest son; the wife massaged his shoulders; a middle-aged auntie sipped Jjigae soup. The auntie had a slight mustache and her stark skinny legs splayed beneath the table. Her petite body supported large breasts, and her side-gaze put her in portfolio. It took months for Skyler to learn that in Korea, a person turning to you, not looking, not giving a hint of interest, but showing you their side like a fashion model, meant something.

He retreated to the locker room, throwing wax into his hair and rummaging through his tiny locker for musk, hoping to woo her from afar. His cell phone vibrated again.

KingArthur: Skyler!! Where are you tranny faggot

A year before, only Sophea dared call him those names—
faggot, tranny, whore, island hopper, chink. He brought
it upon himself, letting her say it, letting others repeat it,
until that's what he was. But the last time Skyler saw her,
at the bar, she didn't call him any of those names. She was
quiet, alone, slouching in her usual head-in-hands position. When the music changed to the next song, Skyler
heard her let out a long groan. So long it wrenched the
gut, curdled the bones. Long enough, perhaps, for someone to knock on her door, for the sound of a siren. Arthur
laughed, then Winston, then Skyler himself, as if the groan
was a burp or sudden fart. Silent, Sophea sat upright, her
knees to her eyes.

The groan was a scream. A surrender. A yielding to them,
to Skyler himself, a person who had never in his life had
power over anyone.

Skyler put the phone away and added another layer of lotion to his cheeks. He took the stairway to the restaurant,
hoping to entice the auntie with his meager Korean language skills. Passing the barrier from stranger to boy-toy
came in four syllables: *Cheep-ae upsoyo*, I have no home.

June 14th 2008

Skyler spent the first four hours of the morning inside the
top floor's warehouse of bunk beds, on a top bunk, covered
in a teal sheet and reading Eric Fromm's *To Have or to Be*,

the only English book in the sauna's lounge. In the sauna mirror he found a nascent pimple tainting the right-side of his face, and he instantly flung the book in the trash, along with its dust and dirt and easy-to-grasp existentialism. He went for a pre-natal pop, but his skin swelled like a banana bruise. Recoiling, he felt a slight roughness in his hair, a slight rub of stubble upon his chin, a touch of rolled dirt on his forehead. He felt thankful that he was never expected to get eye surgery, or use cleansing lotion, or wear facial masks. And his face in the mirror—the face of a butch lesbian, a petite tomboy, a riot grrrl drummer. His hair, now black and well past his ears, was an either-or, a tantalizing question mark hovering above him, the kind followed by an ellipsis or redaction. He could have gone all the way, but he shuddered at the thought of being trapped in a woman's body. His look was a temporary refuge, a place to leap in and out like two selves, one ruled by the sun, the other the moon.

He laboriously scrubbed himself in the sauna with a pink grated towel until his arms singed in bright red. The pain seethed, covered him in a prickly calm.

In the lounge he watched a news program at Seoul's City Hall, where young protestors marched with signs, some in orange T-shirts performing synchronized dance. He brought his legs onto the cushion and watched, the story growing duller. The signs reading *No Free Trade* and *Despicable America* made him drowsy. He found sweetness in the silence that followed, when a gaunt Ajusshi turned off the television. His body entered the cushioned seat like a ship into a harbor.

He awoke some hours later, gripping a small pillow to his torso. Advertisements flashed on screen of half-dressed race-car women making cute faces.

I can't show my own face out there, Skyler thought. I won't be caught again.

June 20th 2008

A week passed in the sauna. At four in the morning, Skyler sat on the small stairway nearby the fake caverns, watching a crowd of sleeping bodies, some on individual mats, some in awkward positions upon the rocks and leather massage chairs. Some slept upon six mats and five rectangular pillows, some toppled on top of each other, while some snoozed directly upon the black tiled floor of the PC room amid the cacophony of loud music, gun shots and keyboard taps. It looked like the conclusion of either an orgy or a massacre: bodies with hands beneath their pants, bodies in the cold stairwell positioned like fresh corpses. Skyler returned to his bunk-bed. With nothing left to do he took out his pen, hoping to settle that urge in him to say something grand that came from living overseas. Something to justify all the time he'd wasted, all the money he'd spent, all the people he'd betrayed. But what could he say? If his life in America was a myth, a grand fantasy prefaced by seductive lies, the past year had been a caressing silence, a page better left blank.

June 25th 2008

After two weeks in the sauna Skyler noticed people, again and again, moving through the same catacomb-like sleeping caves, one after another, each time stopping to catch a glimpse of him, the unexplained foreigner in their midst. He drifted, they cruised, enticing him to follow.

July 1st 2008

Finally, that large-breasted mustached auntie reappeared. She looked at Skyler with a coy grin. He chased her up a stairwell with no way out but by retreat. He folded into her, into the cavern, felt her need for touch.

July 11th 2008

If one desired to make a middle-aged woman as palatable as possible, they could do little better than to put her in a bright orange, elastic, one size fits all jump suit, as the saunas had done. She visited him again, letting him grip her shampoo-scented hair and kiss her speckled face, still moist from the steam of the firewood sauna room. Journeys emitted from her pupils. He felt all of life's solids chip away. Everything seemed perishable, removed, unencumbered, running downstream. Her moans in the sauna's small sleeping cavern bewitched him, the way her echo settled as he pulled her curly hair. He felt himself disappear, caught in her womb.

July 15th 2008

A month of reflection within the sauna's walls, time enough, Skyler thought, to start writing something to wrap it up. Not like those travel blogs, but a real story, one about empire and torture and struggle and domination without hope. He imagined the last days of that Korean heroine, the martyr from Ewha. He saw her as her reputation had her: a model of resistance against the Japanese, a school girl who had never turned old.

PART TWO: RESSENTIMENT

September 15ᵗʰ, 1920, Seodaemun Prison

The girl is silent as Captain Sasaki inspects her papers for a third time, looking for something to spark the uncivil, tribal rage that he felt the first time he beat her. He finds only obnoxious information. Her name, Yo Kwan-Sun, age seventeen, high school student.

"You claim you get no food in detention," Sasaki scolds, "but look at your cheeks!" He pinches and slaps her face.

You know nothing about her except what you were told: a village girl from Ewha School rousing nationalist sentiment. The only sounds Sasaki can get out of her are odd, drawn-out groans.

At Sasaki's signal, you splash her eyes with pepper water. The sunlight still comes through the prison block and you wonder if the other nationalists can hear her muffled screaming. Sasaki's voice is loud enough: "You call this a flag?! You war mongers. Entire Asia is behind us! I piss on it."

You wish it was all over, that Sasaki wouldn't bother reviving the girl again and again. But someone had to be responsible for the paintings of Korean myths circulating among the other inmates. Whenever she speaks, her tongue bleeding from her own teeth, she only coughs out words in Korean. Sasaki fists that red pinched cheek. Her jaw cracks like a smashed beetle. Her cheeks puff even more, her face red like a balloon. She keeps whimpering in Korean.

"You think this is honor?" Sasaki screams at her as she crawls, a heaping mass, toward the center of the floor, her blood following her like slime.

July 20th 2008

Skyler floated sweetly in a deferred abyss, a life of limbo, of shaving cream and hair-wax. Dreary when he woke, he no longer found even a microscopic remnant of a pimple, or a scar, or even a blackhead.

In the PC room he thought of contacting someone. His ex-girlfriend Kiera, his family, his old church mates, all those he abandoned. The phone calls and emails had long stopped coming. Those back home had finally given up on him. He recalled every moment of impulse, every hurt, until he was overcome by the sheer number of flaws to be scrubbed out. To be clean, in total, was to be like the moon. Germless, weightless, and somewhere out there. He longed to float above the world, showing only the side of himself he wanted to show. The rest, permanently shrouded in black.

July 23rd, 2008

His Korean students once told him that showering before a test would wash away all knowledge. Knowledge of books, of history, of all those ridiculous fantasies.

When he showered he slapped himself, increasingly harder. He leaned against the tiled walls, water drowning out his sobbing. His cheeks throbbed. The water slickened his palms so that each slap felt like a boxing glove. Another slap and he felt blood vessels pulse in raw panic. Another slap and his eyes saw white space. He slapped like a battering ram pounding the doors of an overgrown keep.

July 27th, 2008

He returned to the woman's sauna, this time, five pounds lighter, hair at his shoulders, and a spotless face. Still, he was by no means the best looker, nor was he the only woman who kept a towel hiding his crotch and flat chest. He used the beauty products, trotting in and out. Nobody seemed to care.

He thought of how he might negotiate his belonging: he could try to spend an equal time in each, half in the women's sauna, half in the men's. He could try to kiss an equal number. He could try to maintain symmetry like two halves of a body reflecting each other.

An elderly auntie in the woman's sauna smiled at him, a perfunctory, *are-you-done-with-that-hair-dryer-yet* smile. He moved over. She combed her hair, carefully drying its roots. When he returned to his locker, he realized nobody had even noticed his dick, drooping below his towel.

September 20th, 1920, Seodaemun Prison

You flush her again with cold water. Her third resurrection of the day. Beating her has tired all three of you: Sasaki, Hakamata the interpreter, and yourself. You gasp when the terrorist's limbs move again. Her head rolls to look at you all, her eyes making out figures in a dream.

Sasaki has had enough. He strangles her with his boot. The interpreter scrambles to get him off. The stone floor sees blood. The interpreter burns his cigarette into the terrorist's right breast, just inches above her nipple. The burn sinks into her skin.

On a smoke break you watch the misty green hills and think of your brother Kenji in the Manchurian outposts. You wonder about his new sights and new girls. And you, stuck in this hell.

Sasaki continues taunting her: "We liberated you, we have given you your honor!" Her voice becomes an instrument of screams played with bamboo sticks.

August 1st 2008

No one spoke when Skyler went with them. No names to the bodies, not even a body—just skin. Hair. Muscle. Pores. Pieces to lie upon, to keep on top, to soften a fall. Everything came down to the kiss: lips, saliva, teeth. The kiss forgets. The kiss is any sex. Tongues any gender. Taste any color. In the steam, everything is made smooth.

August 5th 2008

Skyler re-read Sophea's messages on an empty stomach, to keep from vomiting. He felt her breath still residing somewhere, sometimes foul. Why was her refuge not their refuge? When did he become the thing to run away from? What was she hoping to find that he couldn't give?

September 23rd, 1920, Seodaemun Prison

Captain Sasaki enters with sharp bamboo rulers. "Careful!" the interpreter warns. "You might kill her." At those words her eyes drop; grasping finally that she is still within her own body, still enduring the dearth of existence.

"Before us you lived in ignorance!" Your mouth screeches, but you can't feel yourself say these things. "You open your legs for the Americans, the Christians! But not for your true liberators!" Your arm grips the bamboo and you strike her thighs. You close your eyes as you slap her, unable to watch. You don't want to hurt her—you just want to hurt her until she gives in so you don't have to hurt her. You want her to give in so badly you thrust the bamboo into her stomach, just above her belly button, with all the power you can muster.

August 19ᵗʰ 2008

A tongue moistened Skyler's lips, softly, as he slid out of the man, and curled into his arms. The man asked for a name. Skyler recalled his many names: Nico, the poor Filipino student; Cecil, the studious observer; Richard, the fastidious cosmopolitan critical of anything resembling backwardness; Caravaggio, the partying beast determined to plunge into the depths of debauchery. Kawika, a name he could never earn, the kernel of his heart.

September 25ᵗʰ, 1920, Seodaemun Prison

"You want to cut her in half?!" Captain Sasaki barks.

Two orderlies bring in a stone pot. Sasaki hands you an iron stick, heavy and white-hot at the tip. "Under torture women can sometimes be more resilient than men," Sasaki says. "She hopes to die before the worst."

The Captain chose you, the most brutal of men. Now, to unsee your body, you don't even have to close your eyes.

August 23rd 2008

Skyler scrubbed himself with the pink grated towel. Redden the skin, force it to grow anew.

Sophea pursued a forlorn dream. She wouldn't wait, didn't care to save money. Disappearing called her, its gravity too intense to ignore. Chatroom messages could never capture her aggressive, slightly threatening, slightly enticing tone. He remembered how she tossed her dark eyes around a room, the way she flung them like rocks from a slingshot. He remembered the smell of her body odor at the day's end, the feeling of sitting with her on the roadside, arm in arm, leaning on each other, the sun turning everything blue.

He remembered the first night they wandered into the women's change room together, bottles of soju blocking their privates. Sophea had pulled him into the women's jacuzzi and bolts shot up his nerves. Even in the steam, his skin turned cold.

"Kawika," she had called him. "Get in!"

The name was a lie. He was a fake, anyone could see it. But Sophea didn't think so.

Blood streamed down Skyler's arm. It collected in his palm and trickled toward a dark drain. The pain felt surreal, pinching, erotic. His heart relaxed; the sting rippled through his limbs. He drew away the grated pink towel where the blood had thickened into the shape of an archipelago.

September 28, 1920, Seodaemun Prison

Sasaki holds the terrorist's soft arms as the saw grinds apart her bones. Those final words still sit upon her lips, that declaration still inducted into your brain. You sip warm sake, listening to them cutting.

"See how they need us!" Sasaki shouts to a group of guards, the sounds of cracking bone testing their resolve. "How they are so oblivious, caught in the web of ideas, spreading their Gods. That is why we must change them, why we must educate our brethren. We must pull these weeds! We must release them forever from the imperialists of the West!"

Cleaning out her cell for the next inmate, you find a drawing of a paper flag, a simple cross on paper, drawn in blood.

Skyler didn't know where this story was going. The words just drifted into him, pushing down pain, only to see it bubble up again. He thought he should say something, anything, to unmake the blank page. But what were words written in the single-framed pause of an air conditioned bathhouse?

The auntie returned, sitting across from him in the pine tree firewood sauna, telling jokes to her nephew. When Skyler left, she followed him into a cave cubby. The soft slow touch of skin connected them. He kissed the cracks of her skin, the blood veins on her wrists and palms, the spots on her calves covered by translucent layers of soap. His fingers entered her and he felt her hymen, webbed like taut thread. He pushed in, massaging deeper.

"Speak English," she whispered into his ear. "Please. English so sexy."

"I don't know what to say," he whispered in barely audible words.

"Please-eh. English."

He rotated his finger around her frail cone. "I don't know what to say."

"ugh. Yes. More." She bit his ear.

"I don't know what to say," he whispered again.

She squeezed his penis. Her body spread on top of him. Despite her hymen it went in easily.

"Keep English!" she moaned loud enough for the entire sauna to hear.

"I don't know what to say." He closed his eyes in the darkness and let the feeling of being inside her the only sign of being there at all.

September 1st 2008

He woke in the sauna's rock-shaped cavern, where the temperature rising from the ground was a dizzying forty-five degrees Celsius. His body had no more sweat to release. Strangers rotated in and out; their language fled the atmosphere of heat and bodies, pleasure and cleanliness. From there he went to the cold room and sat upon a bench of cracked ice. He went back and forth, hot and cold. Visitors sighed with pity and avoided his eyes, but they were only tourists in his land.

In the small cavern bed he began another story, as true as he could make it, about empire and torture and struggle and domination without hope.

One day you escape into a new world. You find your military in every place you visit. Everyone speaks your own language to you. Everyone admires you. You try to hide from them, ashamed of your place. But in time, after a year or so, after feeding off their excitement and delight, you allow yourself to pretend that you had done something to earn it.

September 6th 2008

Nearly three months had passed since Skyler entered the sauna. But here he was outside, blinking in the sunlight of the humid summer. He walked to the Han River, legs tense with every step. No one bothered to look at the water lapping against a beach of discarded soju bottles, cigarette cases, and rice cakes reeking in the sun.

He felt the muggy sweat of the city's pollution. Knee-deep in the river, he shed his shirt to feel the sun's rays bake his skin, his only home.

The Flaneurs Spacechat

Chat log/September 7th 2008

Sophea_S: sup you scrots.

2BWinston: holy shit! Welcome back sophie!

코니: knew youd surface eventually

코니: i kept telling them biotch can take care of
herself

Sophea_S: Yeah. In Goa now.

Sophea_S: Just hung around with a boy toy for a week.
Had the most vanilla-est of intercourses.

2BWinston: how long has it been?

Sophea_S: I don't know, for two and a half months I
was locked up. In Mumbai.

코니: WHAT?

2BWinston: told you it was just a matter of time

Sophea_S: Not for smuggling. Don't wanna talk about
it.

2BWinston: indian jail ... never been there ... what was it
like?

Sophea_S: Oh boy—a lot of people from all walks of
life. It must have been a special foreigner-
only jail. There were Sikhs, Brits, Aussies,
Israelis, etc. all foreigners, mostly collared
for just being dumb tourists like me, or
not paying taxes. Bars on the window
and doors but mostly people curled up in

blankets on the floor trying to sleep it off between meals. I just curled up in my green wool blanket like everyone else and waited for lunch. Then back to the blanket until dinner. After dinner, back to the blanket until the canteen vendor who sold us chips and pepsis.

2BWinston: sounds galaxies better than thai jail ... no maggot-infested rice?

Sophea_S: No—but sometimes I looked around for a bathroom fixture high enough to tie a noose.

Sophea_S: Sorry got morbid.

Sophea_S: How is everyone?

코니: Mel's the same keeps herself busy

2BWinston: Arthur's away ... still being paid for being white

코니: but no one actually misses him

2BWinston: ... he has a kid you know

코니: christ of course he does

Sophea_S: What about Sky?

2BWinston: he's still ... around

2BWinston: going through some karma chameleon shit

Sky4Flaneur: Im right here

Sky4Flaneur: still in seoul

코니: he says nothing for months until sophie
                shows up

2BWinston: yeah we see what's going on ... brown only
                loves other browns

Sky4Flaneur: sophea are you staying in goa? Im checking
                flights from seoul right now

Sophea_S: You want to join me?

Sky4Flaneur: I do

코니: aw

Sophea_S: Fine, but only on one condition.

Sky4Flaneur: I know none of that travel-helps-you-find-
                yourself bullshit

Sophea_S: :)

THREE

Chora

ThinkTravel! Blogbook

Post Date: 2008 SEPT 8

User: SkyFaralan

You again leave your no-life for the dark blot of unknown, searching for what? You are done searching. Now you move out of habit, to get away from repetition, which is despair. To escape recognition, to escape belonging, which is to belong to them.

At a bar in Goa you are nudged awake by a martial arts teacher high on LSD. He tears apart little bits of napkins onto his leg. Behind him naked Israelis run into the hills, crazed out on ecstasy, tripping on stumps, too impaired to notice the blood running down their ankles. You warn them to be careful of the coconuts—because if one hits them on its way down, there will be nothing but a convulsing carcass.

The women selling bangles on the beach join you for a chai; one tells you her husband always goes out to play with his whores, leaving her to work. As you bargain for a price, she tells you: "If you buy at this price, my husband get angry, beat me beat me!" The complaints are cut-off by an Indian man who comes to survey them. He shouts something in a scolding voice and they scatter off.

You assume it's all a ruse to sell you bangles.

On the beach, the Kathans from the south of Hampi sell trinkets handmade by their families in the villages. At night these former Adivasis sell ecstasy and acid. They hail you in German, English, Hebrew, Hindi, Tamil, French, Spanish and Portuguese. But they mostly know the curse words picked up from foul mouthed backpackers. What would be trashy be-

havior in any other country has become everyday parlance for the Goan locals.

"Goa collects the profanity of the traveler," Sophea tells you. "Shize, panpcha, baka na, merde, madar chod."

You walk behind Sophea on a beach of black sand, stepping in her footprints to erase your being here. She lets the lukewarm ocean lap at her heels. A cigarette butt flirts with her toes in the surf. She says the foam makes her thirsty for a cold one. She passes a group of Indian women with their bags full of bangles and says Apkiya hay and you repeat the same words with the same squinty smile.

You stare at the ripening coconuts at the top of a palm tree. The man selling cashew alcohol was the first of many to tell you never to stand beneath the palm trees on a windy day, that when the coconuts fall there is rarely a head left to recognize. You stand below these trees in doubt, wondering if these warnings were just another way to build rapport. Not even you have that much interest in your own wellbeing.

You tell Sophea to kick the tree. She seems distracted, a bangle-selling Kathan next to her. "I'm going to kick the tree then," you say. Sophea smiles at you, but listens to the bangle seller. You kick the tree anyway.

You smoke before and after sex, always hash mixed with tobacco. You welcome her habit of smoking before sex, to phase-shift before tossing about between the sheets.

Sophea looks Hindi. One wouldn't think she was a tourist. She claims all Cambodians have Indian blood. The way she wears her short frizzed hair must be your type, because it's giving you far more erections than those bikini-clad French tourists. You wonder why she let you join her here. You thought that maybe she needed you to protect her from rapey Indian men. But you have yet to see one.

When you found her at the fish market she burst into laughter at your suspicions. She had only invited you because of you: you seemed so lonely, so pathetically lost, and you were doing nothing in Korea but taking up space. She speaks to you with vast eyes, a cigarette clutched between her teeth.

You stick around to watch her send stern glares of reproach to the Indian men cajoling her in Konkani. You watch her gossip with a brightly clad Indian woman who holds her hand. You don't know if you're a couple or just spun together. Two brown Americans traveling Asia, seeking that spectacular anarchy—that rapturous wanderlust that makes your lovemaking so much fresher. But she's no loser like you. You, a self-titled sojourner consuming places without purpose, a drunk kicking coconut trees, a hippie who knocks off in Goa as if it were a puritanical duty. Now you no longer hold any pretense to adventure, to learning other cultures, to challenging yourself. You're not a traveler, just an escaped convict. You ran when you knew that the next time someone crossed you, called you a fag or a sissy or tried to nudge you into their religion, their fragrant white fantasy, you were either heading to jail or you would be found killed. You became so certain of this that on the way to the airport you closed your eyes.

In the morning you see Sophea in the field outside the hotel, staring at a dead cow. The animal seems at peace, its head broken in by a stray coconut. Her fingers make a cone to light a blunt against the ocean wind. Next to the animal a young shop owner paints her nails white.

"Where's Sky now?" asks no one anywhere.

Let them put your story to the grave.

The concert after-party had somehow turned the scattered disarray of fans and musicians into a single swarm of unified degeneracy, a raucous, multistoried affair. The three bands, their groupies, managers and fans, had all packed into the first six floors of a downtown high-rise, a tower of shoddy bars, pool clubs, and karaoke rooms. Every minute more joined, culled by the free jello shots and clanking soju bottles.

Melanie strolled through the third-story bar, her fingers tracing the burnished beer bottles that decorated the booths and pillars, encircling the musicians who were sprawled across stain-ridden sofas holding bottles of Gatorade mixed with soju. She munched on dried seaweed, waiting for Jack Synyster, the lead singer of Photobook, to return from the bathroom. When one of Jack's bandmates approached her, she feigned a buzz by acting mesmerized with the detailed design of a Go-Stop card between her fingers. The man was Photobook's bassist, Vince, a thin man with a glued green Mohawk whose only bearable mode of expression was his instrument. Vince's acne-ridden face bobbled up and down like a protruding Adam's apple as he soberly gave her his personal confessions, the kind only permissibly told while drunk: "You can never know just how much you want to be a father until you are told by some girl that you're the father."

"Huh," Melanie said.

"And you know what? Having a daughter only made me want to have more."

Melanie wove passed him, nodding her way through more musicians and fans until she reached the pool table at the back of the bar. Just as she was about to land an angle shot for the eight ball, Jack nudged her, his spiky black hair knocking back a chandelier. "Is there any blood on my face?" he asked. "Nosebleed again."

"All over. Jus' kiddin', actually." She swayed her hips toward him, inviting him to grab her ass, which he did. Like most foreigners teaching in Korea, she had gained at least ten pounds from the fried chicken, the widely available fast food, and the late night rice cakes drowned in honey.

Jack was checking himself in the glossy mirror wall when two Korean fans hooked themselves to him with officious greetings: "Your band was a-mai-zing!" one said slowly and loudly. "We very en-thu-sed!" They gripped him by the elbow as they shook his hand.

Jack held his left arm around Melanie as if to anchor himself. The two made a photogenic couple. Both were English teachers in Korea who agreed to star in made-up bands—her Dark Rose, him Photobook—and they were both instructed by their managers to wear the same black leather jackets with denim jeans, a type of fashion that Melanie only knew from biker movies. Though she didn't look near as ridiculous as the lead guitarist and singer of her band (they wore little red riding hood uniforms), Melanie liked to mix her outfit with the gold and silver bangles she had picked up in Malaysia. Jack's attire, on the other hand, seemed far less planned out. The chains hanging from his belt rung like wind chimes when he walked. His pants hung so low that his dark brown boxers were exposed, confirming the stereotype that white Americans had no ass whatsoever.

Vince reappeared. "You know, Titus Andronicus was by far Shakespeare's best," he said, and a sip of beer later: "did you see the movie?"

"Too long," Melanie said. "I didn't get it." She tipped herself away from Jack's grip.

"Don't ya love that?" Jack said. "Doesn't get Shakespeare!"

Melanie hadn't had a drink that night, but made an effort to appear too wasted to communicate with. Usually she would hide beneath her cigarettes and books, but all these foreigners liked to smoke, and pretended to be well read.

One of the members of Photobook plunged into a neighboring jacuzzi, screaming as he did so: "My Giraffe wears sooo many scarves!" The scream was followed by the distant smack that Melanie thought was either a lackluster belly flop or the snap of a bra from the fifth floor stairway where her all-female band mates were masochistically yanking each other's straps. Vince laughed like a hyena and then said something she selectively misheard.

"That's really interesting," she responded in a monotone voice, the only way she knew to make her disinterest explicit, before turning to lumber her way through a tightly packed hallway. She sought out Jack, addicted by now to staring at his chest while blocking out his words. He had left as soon as he came, like a trauma-inducing object flashing in and out of a dream. As her shoes stuck to a red candy substance on the floor, she heard a surge of pops, then Jack's unmistakable voice coming from a nearby karaoke room, Photobook's whiny, high-toned screech.

Hard beats hit her the instant she entered. A table full of hollow chips and cans of Cass beer stood on a black couch, leaving the center of the room open for a ten-man mosh-pit. The only non-Korean was Jack, who was thrusting fans around the room like tossing children up in the air. Not caring to stay and witness the inevitable moment when, in show-stopping bravura, Jack would accidentally crush one of them with his heavy black boots and all the beer bottles would go crashing to the floor, Melanie withdrew into a stairway, un-doing her long pigtails. The crash, when it came, sounded like a power cord through a distorted amp.

She followed the scent of red pepper to a vat of dukbokki, the best food she could ever remember eating. She had eaten so many of those red-peppery rice cakes that her jeans nearly burst (thus making her fatness official). She peered at the juicy goodness, but her stomach retched, and she retreated to the bathroom. She heard the sound of a girl vomiting and entered to find the drummer of her band, Connie, on the bathroom counter, pretending to vomit in order to chase away fans.

"Oh it's you," Connie said, spitting twice into the sink. "Do you usually cut yourself when you shave your legs?"

"Mmm-hmm," Melanie said, eyeing herself in the mirror. "I can't walk for days sometimes." She glanced at her body fat, bulging from her waist like pudding left in the sun. She had probably looked ridiculous on stage, throwing peace signs to the crowd, spreading her legs and staring at them from between her disproportional thighs. Though she was selected to go on-tour with this makeshift commercial band only because of her foreigner body and farmer's-daughter face, she never felt used. In her mind, she was always the exploiter.

She drew out a set of three hexagonal pills. They were the last set of the day, the ones that would tear out the marble-sized embryo growing inside her.

"Dude, it's so much easier to shave in this dank bathroom," Connie said, wiping sweat from her tank top. "Like, not a scrape. It must be the humidity. Or, like, my sweat."

"We sweat for music." Melanie lapped water into her mouth and took two ibuprofen tablets, in case the pain started early. "We are *the* great American Rock Bay-and."

"Please tell me you're not in here to avoid telling Jack."

"That guy. So glad he ain't gonna be my baby's daddy. Idiocy and certainty, bad combo."

"He's probably too thick to even know what's going on."

"But he's thinner than a rail. I'm the thick one, hello!"

"No, dude, thick as in *stupid*." Connie fixed her blonde hair into tight buns. To be part of their fake band, she had to go blonde, and decorate her hair with chopsticks like a weeb.

"I was gonna name her after you," Melanie said from atop the bathroom counter, chin to her knees. "Guess I still can."

"Aw!" Connie squealed in laughter. She placed her palm on Melanie's abdomen, just below the biker shirt where the words 'Wild Rose' were spelled in thorny vines. "Little baby Connie," Connie chirred. "Fortune did not favor either of us, did it?"

They hid in the bathroom for hours, first sitting on the counter, then lying placid on the floor as Connie talked Melanie through the pain, helping her decide when to increase her dosage and when to switch from ibuprofen to codeine. After Connie finally fell asleep on the counter, Melanie found that the painkillers had given her a hazy dream-like confidence. She strapped on a pad and unsteadily slipped out of the bathroom, spelunking into the cavernous party still raging on.

Her fingers traced the pulpy paint along the walls as the painkillers pulled her along in an undertow. The sharp pain woke her up to a higher plane and she watched herself moving along the walls slowly, inches at a time. The Korean written characters gaped at her like open mouths, then assorted themselves into colorful Tetris blocks. She smelled cooked rice from an open door and heard a dozen Korean tongues through another, excited to kill each other in a video game. She went toward an open window only to recall the smell of sewer. She clutched her stomach like it was her only chain to the ground. She found herself face-to-face with the second guitarist for the cover band, Counterfeit, whose name she had forgotten. The other band mates popped out, grinning at her in surreal Whack-a-Mole glee. She gave a cute blush and leaned toward the lead singer, a dark man in glasses. "Hi, um," she said, pleading for a rescue from the pain welling in her torso. "Ya'll got the time?"

"Only if you've got the energy."

She pushed past their laughter, feeling pain come in bursts of static. She found herself alone again, wandering the halls and stairwells, keeping her eyes on the red-tiled floor to step over passed-out bodies and empty soju bottles.

She found another large karaoke room full of dancing fans pleading for her to join them. Her wooziness must have made her look drunk, because the Korean men started grabbing at her waist and touching her legs, saying "mass-ag-ae, mass-ag-ae" to appease her. When the stomach pain woke her, she smacked them away, hard, her skull-rings cutting their cheeks. She waddled best she could into a lobby full of plastic surgery advertisements, and then down a stairwell, descending into an industrial dystopia of bottles and crushed ramen packets.

In another karaoke room, she finally found Jack, richly garlanded with soju bottle caps. In the middle of the room a young woman in a short skirt sang an oddly worded techno song: "I'm horny, horny horny horny in the ni-ig-ht." The girl pleaded for a dance partner, blowing kisses at the shy men.

Melanie stood next to Jack but felt another person's hand on her shoulder. Some Cass-smelling fan, dancing with his arms in chopping motions. "Your band, your band very good!" the man shouted, tossing his hands at her.

Melanie chewed on an imaginary piece of gum. "We suck. We wrote all our songs in a month."

"You were great!" he yelled above the music's increasing volume.

"I only just learned to play base over the summer."

"You rocked us out! Best American rock band!"

"No one knows who we are in America." She bent to silence the pain in her abdomen. "We're just pretending because for some reason ya'll think America's cool. Every one of us here's faking it. Like, for real, I'm pregnant. I just took the abortion pills! Ha! So—there is a child inside me dying right now."

Jack looked stunned, finally his eye-shadowed eyes on her. The Korean fan slowed his dance movements. "I just— was very curious, and had some free time," he said. "I'm sorry."

Melanie managed a half-hearted chuckle, grating her teeth through the pain, and held her hand to his face, sweet with sweat.

Three hours later Melanie woke to the sunrise, her abdomen pain roused by the buckling of the bands' large tour bus. She looked outside from her seat in the back row, layered with blankets, and saw a blur of glossy foliage. The still awake members of Counterfeit, Dark Rose and Photobook, watched a subtitled Korean drama playing on the display screens molded into the back of every seat. The large group of hung-over band members watched the soap operas with their faces in dismay, as if watching snakes have sex. It was difficult to sympathize with Korean melodramas, especially when the actors looked so different from them, and when every argument seemed to be about finding the right marriage partner. Connie, the only band member who spoke Korean, informed Melanie that in the drama a Chosŏn ruler had just caught his wife cheating and her girlfriends were already spreading rumors.

"So why is that old woman slapping that girl?" Melanie asked.

"Cuz she can," Connie replied, trying to roll up a cigarette on the rumbling bus.

Since climbing into the bus that morning, Melanie had lingered in the back, her body strewn across three seats, a blanket on top of her and a bottle of water on her abdomen to massage her stomach, the liquid inside wavering back and forth. The pain was finally beginning to subside, and the painkiller skin-patches that Connie had retrieved from a Korean bodega gave Melanie a pleasing buzz.

To pass the time, Melanie sharpied up her arm in a henna, an Indian tattoo that she learned to draw from her Malay roommate in Kuala Lumpur. When the sharpie ran out of ink, she studied the Korean characters on the pen. When bored with that, she watched Jack sitting across the aisle, writing in his lyric book. Since she had told him about the abortion, he was in a blaze of inspiration, jotting down words in an exaggerated cursive, his notebook inches from his face. Why did she have to tell him? she wondered. After she had already gone through most of the pain, after she had paid for the pills, when there was nothing left to do. Perhaps she was giving him an unspoken invitation to more unprotected sex. Or perhaps she was merely settling, in her own mind, that he was the father.

A flopping sound came from the right side of the bus, and the Korean driver's austere expression gave no hint of emergency as he pulled over. The passengers watched from the air conditioned bus as the driver plunged like a dolphin into the side hatch.

"Should we help him?" Dark Rose's bald manager said. "You think he knows what he's doing?"

"Didn't they all just recently start buying cars?" someone said.

The soy fields reached beyond the mountains. A thick mist crawled over green hills. The countryside reminded Melanie of when she was young, playing house in her backyard. Those days in the muggy Florida sunshine, she liked to wallow in the dank humidity, to feel beads of sweat rain down her skin. She imagined little monsters growing out of her sweat. The gusts of wind would blow drops into the soil, where they would form eggs, waiting for her to dig them out. Some did not survive. She dug holes all over the backyard, pretending that the rocks she found were her demonic children. Then she would bury them again to keep them safe, but leave a small hole so they could breathe. She imagined the little devils growing strong in the dirt, far enough underground so the tarantulas and scorpions could nurture them.

"Rrrrrgh!" Vince growled from the seat just in front of Melanie. It seemed all the band members were equally inspired by her abortion. Vince struggled in a combat with his own creativity, his weapons an ink pen and a sketchbook. Melanie didn't possess the audacity to ask what he was doing, and neither did anyone else. Still, without provocation, he answered her concerned eyes. "Ok, so I've come to accept that I'm a great song writer, it's just part of me. But I just hate—*hate* the process."

"Please," Melanie said, gripping her stomach. "I don't know what's worse, the pain in my abdomen or the pain of listening to ya'll talk about it."

"Wow!" Vince laughed. "Let me write that down."

Gripping the iron handrail, Melanie peered over Connie's shoulder, at a new Korean drama where a woman cried into her coffee cup. Melanie whistled but couldn't get

Connie's attention and then refused a cigarette that Jack came to share with her. He lit it up anyway while she lied back and placed her arms on her stomach, wondering if the constant cigarettes and booze would have killed the fetus anyway. Only a day before there grew a seed, a beginning of what would have been her only true company. Now it was just a popped zit inside of her, a virus escaping from her one squat at a time.

Outside, the mist on the rolling hills had given way to a wind that grazed the fields in wavy swathes.

"You know what I did in Florida?"

Jack smiled cordially, then gave a slight laugh, as if he had come up with a witty response but only shared it with himself. "What?" he said.

"I photographed marriages." She quoted the advertisement, "Sunset Gardens Wedding Chapel. Where couples go to find happiness and truth, for eternity."

Jack gave a laugh that petered out into silence. The bus kicked up and Melanie saw three Korean middle school girls waving at her as the bus plodded forward.

The bus stopped for lunch at a ramshackle Korean barbecue restaurant at the top of a hill. The three bands and their managers ate pieces of grilled meat coated with soybean sauce wrapped in lettuce, an entrée that Jack crammed into Melanie's mouth, his fingers rubbing the lip gloss off her lips. She nodded to him slowly so he didn't think her grateful. As if, because of the pills, she was unable to pick up a fork.

"Titus Andronicus," Vince pontificated, "is the only good thing Shakespeare ever wrote. Other than that they should have just shot the bastard." The men at the table all nodded. Melanie watched Connie at the table outside, joking with the cook's family in Korean, smoking and picking rice cake out of a vat. Just as Melanie turned her head back to her table, Jack's hand stuck another jumble of lettuce and meat into her mouth. By the way he was looking at the steaming pork belly, he wanted her to make a similar piece for him.

She took to the bathroom instead, feeling a new pain now working through the patches and the pills, like sharp soju bottlecaps lodged in her intestines, piling up into a crushing, squeezing, stabbing strain. She screamed "shit shit shit!" when she saw only squat toilets. Her *shits!* turned to *fucks!* when, inside a stall, she observed the terrifying absence of toilet paper. Keeping her body squat, she glanced beneath the stall walls to find something—a pad, a tampon, layers of napkins or paper towels, *anything*. She punched the door in anger, cursing: "Damn, backwards country-town shit hole!" She wiped sweat from her face and dragged her purse across the muddy floor with her finger, searching for some paper item to waste. She found an electric English-Korean dictionary, anti-histamine, abortion pills, painkiller patches, a make-up kit, gold and silver bangles, and nothing else—not even that colorful Korean currency.

Then she came across her blue American passport. She flipped through it. Not one page unstamped. She tore off the page that held eight stamps from Japan: her trips to Tokyo, Sapporo, Kyoto, and Fukuoka. She extracted her shit into a roll and plunked it into the rusted bowl. She kept going. Indonesia next. She stopped to study the result of coagulated blood that stained her Vietnam visa, then worked her way down her travels, using two or three pages at a time, from China to Cambodia to The Philippines to Thailand to Malaysia to Singapore. Each page swept up the remnants of an infinite amount of time and life and love that she had imagined was inside of her. Finally she had only the cover, where she saw herself, a blonde girl of twenty, smiling in exuberance, with those eyes that had never seen chickens piled into the back of a motorbike, that mouth that had never tasted Malay cakes, those ears that had never heard the songs coming from three Mosques at the same time, merging with the music of jackhammers, buses, and people jabbering on their cell phones. She used the passport picture to wipe the tears from her eyes, then let it fall into the depths of the Korean sewer system. She stood up, the pain nearly gone now, and flushed the scraps down to mix with the underground streams and then into the rice fields and then into the rice.

When she returned, Jack and his band mates were alive with neighing laughter, their boyish chuckles echoing down the bathroom hall. She overheard Vince, his voice charging down the hallway toward her: "Well there's certainly something to be said for cheating on your girlfriend! And no one ever found out, right?"

"Nope," Jack said.

"You gae-sagee!" Melanie heard Connie scream from across the room. "Piece of shit! I heard what you just said! Your secret's out now, fuckhead!"

Melanie left them alone, disinterested in whatever drama was going on, and felt the rush of a painkiller-high dragging her back into the tide. She wavered through the restaurant and found herself in the sun, standing next to a Korean child who said: "Hello, how are you? I am fine," and then exploded in laughter. She continued moving through what she thought was a market, but ended up being a passageway to a large Buddha statue and towers of stacked rocks overlooking a small lake.

The solid terrain appeared to her like a small industrial city, with piles of sharply stacked stones stretching as wide as a city block. Hundreds of rocks stacked upon rocks, a makeshift metropolis. The small Korean bus driver appeared behind a tower nearly twice his size.

"Annyeong haseyo," she struggled to say.

"Naaaye, Annyeong haseyo," he said, smiling through his dark wrinkled skin. Then, casually, "build rocks, make wish."

"Stack rock?"

"Ah yes." Squinting, affable eyes. "Stack rock, make wish, aha."

She stepped carefully into the city of pagodas, her steps slightly vibrating the stones around her. Thousands of people had contributed to it, each hoping that their miniature obelisks would last. She picked up a rock the size of her hand and used that as her cornerstone, placing it on the ground between two other stacks. She leapt over a row of sharp stones and found two other rocks, one like a saucer, and a thicker one shaped like a small cast weight. She stopped to breathe, her heart pulsing from the wetness of the air, the heat of midday. Her tongue began to salivate. The smell of sewage crept through her and she gasped in disgust. The towers of rocks looked hazy and the ground seemed like a sharp drop-off as she swayed her tall body, holding onto her legs like the sides of a rope-bridge fifty stories in the air. Her body edged past each tower with cautious steps. A sudden current whisked her, trembling the rock stacks as if seeking to shuck off each pilgrim's offering. But the rocks held firm. She made a quick hop and placed the two rocks she had retrieved on top of the cornerstone. She tilted and let out a shriek, leaping just before falling, finally out of the stone complex. Heaving, she felt the air conditioning of the restaurant whisper to her. She left the pile as it was, and when she looked back, she couldn't tell which tower was hers. She knew she had contributed to the stone city somehow.

She felt the bus driver's eyes as she headed back indoors.

"Small wish," she explained.

"Ah, small wish." He laughed, clapping once with his hands, as if to make it true.

ThinkTravel! Blogbook

Post Date: 2008 OCT 2

User: SkyFaralan

In Mumbai, Sophea gets a mani while you patronize a barber shop aptly named "The Imperialist's Salon." The barber can't be more than nineteen. He wears a purple collared shirt and a robust seriousness as he sprays a loosely shaken concoction into your shaggy and unkempt hair. He slaps at your head as if he were flattening dough to make a roti, pushing so forceful-ly against the bumps that your neck shifts from beneath his palms. When the cutting begins his concentration remains. Latched there, plunging in, he lets the precise movements of his fingers carry him into that sublime sonata of the mind. The snips of his scissors refuse error, his hands listen to the curves of your scalp, tracing its bumps and patches. He wields a shav-ing puff dipped in white powder, ices it over your face and neck, then snaps open a large razor blade. He measures the symmetry of your face with the length of your sideburns and saws at your head, stroking the razor back and forth, letting fall tufts of hair. The sweat of your palms makes your hands clammy, but the concentration of his eyes infects you with his confidence. Even as he runs his hand through your hair, toss-ing about the spare pieces, slapping your hair as if slapping the dust out of an old quilt, you still cheer him on. You want it dead, not a single hair standing. You want him to beat it out. From the world, your visions turn inward, to the freely carved metal bracelet around your wrist, the succulent pastries at the ubiquitous corner shops near every intersection. The young barber subjects your hairline to careful examination, his eyes undeterred by the game of cricket on the television just above the mirror, his ears unbent by the meddlesome gossip of his friends watching the match. As he yanks at your hair, pulling your head back up, your body goes numb. Even when he beats your neck with a long white hand towel, just the numbness remains. The dumb docility. You are a corpse feeling only the plush velvet of your own coffin.

For days his umbrage haunts you. Skin the color of a black bull, his hair a sideways crease of perfect symmetry. You think of his color as you wash your running shoes in the hostel kitchen at two in the morning. The dirt crud falls in chunks from the bottom, the fine bark of his skin. You hear the snip of his scissors as you scrub the black soot.

The Flaneurs Spacechat

Chat log/October 1ˢᵗ 2008

코니: its official! Total stock market craaaash

코니: servesem right greedy fucks hope they all die

2BWinston: so now what ... we stay here and rise with new Asia?

2BWinston: melanie our spokeswoman hasnt learned two words of korean

코니: is it weird that part of me just wants to toast and get hammered? its the fall of the empire—lez get loaded!

2BWinston: its enough to make you want to marry a white girl and move to the suburbs (i almost did this)

코니: im disappointed in you and your ressentiment

2BWinston: revenge against whitey has led me to date some white ass women in my life

@Melz: stoooaaawwwpp mel still sick lah

2BWinston: speaking of which

@Melz: wowie this chat is still a thing lol

@Melz: so anyone heard from skyler arthur sophie?

2BWinston: all too good for us ... that was a while ago ... nothing wounded nothing the matter

@Melz: i too want to join them! eat curry with pretty
              people in garters and only minimally offend
              locals aand learn how ta pole d@nce

2BWinston: we're expats ... people come and go ...
              thats the gist

@Melz: fuuuuck this. place. it settles. til you upp the
              dosAge. Lol

2BWinston: we're just a bunch of flies who got caught
              in the same web ... paralyzed in every way
              except for our big fat mouths

@Melz: they culd least text back

2BWinston: people do not keep in touch ... now getting
              attached to people ... letting those neurons
              in your brain fire in their direction ... that's
              when youre doing the expat gig all wrong

@Melz: love is about the spirit mnot the vessel
              carrying it

@Melz: gawd I gonna puke

@Melz: Hooooly shit

@Melz: I SERIOSLY UST FUCKIG PUTKE D GUYS

@Melz: wiping it off the floor now GODthat felt good

@Melz: shoud really do that more often

코니: hey winston those happy pills impairin your
              dick?

2BWinston: they're saving me ok

2BWinston: fluoxetine does wonders

@Melz: hisstory never ends you know

2BWinston: no I dont ... please explain to me

@Melz: history

@Melz: it never ends

@Melz: not with you

@Melz: like thes stock market crsh

@Melz: its all staged yes i indeed subscribed to the
                    illuminatis email list ive ruined 70% of the
                    world for myself via conspiracy theories—
                    you know i ue to plaster walls w/ conspiracy
                    theories JFKs assassination was an inside
                    job etc

2BWinston: you all might think you're out of it but
                    float around here for a year ... maybe two
                    ... you'll go right back to your wombs ...
                    your stupid national ... imperial ... racist ...
                    spiritual ... whatever

@Melz: I juss miss em

2BWinston: Mel you never knew them ... did any of you
                    know I have an older brother?

2BWinston: he grew up on the bases like me ... we're
                    both blasian

@Melz: what was his name

2BWinston: youre not gonna remember so who gives a
                    shit.

2BWinston: long story short one day they found out
                    about his HIV

2BWinston:	one call from the wrong man and he was out ... no korea ... no taiwan ... no china
@Melz:	im sorry its terrible
2BWinston:	oh GOOD! Thats all I've been looking for!
2BWinston:	I guess a SORRY from a SPOILED WHITE WOMAN is all I really needed.
2BWinston:	wow GEE GOLLY I suddenly feel tremendous!
2BWinston:	Yo' brotha' sure I said sure musta beeen a real friendly feller to 'ave gotten HIV
2BWinston:	o' fo' sho' he musta' done the wild thang with such and such girls and done this and thaaat
2BWinston:	fucking DEATH to all traveling pretenders

2BWinston has left the group.

@Melz:	he not happy
코니:	happy pills make limp egos
@Melz:	this flu ... is making me crave ... bread
@Melz:	no...potatoes
@Melz:	somthinh startchy & floury
@Melz:	you know what would hit the spot ... double cheeseburger FTW
코니:	the burger joint downtown is still open
@Melz:	naaaw just wanna dream-taste it

코니: dude why are we still on this chat? Just text
me.

ThinkTravel! Blogbook

Post Date: 2008 OCT 4

User: SkyFaralan

There's nothing quite like waking up on the top bunk of a train cabin. The clanking of rails, the train whistle blare announcing your arrival. It helps you forget the Mumbai train station where you watched a man help his daughter take a dump in a public trashcan (a long, frothy mudslide).

In Chennai an elderly Sikh invites you and Sophea into his small apartment to watch WWF wrestling. He feeds you Tandoori chicken, egg curry and tomatoes. He doesn't speak a word of English, but you drink whisky and speak in your mother tongues as if you understand each other. Your hand goes around Sophea as you watch Triple H take down Mysterio. During the commercials, you watch the stock market meltdown.

Panic has gripped Bangalore, aka ITocracy, aka calltopia, which houses one out of every three office buildings in India. Perhaps that's why it's the center for obesity and diabetes. At 3am, when the American workday ends, Bangalorians drink off the global crisis in jam-packed pubs with rooms full of belly dancers. Here, in the IT revolution city, the economic plunge has hit hardest. Anxious young Indians in collared shirts jabber on headset headphones in a desperate, panicky English. The city is a surreal desert of nascent buildings still undergoing construction, and the only movement comes from migrant workers living in tent cities on every roadside. American multinationals aggregate in industrial parks; their incomplete buildings cast foreboding shadows that stretch from the rocky hills of HITECH City to Hyderabad.

The news of the stock market crash disappears in the six-teen-hour train ride, sleeper class, where you and Sophea rest on the upper berth of a crowded cabin, folded into each other beneath a rusted fan. You easily grasp onto passing soft drinks, samosas, and the coarse hair of children with sticky fingers. Outside the train, the sunset straddles the horizon of electrical towers that stand like steel angels in the dark. She sweats through sleep.

Expats flee New Delhi to protect their assets, leaving you and Sophea to chase the red-tape fairy around the train station from one ticket counter to another. You fill out forms, get tickets stamped, protect the luggage on your backs. You new colonials suffer through the old colonials' leftovers, foremost among them, the bureaucratic obsession with identifying you, sorting you out, helping you decide where you belong. But you and Sophea fit no stamp, you've both been gone too long, re-jected America, Asia, love, happiness. Boats without anchors, but in the end tethered together.

After hours of confusion at the train station you discover that there is no train left for Jaipur. Why go to Jaipur? A British man asks. Why travel when the world is melting?

We are poor, you answer. Too poor to care about an economic crisis. At home, nothing would change for us. We would still be eating ramen noodles and french fries. This crisis is just about you becoming like us.

Just to spite the recession, you buy first class.

In Chandigarh two high school boys chat with you in line for a Bollywood film: She your girlfriend? You kiss her? You fuck her? How many girls you do this with? Very common in America? They are obsessed with foreign women. Very naughty, very sexy they say. You ask them about Indian women. Very naughty, very sexy, they say.

The crisis fades to background noise when you reach Amritsar, where Sikh pilgrims lie scattered on the white marble of the Golden Temple. Sophea invites a young Indian from Canada to share a Thali, and you can't help scooting into his space.

She sits him between you both on the bed of your hotel room. She places your hand onto his thin jeans. You trace his thigh. He is the first to kiss you. You kiss back, until you are all drunk on wine, listening to the allahu akbar chant from a nearby mosque. Amritsar becomes your sacred space too.

The first night in Jaipur, the capital of Rajasthan, a fuse blows out in your five-dollar hotel room. You and Sophea move to another room and that fuse blows out too. No money left, a man says. No electricity. The next day you relocate to another hotel for three dollars a night. It is ridden with ants, spiders, fleas, mosquitos, cockroaches. The mattress is a cot on wooden planks. It reminds you of your first cockroach-ridden apartment in Las Vegas. You wake up with new places to scratch.

To find yourselves in a new city means you must survey the perimeter, ridding yourselves of the tourist monuments like passing difficult excrement. And after the tourist sites you pace toward whatever seems exigent—a broken down building, a gathering of Indians around a well-lit street, a strange figure in the dark. You and Sophea simply float within the crowd, you unthinking and unassuming defectors, trusting the void wherever it leads.

And Jaipur is a city full of Gods, Kings, monkeys, and street children. The latter work in groups, perhaps. Although the *world is melting, Sophea still gives rupees. You try to give food, but the street children won't take it. They scream "fuck you, cheap America!"*

The train takes you across Rajasthan, where men follow Sophea with their eyes. In the Guide it warns that "Indians are known for harassing women in Western style clothing." This means asking for kisses, asking how many people Sophea has been with and whether nor not she uses condoms. It means constant whistles, taunts, and hands falling upon different parts of her skin. When Sophea orders a beer the waiter gives it to you.

In Udaipur, breezes compensate for overhead fans. You can spot the scattering colors over Badi Lake. Back-up generators may fail the people, but never the tourist. You inhabit landmarks for three dollars a night. In the hotel bathroom you only find a squat toilet. You're used to it now, and when you can't find any tissue in your backpack, you accept the excrement into your left hand. After a year of wandering around Asia, this is what you've learned. No more fantasies. No more armor. Just a left-hand wiping the shit off.

The inflatable penguin's long stalky feet waddled past Arthur's leather loafers, toward the fountain spewing winter snow. Christmas, Christmas in Fukuoka's circular Canal City Mall.

A robot made of yellow blocks approached, wiping the floor with its sponged rear-end, its small arms decorated in Christmas ornaments. "May-I-Help-You?" it spoke in English. Arthur took a selfie with the robot's touch-screen face. *Click-click*—capturing himself in a blue Yukata with the Christmas robot. The penguin joined. *Click-click*—the *kawaii* posse. His friends in Seoul would see it posted on his travel blog and split a gut. *Crazy bastard*, they would say. *What an asshole*, they would say.

Water spurt from the oval fountain, and then plunged into refracted blue and purple, waltzing to a song: "let every heart, prepare him room, and heaven and nature sing!" *Click-click*—cosplay customers shopping for cat sweaters. *Click-click*—capturing that pink ribbon on the storefront. *Click-click*—those snow-tipped hills painted on the walls.

Blue bursts of snow came from high turbines. The crowd of shoppers lifted their gasping children.

"Heaven and nature sing!"

Click-click—nutcracker soldiers in stilts with candy-cane rifles, marching in delicate rhythm. *Click-click*—winter snow. *Click-click*—joy to the world.

With nothing left to photograph, Arthur touched the Christmas robot's screen to bring up a schedule of events. He scratched the robot's rimless plastic, the cold, scratch-proof anti-glare. The next parade of Christmas cheer was scheduled for an hour later. Arthur would be back for it. Higher floors, undiscovered vantage points.

Exiting the mall, Arthur followed the suggested route on his tourist map to a night market along the Nakagawa River, a glittering grid coated with tourists and the smell of street ramen. Blurs of neon rubbed out the river below in the pinkish sunset. He walked as if he had a purpose on those nub-tiled streets that massaged his feet with every step. *Click, click*—streets sparkling with cosplay girls.

A group of inebriated businessmen stumbled from a convenience store and stared at him, sharing jokes in Japanese. Arthur nodded, patting his blue Yukata, wondering if it was the object of their ridicule. "Nazi xenophobes," Arthur whispered to himself.

After half a year of shaking hands, passing out business cards, and working toward a $2,000 a week salary, Arthur no longer saw himself as a pretend businessman, but just a businessman. He paid for sushi, sake, and women, just as they did all around Japan, though he still couldn't put together a sentence in Japanese. And like any self-starter, he was desperately lonely, skipping from one diminutive hotel room to another, every day another set of neatly turned out sheets, another bashful housekeeper to squeeze into his mind reel before bed. He walked the streets of the busy but quiet city admiring the youth in their groups of five, and felt devastated by their laughter. For a man traveling alone, the camera was his lone witness.

He looked over the prices at a fast food vending machine for a good ten minutes before deciding to just eat convenience store ramen again—with its three packages of dried vegetables and powders, it still tasted like an exotic luxury. On the magazine rack he found pictures of anime girls in scant clothes and advertisements:

LEARN JAPANESE IN FUKOUKA—ONE OF THE MOST COSMOPOLITAN CITIES IN JAPAN

Fukuoka, Arthur thought. *Fuk u, ok*?

When the sun set, Arthur took a taxi to Hakata Station, where Christmas wreathes lined the hallways above homeless men sitting in small cardboard boxes. Panic found him when he heard his train number called. At the gate Arthur simply presented his Japan Rail pass, available only to foreigners, and was waved into a train headed for Osaka.

The doors slid shut with the suction of a space port and the train plodded forward, passing snow-covered trees. It built speed quickly, shooting by darkened five-story buildings, as the passengers took off their shoes and the cabin lights flicked off. He sat aloof, spreading himself over two seats and flipping through pictures on his digital camera. Though he always took two photos at once, most were blurred from his shaky, over-eager hands. Smears of red and white taxi brake lights, rotating pink tubes in ultraviolet-sensitive phosphors. Then pictures he took of himself wearing that dark blue Yukata, smiling in a tired squint—*delete, delete*. All the pictures were plagued by Japanese men, not a woman in sight. The guidebook had promised geishas wearing television goggles.

Slipping off his shoes, he used his smartphone to log into the Flaneurs Spacechat group. He wrote a message to wake them.

KingArthur:	you won't believe this bimbo across the bar from me. Mother gave her a stripper's face for sure.
@Melz:	you're wrting this in a BAR??? omg put away yiur phne and talk to peeple
KingArthur:	she's winking at me. Sweet sexy jap eyes enticing me to follow
@Melz:	she's gonna stab you in the barfroom (wehat we call it in FL)
코니:	fucking inbred piece of shit (what we call Arthur when he's not around)
KingArthur:	just you two on this chat huh?
코니:	yeah no more male conniving to protect your fragile racist ego
@Melz:	arthur doesn't condone racism he has ONE black friend
KingArthur:	hold on Im honing in on this piece of street meat

That should rile them up for a while, Arthur thought, chuckling to himself. He listened to the snores of an older Japanese man and watched the snow dissipate onto wet rooftops. He focused his camera on a young girl lying across two seats with her arms spread about in an exhausted surrender to sleep. He waited until the train curved and the moonlight exposed just a slice of her hands and the wavy black skirt below, where the skin of her inner thigh showed ever so sweetly, with her feet lodged in-between the arms of the seat in front of her. He followed the bottom of her dark shirt to her still neck. As she breathed, her chest expanded and the wind blew out of her in a slow tide. Her eyes moved just noticeably beneath her eyelids; her mouth opened a slight gap between thick burgundy lips.

Click—the flash woke half the cabin. After a moment the fidgeting ceased and the snoring returned. Outside they had reached a high elevation and the moonlight revealed a blanket of snow.

The picture on his camera looked nothing like the girl in front of him. The girl in the photograph did not look Japanese, but had dark brown skin. Her white leggings were stained with dirt, and her ankle-length skirt was green and rumpled, as if it had been unwashed for weeks. He looked at the real girl again, fixing his gaze on her silhouette until the train shifted into the moonlight. He saw neither the supple young Japanese girl nor the colorful girl in the photograph, but a pair of opened eyes placed on him. He canted his head and feigned sleep. Silently, he lowered the contrast on the camera and pointed it in her direction, watching her through the small video screen. She was still staring at him. As his eyes traced the curve of her arm, he found two watches on the same wrist.

"What do you want?" she asked in English.

"Hey, I couldn't help but ask…" he whispered, shutting the camera off. "I was wondering, about the watches?"

She leaned in to whisper. "One is my time. One is your time."

"Your time? What is your time?"

"Time is relative."

"Well, of course. Einstein, right? But—"

"—I remind myself, to be myself to myself."

Out of responses, Arthur leaned toward her and whispered: "I can't really hear you. Do you mind?" He used the moonlight to guide him to the window seat next to her, just before the train propelled into another tunnel and all went black.

"My name's Arthur."

"Yen," she whispered.

"Yen? Like Japanese money?"

"Yes."

"But you don't look Japanese."

"I know."

"I'm American."

"I know."

"So obvious?"

"Yes."

They came out of the tunnel and Arthur lurched back. Her sleepy eyes never left his.

"You're going to a business meeting," she said as if reading the words from a newspaper.

"Yup!" He was proud to declare himself of the business class. "First to Osaka, then Tokyo, then, who knows? New York, Paris, London."

"Ok."

"Well, where are you from?"

"I don't know." She gave a soft shrug. "Down South."

"Yeah, but—when we say 'where are you from?' we usually just mean which country."

"I know."

"So which country are you from?"

"I don't know." She turned from his gaze. It was as if she had anticipated his every word and was now bored, running through the usual lines. "The Republic of Vietnam."

"See? Was that so hard?"

She sat up and leaned her arms against the seat in front of her. Her ponytail hit his nose. "You ever notice how often people interrupt?" she said abruptly, facing him again. "How unsure of themselves they are when they speak? How little they make eye-contact with you? How much they don't really pay attention to each other?"

"Yeah, yeah I do notice that." He fished a Christmas-tree shaped rice cake from his bag, the wrapper crinkling as he split it open.

"They don't like to hug either. Suchlike, not a real hug or a human hug."

Arthur figured that since she was telling him this, he must have been part of her strange world. And perhaps now, in a Japanese train where snow flew by at three hundred kilometers per hour, he too could feel it—that illusive wonder that had always cast him aside.

"I'm in exile," he told her, putting his arm on her shoulder. Certainly it was true: no family, no friends, alienating everyone. He told her bits of this, getting to the details about how his wife had left him in Shanghai, how she stole away Joey, their only son.

"I tried to forgive," he whispered. "Some people are just so evil you can't wonder why they do things. I was married to this evil Chinese woman. Took me for all I had. Chinese, they really only care about strengthening their own nation."

"Hmm," her voice came in the dark.

"Yeah. I got some problems, who doesn't?" He prepared himself for the typical questions—where was his wife? Didn't he care about his son? Why wasn't he looking for them? For which he would declare: "As a man, I respect their choice."

But she remained silent, her head moving from his shoulder to his chest, comforted perhaps by his breathing. "I was sleeping before you woke me." With her head there, he found himself too drifting off.

He awoke as they arrived in Osaka. He couldn't find her in his daydream haze. Perhaps she had gotten off earlier and didn't want to wake him. As he exited the train, he felt mildly relieved that she hadn't.

Arthur had no formal meeting in Osaka, only a midnight rendezvous with a foreign client to meet for sushi, sake, and women, each task taking a firm hour and a half to complete. Arthur's life of late had been to bullet around Japan in this fashion, to act as liaison, consultant, and chief advisor to all foreigner affairs. When the job required a native English speaker, Arthur was the only qualified candidate in his entire company.

A taxi took him through shopping centers of shoulder-to-shoulder crowds and dropped him off at a six-story building of arcades, pubs, and karaoke rooms. *Click-click*—life-sized robotic Santa-Clause playing drums.

He threaded his way through a restaurant of small wooden booths, tight doorways and translucent curtains that gave privacy to small karaoke rooms. Inside Room #406 he found his company's client, a bald and bearded Arab man in a black suit, who had already hired three karaoke girls to latch onto. Although Arthur repeated the man's name to himself, he forgot it after shaking his hand.

"What music you like?" the man said.

"Right now?" Arthur took a seat next to a short red-haired woman in a glittery cut-off. "Grunge, old school."

The man's face was planted in his busty karaoke girl's cleavage. He set the microphone handle between her breasts, balancing the tip in her school girl top. "Pop it out!" he exclaimed. "Look, my man. Her breasts are like two firm cantaloupes." He grabbed her left breast like testing an avocado's firmness. "I just want to bite'em."

"Hell. Yes." Arthur said, opening and shutting the red translucent curtain, wishing the waitress would bring him a drink. Without alcohol, he never knew what to say.

"But she's Sailor Moon!" The man fingered his girl's hair. "Look, she thinks she's blonde! Like you, my man!"

"Where is the waitress? Excuse me." Arthur left to the lobby bar and ordered a white Russian, eyeing a woman leaned over her barstool, chewing on edamame skin. She turned around, her face thin and slightly cracked in places, and started clapping jubilantly for her friends playing darts. Arthur stirred his drink carefully, watching her. When she turned around he drank it in one gulp, ordered two more and checked his phone.

@Melz:	sold some art today! my first piece since may, but still
KingArthur:	aw, how much they paying you for your purty piece?
@Melz:	20k, not my piece ... just helping sell for a friend.
KingArthur:	can't do it themselves?
@Melz:	they're korean lah...
코니:	why are you still on here, 개새끼?
KingArthur:	in osaka, just needed to get on my phone, show the ho next to me I'm typing in English. Surefire way into their panties
코니:	if only you had some other redeeming quality
@Melz:	arthur maybe your ghost is there ... Osaka is SUPER haunted ya know
KingArthur:	my ghost is in china. anyway she saw my

english skills, tongue in my mouth, hopefully it won't be too expensive

@Melz: she's A JAPANESE GOHST. what she look like?

The real woman across from him was gone. He flipped through the women in his mind and tried to make someone up fast. He remembered the girl on the train. Was her skirt green or black?

KingArthur: Dis girl in a green skirt. Said she's from vietnam, republic of vietnam.

@Melz: HOLY SHIT....REPUBLIC OF VIETNAM IS NOT A COUNTRY your fucked now RIP

KingArthur: vietnam is a country

@Melz: yeah...but the REPUBLIC has been gone since the vietnam war...

코니: probably a descendent of the boat people or trafficked

@Melz: NOO IT'S A GHOST!!

Arthur felt the buzz, his mind like a ship suddenly pulling anchor. His heartbeat quickened, his hand jittered. He typed a quick exit:

KingArthur: my tongue is in her mouth now later ~~

He returned to the karaoke room with an exaggerated

stumble, a bottle of Jack Daniels in his hand. "I trust you're still thirsty!" he exclaimed. The women's forced grins tantalized him.

"You been with one of these girls yet?" said the Arab man, lighting a cigarette. Arthur didn't have to ask to know he meant Japanese girls.

"Yeah!" Arthur sipped from his drink. "All goddamn bitches. Because—" singing, "—Asian girls want money! Those evil goddamn prudes! I'll tell ya what they do— they cry as you do it," he scrunched his face and nodded, "you think a guy can get it on when a bitch be balling?" nodding his head. "Yeah man it makes a guy feel sick. Ya'll doing yo thang, then—uh … uh …—like, bitch who you think this is? It ain't that big, know what I'm sayin'? You all used to your boyfriend's teenie weenies. You never known no American dick, right? I mean do you know what I be sayin' to *you*?"

"You are crazy man!" The man clinked a glass full of brandy. He sipped greedily, spilling an ounce or two onto his white shirt. "Which girl you want tonight? Green skirt? Black skirt?"

Arthur eyed the three girls in front of him. One in a white collar, the other in black. One in a sparkling red.

"I'm just gonna sing, yo. You go, pop dat ass open."

Another drink in and Arthur couldn't stop singing. When the lights and music shut off he realized it was only him and the red-haired karaoke girl, who blobbed bits of Vaseline on her chapped lips. He kissed her on the neck while she fake-laughed and said something in Japanese and pushed him out.

Sometime in his stupor, he found himself alone and lost among the neon lights and yellow cabs. He stepped on a bulb, crushing it and diffusing the Christmas lights that spread about a small shopping village. The village was a small version of Osaka inhabited by miniature *kawaii* characters in red and green hats. A familiar song came on an overhead stereo: "Everybody knows, a turkey and some mistletoe ..."

In the late afternoon Arthur trudged to Osaka station, following a dense crowd into the train. It hardly seemed shocking that he saw her then, those same curious pair of detached eyes looking in his direction, though there was no sign that she recognized him.

"Yen," he gasped.

A life sprang into her eyes. "Arthur," she said, smiling back. She was in the same wrinkled skirt that she wore the day before. *Green*, Arthur thought.

"Talk about a coincidence." He plopped into the seat next to her. "Where are you off to?"

"Not sure." Her hazel eyes remained on the snow breezing past the windows.

"I can't believe this. What are the chances?"

She looked out the window, at winter's early frost.

The Japanese crowd began to lessen a little more at every stop, until eventually they were almost alone, the train whisking them through clouds of snow. Arthur watched her with a growing intensity, rattling coins in his pockets to keep from losing his grip on reality. The chances of finding her in the same train, the same cabin, sitting across from him—the chances were supernatural.

"What are you looking at?" he asked, to no answer.

Her presence seemed scarce, as if she were to fade into that passing landscape of snow. "Do you know chora?" she asked. "It's a passive state of receptiveness, a perception without prejudice. Everything is as it is, unburdened by knowledge or experience. Like a baby before they've learned to speak. I've been thinking. I feel that way here, in the chora."

"On the train?"

"Somewhat."

"Sounds ancient." He wondered what Vietnamese sage had invented the word. "Chora. You know, I think there's something like that in Native American culture." He stretched his arms to cradle her again like when she slept on his chest. "You know, in Bali, they believe in Hinduism. Cycles of life."

She receded from him and stared out the window. "I feel it in the train. Chora. A lack of prejudices, a place before hierarchy, before values. So it's more fun, not to leave."

"How long have you been on the train?"

"All this time."

They emerged from another tunnel and Arthur prepared his camera for the mountains, but not even the hills were visible—no picturesque view of Mount Fuji, no neon lights—they might as well have been in Siberia. The only objects visible through the snow were the tattered homes near the tracks. "Can't see a thing," he said, putting the camera back in his pack.

"It's nice. No God beneath the clouds. Only man."

Was this the strangeness he had been seeking? Her eyes, adrift upon the clouds of snow, her voice, remote but quaint as it touched his ears. Was this the strange, the foreign, the outlandish, the exotic, the thing he had been searching for—the reason for all this? He glared at the snow caking onto the window as the train pulled to a whimpered stop.

They arrived in Tokyo. This was his stop. He stayed on board. Hell, he had a pass.

They talked though Fukushima, Sendai. She went on for hours about how death was always there, how she could sense it coming and on the train it was like she had stopped retreating and was finally on her way. She never once asked where he was going. At some point his hand slipped into hers. Her palms felt rough and cold and her tense smile caused him to grip her tighter, as if she might float away through the passing snow. The clouds outside turned into fine sharp wisps streaking across the hills like suspended electric volts. The train passed the face of a mountain where a large graveyard stood half blanketed in snow. Only after they went into a tunnel did he remember his camera.

She whispered to him: "this is my first time doing this. Holding hands." She clutched him tight. Her skin felt resistant, a layer of bread crust. But the longer he held her hand the softer the touch, until he felt he was committing an illicit act.

"What are you looking for?" she asked.

"I'm just on vacation."

"I don't think that's it."

"Well, to take a break."

"From whom?"

"Just—people. Ignorant people, who can't handle my energy. I'm just off for a while. Why are *you* here?"

"I asked you first."

"And I answered."

"No, you didn't really answer."

"Well, what do you want me to say?" His voice grew tense. Her eyes went back to the snow and he knew he was doing something wrong. He thought of all the stories about him circulating on the tourist grapevine—lost his wife and son, hunting a ghost, the misogynist, white American racist drunken expat *par excellence*, a role he took immense pleasure in bringing to life. The man was an institution of fuck-ups and fuck-offs.

He tried again: "travel is a spiritual journey to me." His cheeks tensed up. "Feeling lost in large cities, surrounded by the unfamiliar—"

"—being estranged, a stranger to yourself." He could barely follow her soft voice. "You move around searching for tragedy. But something remains unfinished, Arthur."

"I don't get you." He watched another set of gravestones.

Looking as if speech had drained her, she managed a smile. "Good."

They had three hours at the northernmost train station, Wakkanai, on the edge of Hokkaido, before the train would head southwards again. Not a foreigner was in sight, just the city and the deep sea of snow. Yen grasped tightly onto Arthur's hand as they followed signs pointing them inside the small hilly city. She carried a square camoflauge backpack hiked up to her neck and wore an overcoat that only reached her waist. Her shivering hands grasped his and she kept her head ducked to protect her neck.

"I've never felt such cold before!" She laughed a mad, unhinged laugh. "Look! My thighs feel numb!"

Not a word of English was visible throughout the city's small shopping arcades. Hunger pulled them from one sweet smell to another. They stood at a ramen shop entrance where the only places to sit were in high stools facing red brick. They waited for someone to seat them, but even the busboy ignored them. They went instead to a small convenience store to buy katsu chicken sandwiches and ate them in the nearby stairwell. Arthur sat on the stairs and Yen stood tracing the wallpaper's circles.

"Where to now?" he said.

"Um, you lead the way, why not?" Then, staring at the wall: "I think the Japanese are affable people."

"They're what? We just got stared out of a ramen stall."

"We should presume the best in their actions."

"They're xenophobes! Plus—Do you have any idea how many Chinese people they massacred and raped? Have you been to Nanjing?"

"Every country has good and evil," chewing the sandwich. "You're one or the other. You either bring life or you take it away."

She sat on the stairway, mouth full, and her eyes turned pensive. "I thought you hated Christmas music."

He realized that he had been humming a Christmas song, but couldn't remember the lyrics. "That's why I hate those songs. They get stuck in your head."

"Why?"

"You can't stop thinking about them."

"Why?"

"It's *aggravating*." He wanted to curse at her but bit into his sandwich instead. "It's like every time they come on they just automatically start playing in your head, and they won't ever stop. They're always in the background, until you break away for good."

"But they're fun. I love Christmas music." She hummed Joy to the World, her face a cheery apparition of an anime doll.

He could only stare back at her, his mouth agape. Wasn't she different from the herd? Wasn't she the one who spoke of the chora in a quiet, unearthly voice?

"Tell me about the chora," he said.

"The Julia Kristeva term?" she said, pausing her song. "I'll give you her book on the train." She continued in a bubbly voice, "and heaven and nature sing!"

On their return to the train, the night thrust upon them a new type of cold. It numbed Arthur's face and hands. They took turns biting into a Fuji apple as they entered a park with snow covered trees and ice statues. Some looked like demonic dogs, with their tongues twisting around their bodies. *Click-click.* Beside them were *kawaii* characters missing distinctive facial features: a bear without ears, a cat without a mouth, an old woman without a nose. *Click-click.* Their simple faces made Arthur want to smile back.

He sat with Yen on the brick wall surrounding the park, his arm around her, their bodies bathed in the yellow haze of another convenience store.

"Why do you do that?" Yen asked. "Take pictures."

"*Why?*" He shook his head, sputtered "khk." Then: "I'm just taking pictures."

"But why?"

"It's just pictures!" he squeezed her hand though it felt slim and lifeless—a vine that had withered in the freeze. He let go and let her follow him until they reached a small plaque that had the only English words they had seen in the entire city: <u>Good Dragon Sauna</u>. Below the sign was a picture of light-skinned feet dipped into a pool of small fish.

A stone walkway led inside a large sauna with no receptionist. Arthur wandered the grounds and approached a large steam-marked glass wall. Peeking through an unstained portion of glass, he saw a thin canopy of leaves shaded over a crystalline blue bath. Further inside he saw small colored pools—bright red, murky white, and blueberry blue. He spotted a nude family in a clear bath: a mother rubbing oils onto her son, a father playing with his wife's feet.

"Just a second," he said to Yen, pointing his camera toward the nude woman splashing water onto her son. *Click-*

click—it would make for a picturesque blogpost.

"I think I'm gonna go now," Yen said, bored. "Train's about to come."

"See you there?"

She shrugged.

He closed the camera. When did he lose her attention? When had their brief fire died? He watched her tramp through the snow. Her rumpled greet skirt, her fluffy jacket, her scarf trailing behind her in the blanket of white. Nothing seemed special, unique, or interesting—just another human being.

He waited for a moment and then moved to the automatic doors. A burst of snow and cold tossed him back, and he had to shield himself from the wind until the doors automatically closed themselves.

Inside the sauna, there was not a single white person in sight, only Japanese families—children, elderly, and adults well over forty. The counters in the locker-room displayed male beauty products and utensils, eye curlers and spray-on hair-dye. It seemed unfair that they would separate him from the women by segregating the male and female bathing sections.

The chairs in the sleeping hall were all taken by families lounging and watching TV. Arthur scoped out the older daughters, though they were all covered up in layers of blankets, their minds in peaceful slumber.

On the lower floors Arthur found a small PC room where he uploaded his pictures of Fukuoka, Osaka, and Wakkanai to his travel blog: the fake snow of Fukuoka, the drunken debauchery of Osaka, the mouthless ice statues of Wakkanai. He removed the pictures of himself in bars, at karaoke, of his inebriated, mouth-half-open, asinine stare that seemed to follow him everywhere. He found the picture of Yen. The unkempt clothes, the unmatched colors, her gaze, spiritual and contemplative and dumb and docile. Then the picture of the nude Japanese woman with her family. A message popped up.

@Melz:	hey arthur, didz your ghost haz killz youz yetz?
@Melz:	okie artie dead
코니:	KingConnie long live the king
KingArthur:	Im still alive dingbats
@Melz:	was she A GOHST?
KingArthur:	I have no idea what that was.

Out of habit he typed something shocking, about booze and jizz and getting it all over a hotel room.

KingArthur:	so long story short long night of sex but missed a meeting in tokyo. Maybe out of a job now
코니:	korea isn't an option for you I've made sure of that
KingArthur:	thinkin of heading back to china anyway

코니: to smuggle dope?

@Melz: ta find your OFFSPRING?

He typed something about Shanghainese girls and three-somes, but deleted it. Staring at him still was all his photographs. Every *click* had been so effortless.

KingArthur: Maybe the latter. Maybe pick up the trail, see where it leads, at least. Just, no idea where to start. Nanjing has millions of people. And my ex has one of the most common Chinese names in the world. And that's it.

@Melz: this guy Im seeing is from china. Send me the name! We can help!

코니: yeah dude the english-speaking world in china is small as hell, and the gay politics… well if there're two lesbians with a white baby shouldnt be too hard to find

@Melz: yippie! a new quest!

코니: is your ex-wife hot btw? I mean just saying a little motivation might make this go faster

@Melz: send a pic!

코니: yes for research purposes

@Melz: aw hold on kid daddy's coming back!

Arthur pushed the power button on the computer, his eyes frozen on the screen until it clicked off. He stood up and, feeling faint, headed to the massage chairs nearby. Each chair stood above a small pool of fish. Instructions in English read:

One takes off shoes

One puts foot in pool

One's feet to be cleaned from fish

He dipped his feet in the cold water, its chill racing up his bloodstream, and felt the small mouths tickle his toes. He closed his eyes and wiped sweat from his forehead. Below, fish snipped off kernels of microscopic bacteria that had clung to him since he was a child.

Something drained him. He felt queasy, repulsed even, like he had smoked a heavy cigar. What was their problem? Why the fuck would they help someone like him? Someone who wrecked everything, everyone, every city he dribbled his drunk appetite through. He held his hand to his mouth to keep from hyperventilating. He leaned his face down so the world could not see.

"Thank you," he whispered, opening and shutting his eyes to cut the power to his own mind. "Thank you" he mumbled, seeing Joey's face in his mind, nearly two years older, but the same eyes, the same laugh.

He let snot and tears fall into the puddle of microscopic fish at his feet.

"Thank you," he repeated, facing the translucent fish in the bubbling water. "Thank you thank you thank you thank you."

ThinkTravel! Blogbook

Post Date: 2008 OCT 25

User: SkyFaralan

In Varanasi a willowy man meets you at the station asking "You want coolie?" His teeth are stained yellow with paan and his eyes are in a maniacal blitzkrieg. Before you or Sophea can answer, he lifts your bags onto his head and marches up three flights of stairs, his aged body nearly giving out under the weight of tourist knick-knacks stockpiled among your belongings.

After a day at the market you visit a small sari shop and change from your black dress into Varanasi silk.

"Is that a man?" a Japanese boy says, pointing at you in your light green sari.

Sophea grips your hand. You turn, bare, ready for their looks.

"I'm sorry," the boy's short-haired mother says. "I hope you do not mind."

"No," you tell him. "It's a funny question."

"He looks so pretty!" says the child. "Could I do that?"

"You can!" says the child's mother. "I'll love you, my baby boy, or my baby girl."

You let loose a chuckle as tears begin to form.

Sophea grips your arm. "This one's all mine," she tells the child.

Along the southern Ghat you see more tourists, silent in their spiritual recovery. You hire a boatman to take you onto the Ganges, the most holy and the most polluted river in the world. Sophea dangles her feet into the brown mixture of feces and decaying organs.

A mustached man commandeers your small boat and gives you a fulsome history of the river. "Those who come here to die need very special wood to burn their bodies with, you understand? This kind of wood, my friend, is extremely expensive. But if they do not have a proper burial they will not go to enlightenment." He points to a pyre belching smoke. "Look, the ghosts tremble the smoke towards you! They are choosing you for rescue. If you give money, you too will go to Enlightenment, no problem!"

The smoke from the burning bodies pinches your nose; the requiems of lamenting families reach out in a chorus; the yellow marigold garlands set your eyes to shame, settling onto the water below. There is still that rattling of a guilty conscience, the desire to help bear the other's burden. It flashes across your mind: the fear that after refusing this chance for redemption, you might never again breath with ease.

"No," you tell him.

"You refuse enlightenment?" he asks.

"Yes," Sophie says.

The tout disembarks at the next pier, shaking his head. The boatman follows, spitting a thin web of saliva onto your garment, then kicks your boat off from the dock. You float alone, without anchor or paddle, a coffin drifting in slow circles. The Ganges is so still, it pulls you nowhere.

"I'm going in," Sophea says, and leaps into the contaminated waters. She comes up for air, laughing, and then takes another dive, her feet bobbing up and down in scissor kicks. Your green sari blows in the wind, rippling up like the ash floating freely in

the air. For the first time you feel lucky to be here, in your body. Only here, drifting without oar, could you see her face smiling up at the smoke-filled sky. Had you given up, you never would have been here to see it. When that sun-shiny face turns to you, wet with river muck, you feel this moment, the here and now you share, the only home you'll ever need.

After two days there was nothing left to do in Vientiane. Winston had taken the walking tour suggested by the guidebook and visited the few Wats nearby until there was nothing more to do but drink coconut shakes on a patio overlooking the slow Mekong river. He watched the muddy banks, the fishing boats towing nets through the brown water, the darkened stream of plastic and industrial waste that seemed to flow through every dark space in the world.

He took out a silver Art Deco pen that he had purchased from a beach tout, along with a hardback journal, snarled back from when he was caught in a monsoon near Saigon. He practiced his Korean script, then his Chinese, then his Japanese. He could spend hours writing in Japanese rapid and sharp lines, terribly burdened in some places, zestful and free in others, but always containing those minute motions that ended in a playful stroke. The Thai and Cambodian scripts were still ugly to him, but he liked the Vietnamese way of putting accents on Romanized letters, giving attitude to overlooked vowels.

In the late morning Winston recognized a young girl walking the beach, wearing the same purple dress and holding the same lonely pink balloon as the day before. She asked him if he wanted to buy the balloon in the same indifferent, sleepy tone. He said no and tried to teach her English.

"Do you remember what I taught you yesterday? How to say how old you are?"

"I am eight years old," she said, rocking on the ball of her feet.

"Good! Now, what are these?" he said, pointing to his Fossil shades. "Sun glasses. Say 'sun glasses.'"

"Sun glaysees," she said, a finger in her mouth.

"Genius!" He fumbled in his pockets for some American coin to give her, but had none. She went on her way to talk to the next tourist. Winston never really liked kids, but after spending the last year teaching English in South Korea, he at least knew how to talk to them. Teaching English, he knew all along, would be the latest in a long series of false starts, abandoned jobs, and forays into boredom. Now a decade of collecting vocations had passed, which saw him as a fledgling architect in Singapore, a web-taught psychiatrist in Thailand, and an intern physicist in Guangzhou. Each prospect seemed to end like this, with the sort of expelled malaise that frequently besets expat brats.

The restaurant servers started to open the shade umbrellas. An Israeli Kibbutz farmer sat near him, also overlooking the river, also keeping a fruit shake suspended near his mouth. Winston asked him about Israel just so he could hear the Hebrew language—the name of his Kibbutz, of the prime minister, of religious rituals.

"But I have not been back in, oh, years, many years now," the man said.

"Years? So what do you do here?" Winston poised his pen.

"Do?" The man looked at the sifting tides of the muddy

Mekong, a serene smile gracing his lips. "This," he said. "I watch this."

When the afternoon came, Winston bought a banana pancake in a plastic bag and walked the muddy alleys to his hostel doors, now blocked by a padlock chained to the bars of a folding metal gate. He rapped the lock until an old Laotian man hazily unlocked the gate, his movement restrained by a limp leg. Though Winston had been trying to taper off his anti-depressants, once inside his musty hotel room he snuck a small dose into his pancake. He let the syrup trickle the pill down his throat as he reclined on his bunk bed, waiting for the feelings to pass.

By late afternoon the hostel's muggy heat chased Winston to the market, a sort-of mall, where he ate from a buffet of overpriced rice and watched the locals read instructions before riding the only escalator in the entire country. When the heat began to lighten up, he went to the bus station to discover that he had mistaken the time on his bus to Luang Prabang. It left at 7am, not 7pm. He went to kill time in a PC room, then a coffee shop.

After sunset he found himself walking aimlessly through a dark back alley when he heard a voice summon him:

"Hay-lo! Black boy! Black American! Come come come! You want drink? Come sit here! You sit here! Where you go-ing?"

Winston tried to put together the accent he heard: an endorphin-induced Thai-Laotian hybrid of spirited long endings mixed with the over-compensating lisp of a British drag queen. He turned to face the hailing voice and found it belonged to a middle-aged Kathoey sitting under a lit tiki umbrella with a table full of young travelers.

"What your name?" the woman said. "Where you from? The States, right? I love the U.S. ... what state you from? My name Jimmy. I'm from Koyat or Nakhon Ratchasima, it has two names, so one is really long so it has kind of like, nickname called Koyat. It's north-eastern part of my country."

"I'm Winston," he said plainly and leaped over a puddle to approach the table. "I'm not from a State."

"Let me guess," one of the travelers chimed in. "You're an army brat who has lived in Korea, the Philippines, and Singapore." The assessment came from a young white American decorated in tattoos and wood earrings.

"Right," Winston said. "How did you know?"

"Your accent," the man said, scratching his week-old guy beard. "Now for your race. You look half Asian, half black. Your mother is Japanese. Wait, part-Japanese, part-Filipino. Am I right, America?"

"You guessed it," Winston said, trying not to give away his shock. The man had him down to a mathematical formula. Would he also know that Winston's mother had died of cancer, and that his father, ridden with guilt and depression, had vanished off the grid?

The American man called himself India because he lived in Dharamshala. India introduced the rest of the group. There was Montreal, who wore three small skulls around his neck that clanked about every time he ashed his cigarette. Then there was a young man they called Liverpool, a couple named Czech Republic, Jimmy the Thai transgender, and Jimmy's cousin, a lithe local girl who could not have been older than fifteen. None of the nationalities bothered to shake Winston's hand as he sat at the table.

"How did you learn English?" Winston asked Jimmy, pushing in his wire-rimmed glasses.

"Me?" She cracked an almond between her molars. "I just learned like, how to write ABC and just, you know, how— sing a song and things like that. Just talk, only talking."

Someone placed a beer in front of Winston. He took a sip.

"Hey, you smoke America?" Montreal asked, lighting a cigarette. The firelight skipped upon his oily face.

"Only cigarettes."

"Yeah, cigarettes, that's what I mean," handing him a pack.

"Only cigarettes, who says, I smoke only cigarettes?" India said with a large smile. "This fucking guy!"

"Take, take," Jimmy said, tossing a small plastic bag on the table. Winston was the first to pull out a giant grasshopper from the bag. It made a crunching noise like a cheese snack, the legs poking at his gums. The travelers continued drinking until Jimmy hailed another man from the street, a short tourist with glasses and a keg belly. In seconds Jimmy was off with him, arm in arm down the muddy alley. Her young cousin stayed behind, preoccupied with setting beers on the table. Montreal spoke to her in Lao, tracing his fingers over his black beard. The girl spoke slowly, and mostly nodded and smiled at him, a bit too eagerly.

"It's disgusting, I can't stand it!" the woman from the Czech Republic said in an outrage. "I like Jimmy, but that old man she went off with looked nasty."

"But you must understand these working girls," said India with a buzzed smile. "Go home with one of these girls, go to the village where they live. Meet their parents, eat with them, drink lao-Lao alcohol with them, spend all night slapping malaria-ridden mosquitos, see the expression on their little brother's face when they arrive from the city bearing food, and you will understand why they come out to the city and sleep with an older, nasty man."

"Well, the girls are one thing," the woman said, drawing back her straight blonde hair. "But who are these men who come here just to buy prostitutes? That is disgusting. If you are sixty years old, do not sleep with your granddaughter."

"They do it because they have a penis," India said.

"But it is disgusting!"

"They cannot get women in their own country," said Montreal, joining the woman. "So they must come here because they're so ugly."

Winston thought of his own sex life, how he had not slept with a woman in nearly a year, how he hated himself for failing whenever he tried to flirt. He thought of how much easier it would be to just pay up and then find himself sleeping with a different girl every night. How many novels, how many love stories, would appear dull once he reached that point? "Every wanderlusting backpacker is one night away from becoming a doped up sexpat," Winston said, rubbing the condensation from his Beerlao. "They're the easiest people in the world to understand."

"They have penises." India nodded in agreement.

Winston wasn't used to taking a side, to having anyone agree with him. "You want to hate someone," he said, testing the waters. "Hate America. They dropped more bombs here than were dropped in all of World War II. Take a walk out there, I dare you, just a couple miles away. We're in a land of unexploded ordinances. Millions of them. Bombs that children play with. See all the people without legs, people riddled with shrapnel. It will take centuries before all the bombs are out of the ground. First they lay waste to a country, then they send in the doctors to patch'em all up, with interest of course, then ..." Realizing he had their full attention, he continued with abandon. Just minutes before, he had been done with expat groups. They never learned the language, avoided local politics, and turned every night into a reckless drunken spectacle with just enough risk to remember themselves as heroes. But here, in Laos of all places, was a group that listened.

Something stopped Winston's tirade: a quick kiss by Jimmy's slender cousin, who drifted around the table like a water petal. She took turns sitting next to the travelers, holding their hands and playfully kissing their cheeks, drinking and chain-smoking. India bought her a beer and gave her another cigarette.

"Hey, America," India said, as if Winston's hatred for the US only made the name stick. "I gotta tell you about this girl. Her name is Lin; she speaks no English. This girl is so young, she's mentally retarded, so these disgusting foreign tourists, they take her and they make her love them. Sometimes they give her no money because she doesn't know any better. So every night we buy her beers, we give her cigarettes, and she fucking chain-smokes man, and she drinks everything we give her, but she never acts any different. She is always ready to go off with some fat tourist. Now this girl, we love this girl man, we protect this girl. If we don't drink with her, you know what happens? She gets bored, she goes into the street and goes to that sexpat bar down the road."

"So you see," Montreal added, cracking his knuckles. "This is what *we* can do. Look at this girl. You want her cheery face to be laid out for some tourist looking to bone a young girl? No. They will never have the chance to laugh when they realize that she is handicapped. *We* will not give them that. We will stumble, and drink, and chain-smoke, and laugh ourselves to death before that happens."

"Yes yes I understand," Winston said, nodding.

"Look at America!" Montreal said with a sly grin. "Obama come to save us all."

When the outdoor bar closed, all the nations marched together in a Dionysian procession down the unpaved streets of Vientiane, inviting anyone they saw to join in their parade, chanting "Come with us!" like a regiment. With Lin in the middle, they trooped through a crowd of friendly young pimps and drug dealers, and entered "the bar," the only visible late-night pub. Inside, loud American music mixed with the sound of tourists rooting for their football teams. Winston ordered a drink from the long bar, squeezing his way through different nationalities: Nigeria (a lanky businessman), New Zealand (a sombre girl with dreadlocks), South Africa (honeymooners in khaki shorts), Australia (three young men shouting at the football game).

"Buffalo Sol-dar!" the bar sang. "In da heart of America!"

"It's not the American people that I got problems with," New Zealand told Winston with a snide smile. "It's your government. Who will you go to war with next?"

"Actually, America is a Democracy, so you should probably hate the people too." Winston gave a smug grin. "They did vote for Bush twice. Don't feel bad if you don't like the American people, or feel disgusted at them, maybe you should."

"But you have Obama running for president now," Nigeria said. "Things will change."

"You think so?" Winston quipped: "Unless it means an end to war, I'm not even casting a vote."

His comments staggered them, as he knew they would. Out of all the expats he ever met, he was the only one with the guts to actually ex-patriotize himself, in paper and in mind, a full severing from the evil empire, black president or no. In their silence, Winston strut to the bar to order another cuba libre, and found himself locking eyes with a petite brown woman leaning on a black table that made an island in the circling carousers. She smiled at him with the enigmatic grin of Buddha statues, her curly hair straddling her breasts.

The bar erupted in an Oasis song. Winston did not know the lyrics and neither did she.

"You must be American," she said.

"I guess. I only lived in America for a couple of years."

"So you are not America?"

"I've been traveling around all my life." He hooked his toes into her bar stool. "Never lived in the same place for more than a couple years."

"So you are Africa?"

"Well, sure, why not. Everyone assumes that anyway."

"But you look like Obama! So you are America!"

Winston pat down his hair, which stood out like the wool of an unshorn sheep. In his mind, he looked nothing like that guy. "What about you? You Laos?"

"No! Me Philippines! From Manila, yeah, but live in many places. Hong Kong, Dubai, Israel. Work and travel. Now I here, just, you know, see Laos."

"You're a tourist?"

"Yes."

"I know some Tagalog," Winston said, testing her. "Kumusta ka, ano ang gin [click] gawa [click] ngayon."

"Oh man. What's with the clicking, yeah?"

"I do that when I don't know the real word!" Winston had to shout over the singing. "Just to fill in empty space!"

The lights and music switched off, erasing their faces.

"Is it a blackout?" someone shouted to an echo of inebriated laughter.

"It's the one a.m. curfew!" a voice answered.

The nationalities stood with drinks in hand, nothing to sooth them but their own singing, while the bar girls escorted them out. The tourists only started their sluggish exit when the bartender announced that the police were coming, though the warning did not seem to worry the pimps and drug-dealers waiting outside. India, Philippines, and Winston huddled around Lin as they walked out, leaving Montreal to haggle with the dealers, while the remaining revelers piled into a tuk-tuk. Letting Lin sit in the center of the seats, Winston hung his body out the back of the three-wheeled tuk-tuk, standing on the ledge along with one of the Aussie boys to avoid the motor's smog.

"Hey, she your girl?" one of the Aussies asked, his eyes on Lin's nape, visible just above her pink shirt.

"She's no one's girl," Winston snarled.

They arrived at the only lit building in the entire city, a bowling alley full of Vientiane youth. Winston sat at a small dining table with India, Montreal, the Czech Republic, and Lin, who had her legs locked into her chest as she watched the Australian boys bowling in their Australian boy bubble.

"Can you believe it?" Montreal said, lighting a joint. "The Aussies really come here to bowl." The Czech girl danced to no music. Winston watched Philippines bring drinks to Australia, who had just made a strike. She started calling the one with fuzzy blonde hair *honey.*

"For beers, give me money," Philippines said, holding out her hand out to the Aussies for cash. She collected slips of money and then joined the table of mixed nations.

"You getting paid this time, Philippines?" Montreal asked.

"I dunno man, they not get it now. They not get me. Why?" she slapped Montreal in the face. "Why you talk like that? You think I'm some you know—prostitute!" laughing.

"Ma chérie, I love only, I have only love."

Winston poured beer into a paper cup and handed it to

her. As a thank you, she scratched the outlying follicles of his receding hairline.

"Those Australian boys, they no cool," Montreal said, then sipped his beer with a grin that showed his stained teeth. "They no cool like us. You cool. Me, I cool too, India cool. Lin cool. America here, see, America really is cool. You cool America. He doesn't know. But he can, how to say, *kick*, kick it."

"Yeah, I see." Philippines' eyes leered into Winston's. He suddenly felt out of place, as if he had been gazing at a room of statues. "But America no notice me."

"Ah," Montreal said. "Therefore, he is cool." He gestured his hands in a 'viola.'

The Czech Republic walked off hand-in-hand. That left India, Montreal, Winston, and Philippines to watch over Lin. The group shared more drinks and smokes as the night wore on. Winston was only half-awake now, keeping his eyes on Lin, who smiled at them like an elder, just happy to be present. She put her plastic cup upside down on her squarish head, meaning that she was ready for more.

"Lin, that was so fucking punk rock," India said, handing her a joint. "This girl, this girl is punk rock number one! Montreal, you can be punk-rock number two. I am punk rock number three, Philippines is number four, and that makes Obama over there number five. So Lin, congrats, you are number one most punk-rock at the Punk Rock UN."

Lin smiled, the cup still balanced on her head, a joint sticking from her lips like an orange lollipop.

The group toasted their cups and cheered. "Number one most punk rock!"

Lin passed the joint to Winston and he only pretended to take a drag, since he hated marijuana.

"Aha, I know you fake!" Philippines said, pointing at him, "You faking, not really getting high." She took a drag. "What's with you? You some American spy?"

"Maybe I should go," Winston said, feeling that impending urge for his happy pill. He could feel his lips tremble, his voice break.

"Stay man," India said. "Lin's going to tire out soon. One more beer, one more smoke. This is how every night ends. She's got one more hour tops." They drank another round and Winston felt their collective relief when Lin let out a yawn. Philippines leaned on his arm and he could smell the perfume in her curly hair. His arm vined around hers and she stroked his inner thigh.

"Come, you come help me," Philippines said. She darted up and gestured for Winston to follow her.

"We'll be back," Winston assured the table. Lin smiled and waved goodbye, her eyes bright and eager. India and Montreal poured more booze.

Outside, Philippines called a tuk-tuk to her hotel. She paid for it, even though the driver drastically overcharged.

"I not pay you anything," Winston told her amid the screeching tuk-tuk engine.

"Man, if you pay I tell you," Philippines said. "I no want your money."

"Ok, but I have to go back later. Make sure Lin is ok."

"You crazy, man!"

Her hotel room was too dark to see how filthy it might be. She used a flashlight to show him a picture of an infant and said, "my baby." She told him she was really thirty-seven. She showed him love letters from a white American man who used to send her money but had died in the war. She told him that she was traveling around Laos because her Philippine passport was no good in Western countries. She told him she really loved him and that because he looked kind of Asian but his skin was black she felt like he was different and that's why he would never have to pay her. All this she did while burning a red pill over a layer of foil and used a straw to inhale the fumes—freebasing, as Winston knew. She offered him the drug.

"I have an early bus tomorrow," he said.

"I like you man. You drive me crazy. I was going to be with Australia but I kept looking at you. I think, 'Ah, I must have him. I really want him to fuck me.'"

"I love you too. I really do. I've never loved anyone. But I love you."

"You drive me crazy." She took a hit and held her head back, allowing her small pot belly to distend. Winston opened the window shades so he could chart her body with his fingers, each wrinkle a different transit point. Dubai, Indonesia, Thailand, Hong Kong. He followed them down to her belly's stretch marks, lit with the light of a streetlamp. He found the phrase 'Noli Me Tángere' tattooed under her left breast.

"I know what that means."

"It can mean a lot of things."

She kissed him and he winced away, staring at her smooth face. She looked like she could have been his sister, though he could offer her nothing. When she looked at him, what did she see? In all his years in Asia, never had his darker, mysterious mixture of skin made him look attractive. Wherever he went, it was local hands grabbing onto his hair. It was nightclub managers asking him to DJ, trying to hire him to dance. No matter how many languages he could speak, it never mattered in the long run. He was always a spectacle. But now the spectacle was a symbol for something more, an untapped natural resource for a nation he had kept as far away as possible.

She felt his deflated penis.

"I can't," he said. She moved on top of him but he could not respond. He hugged her tightly, picking off three bedbugs from her shoulder. She shoved him in anger and he stared at the wooden planks on the ceiling, letting the sadness envelope him.

He thought of Lin, at that bar alone, an old crooked-toothed Aussie smiling back at her.

The thick smoke from a joint wafted to him. Philippines offered it to him; he took a hit.

"Let's just kiss and you can touch me," she told him, leading his fingers onto her. Her hand gripped him. He wondered if he would forget her face. He stared at her, hoping to burn her into his memory, so it would appear wherever he went, whenever he saw the sun's reflection over a muddy river. Somehow, he felt the blood flow to his dick. He listened to where her body shook in certain places and he spoke to her until tears welted in her eyes and she squeezed his back flesh. He confessed that he wanted to try freebasing and that he wanted to do it with her because it was the only way he could make love to her. He took a hit and it was like wind sweeping off the dust in his brain. A new way to see the world, a new script. As he slid on his back, his tongue locked in a dance with hers, and he wondered how many other worlds were out there.

When the drug began to make Winston's body feel numb, an explosion of energy tossed him into a mess of choked breath. *Lin*! He heard her sex moan, saw the Aussie boys having their way with her one by one, calling her retarded, jungle bitch, LBFM. No, he could not abandon her. His head felt like stone as he lifted it off the cushion. He felt his face wet with tears.

"Honey, honey," Philippines called to him.

"Don't call me honey. I'm no John!" He staggered up.

"Where you going?"

"I need to help her." He struggled to stand, his knees shaking, his fingers fidgeting with his zipper. The space between him and the door was a black hole.

"You people crazy, man. What you thinking?"

Winston breathed in forced fits until he vomited all over the wood floor. Part of the greenish yellow liquid expelled in a paint blot on the white unsheeted mattress.

"Ahh!" Philippines shrieked. "What you do?!"

He tossed her a wad of cash from his pocket and slowly walked out, though every step felt like uprooting a tree. He walked into the dark night, hearing her shout obscenities at him. He imagined catching some fat foreigner walking Lin to his hotel. He imagined tearing out the man's Adam's apple.

"Tuk-tuk?" a scrawny mustached driver said. Winston stumbled in. As the motor revved he stared at the concrete ground in a daze. His eyes regained focus on a pack of black dogs running behind him. He stuck his head out and foliage slapped his face. All around, the small city of French architecture seemed to transform into a Hollywood zombie flick, where locals became the undead, touting for blood, in that humming Laotian accent.

In the bowling alley parking lot, the driver tried to bargain for a higher fare. Winston threw bright cash at him and tried to pilot his swaying body toward the entrance, passing stray dogs and cats awakened by his dragging feet.

He mounted the steps from the bright entrance to the alleys. He focused his eyes on the tables and saw India sitting in a small booth, with Lin on the other side, a white flower in her hair. Hail India! He was the last one! The man looked like white Jesus as he turned and smiled toward Winston, eyes bright with whatever he was juiced with.

Winston sat with them and stayed until sunrise, comforted by Lin's pleasing smile. It never seemed to fade, but remained even as she began to doze off on the plastic table, as if her dreams would be just more smoking and drinking. He thought he'd remember her forever, sitting with her legs tucked under her, staring vacantly at a puddle of spilled beer that reflected a yellow stripe of sunlight. When Lin finally fell asleep, head soft on knees, India and America, the last remaining members of the Punk Rock U.N., went their separate ways. On the long walk home Winston felt a heavy feeling coming, one so unlike sadness or anger.

The sun cast glints of brass onto the muddy Mekong. Winston sat at his usual spot on the patio overlooking the river, sipping from a coconut shake. The muddy waters flowed stronger than usual. The green plants and twigs couldn't be seen. When he realized he felt no need to take his pill, he let his bus to Luang Prabang come and go.

The waiters opened up the umbrella shades and Winston used his Art Deco pen to practice Japanese script. He tried to remember last night as plainly as possible. He recalled talking to India at the bowling alley while watching Lin drift to sleep.

"What about when we leave?" Winston had asked him. "Lin will just go right back to that bar, back to the streets."

"When we leave?" India had said. "Hopefully there will be people like us, who will see this girl and spend all night drinking with her and offering her cigarettes."

Winston stared at the muddy Mekong, wondering if the girl from the Philippines was the same. Did they both come from a family in a village? Neither of them made any money that night. Did the tribe of backpackers keep their families hungry? What if their brother, or their grandmother, or their mother, was sick, and needed medicine? He recalled his manhood in the hotel room, but could not remember how far he had gone with her. What good was sex with no memory of its happening?

His pondering was interrupted by that child selling balloons. She wore the same purple dress and her dirt-marked face still hadn't been washed.

"Do you remember our lesson yesterday?" Winston asked her. "Sun glasses?"

"Sun glaysees," she repeated, a finger in her mouth.

"Excellent. Now how about *money*. You know *money*?"

"Yes."

"Hmm," Winston's eyes darted around for an object to teach her. "Oh. How about coin? You know coin?" She looked at him blankly. "No?" He dug in his backpack and pulled out some American change, just pennies and nickels. "Look here. I have two coins. Now these are two more." He lined up four quarters on the table.

"You want peepshi?" the girl said flatly, her eyes on the American change.

"You mean Pepsi? Pep-si."

"No, peepsi." A blank stare.

"Pepsi. *Pepsi.*" He looked about for a Pepsi can.

"Peepshi," she said, finger in mouth. "Peep shew."

"Peep shew?" Winston asked. She shook her head. Winston looked at the single balloon she held, pink. Peep shew, he thought. Oh, *peep show*.

He saw that the girl's hands had lifted the carefully sewn end of her skirt, revealing white panties beneath. The sky darkened around him, shadowing the river and the jungles on the other side.

"No, no," Winston stammered, putting the coins back in his pocket. He turned away and watched the river, listening to the tapping of her shoes echo across the patio.

The muddy Mekong was the color of polished, gaudy wood, of brown pepper, of those ants marching up the table leg. Winston sat and watched the river until the sunset drew over it and it became just a quiet nothingness flowing by in the dark.

ThinkTravel! Blogbook

Post Date: 2008 NOV 5

User: SkyFaralan

A man with flaccid limbs drifts by you at the Varanasi train station. Except for a beard covering half his torso he is completely nude, and just as you see his swaying comportment crossing your path, he plummets into the railroad tracks, tumbling into the heavy iron rails the way one might fall onto a softly pillowed couch after a long, exhausting day.

Aboard the train to Kolkata you can think of little else. The fall, his fall, a fall. It seems he was ... drunk? Poor? Desperate? Demented? You are so out of your senses that when you and Sophea wake up in the middle of the night to find your bags stolen and you are charging through each compartment of sleeping bodies searching for your stolen passport and credit cards, and when the Kolkata police with Rajasthani mustaches and thick eyebrows arrive holding AK-47s, and when you are both left sitting in the Kolkata station wondering if you are ever getting home, and even when, hours later, a hotel clerk throws your only remaining backpack into the floods of the monsoon, refusing to let you in his hotel without your passports and then you have to trudge for hours through a street flood that has risen to your waistline and your tears never show through the pouring rain—during all of that, you are still in that Varanasi train station with the heat slapping you down, still watching that nude man plummet into the train tracks, gravity tugging his skin, making his eye sockets cave like hollow pits.

How does a man, entirely nude, get all the way from the plat-form staircases, through the corridors of the station and the hired guards, to your end of the train? Had he really walked through the entire train station, naked? You wonder this as you and Sophea are rejected from your fifth hotel and sent back into the waters of the monsoon. With everything you own in the world either stolen or damp from the floods, you begin to count the things you still have. The clothes on your backs. Toothbrushes and bones. Defeated eyes. Varanasi silk. The vacant railway. Words that have hibernated for so long in your mouths.

You just have to keep your heads in the right place. You re-peat to yourself an adage: The greatness of a person is not in their achievements, but in the way they react to tragedy. No longer with the privilege of cynicism, deprived of your sense of distance, you are comforted by every cliché that comes to mind.

Another hotel manager refuses to let you in, assuming that she is a vagrant from Orissa or the Northeast, and that you are a ladyboy hoping to find a drunk tourist. It strikes you that this would all be different if you were white. There'd be no denying your story, your Americanness. But in her they just see rabble drifting in from the storm, and in you, a taboo born to life, too strange even for a tourist hotel. When you show them your police report, they snicker at the stamp.

Sick with exhaustion, you wetten the floors of an internet cafe. As Sophea calls her loved ones, reliving the tragedy again and again, you cannot forget where you are and the things you no longer have.

Keep counting: You have mother-of-pearl bangles. A new bed-cover three sizes too large. An ineffable urge to fly.

"We have to keep our heads," Sophea says, plugging away at the keyboard. "This happens to the people who live here every day." Unlike you she's focused, centered, calm. "We must keep our heads, Skyler. It's the only thing we can do. No matter what, keep your head."

You pause, eyes riveted onto the webpage: the American embassy website. Images of that flag. That country's diverse assortments of happy-go-lucky polo-clad military sent overseas to kill people in public, in secret; people like you, brown and poor and unsure of their place. And when all those enlightened ones chose to keep killing despite the massacres, the lies, you too made a choice.

Adjusting her headset, Sophea calls the American emergency services hotline.

"I'm sorry," you tell her, venturing back into the flood. "I just can't."

The street has transformed into a river with a heavy current pushing against you. A black bull has somehow retreated to a rooftop. Children in school uniforms laugh as the rushing flood carries them away. A construction site hole erupts brown water. Unable to see your feet, you take slow, careful steps. In the water you lose your mind, sobbing out loud. But your body does not give. And with it, your mind returns.

You climb into a small hostel inside an old brick building. You meet Phillip, the owner, an Indian man with a British accent and a small mustache. When you tell him what has happened his fists clench in a rage that you are far past. He offers you a room, tells you everything is going to be all right.

You pick up Sophea at the internet café. She says an American duty officer will meet you both in the morning. "But look," tapping the screen. "He won the election." You see pictures of people marching in the street, cheering, holding signs of a rising sun. You know almost nothing about him, only what the Indian locals have told you. A man from Indonesia and Hawaii, they said, a black man, an Asian man.

"Let's go," you tell her.

Back at the hotel, Phillip assesses the situation. You have no copies of your passport. No identification at all. No money. No credit cards. No cell phone. You have nothing. Nothing. Do you know what it means to have nothing? In this country?

Huddled on the hotel room bed, you watch a television screen showing American streets where people parade with banners proclaiming hope and change. You feel like you recognize them. Chinese, Indians, Filipinos. Whites, Blacks, Browns, Reds. Gays, Transgenders, Queers. People too vast and impossible to name. Like you, they were never immigrants. That very word, you realize, was a con. Your family came as cane-pickers and colonial servants. Hers as refugees. America was no city on a hill, but a floating net collecting the debris from the bombs it dropped. And you had forgotten what it was like to be there, clustered in that oddly beautiful concoction of colonial leftovers, slung together over the arm of a stomping giant.

Together you watch, your bodies damp and waiting to be picked up.

The Flaneurs Spacechat

Chat log/November 21ˢᵗ 2008

코니: whoooo the fuck invented all you can drink specials

@Melz: HHA well good morning sunshine

코니: theyre trying to kill us arent they

@Melz: you asking me?

코니: at least it wasnt the worst night I ever had

@Melz: nope ... theres still TONIGHT RIP

코니: Did you stay with me? Why arent you here?

@Melz: teaching now giving a test (little bastards) one is touching himself in class again which is .... something ... im ok?? with

코니: did I call her last night?

@Melz: i deleted her from your phone

코니: what

코니: thank you I guess

코니: you can give me her number now

@Melz: ya gotta earns it

코니: btw who was that guy? from last night? that waegook dancing on the tables?

@Melz:	oooo the man stoned outta his gourd?
코니:	dont tell me
코니:	a new english teacher
코니:	god fucking dammit dude
코니:	we had like two months of peace since Winston left and more are coming already???
@Melz:	its november ... dey been coming
코니:	but it usually takes them a while
코니:	to find our bar
코니:	shit it is November
코니:	every fall like clockwork our bar turns into a hive
코니:	meth-den mentality
코니:	you were at my place all night?
@Melz:	didnt even stop at home to get my toothbrush ... its ok, i had company
코니:	what who?
@Melz:	a book, obvs
코니:	what book
@Melz:	a meditation guide from some burmese monk ... you know theres a meditation center in korea ... was thinking, maybe ... a ten day retreat?

@Melz: no phones, no laptops, no money, nothin ...
          just a lake to stare at

코니: can you just tell me her number now

@Melz: heeaallz no

코니: pleeease have some sympathy you witch

@Melz: you knew the second her boyfriend came
          back from military service she wouldnt see
          you again

코니: I got a funny question

@Melz: what? funny-haha?

코니: you meditate a lot

@Melz: i do ...

코니: do you really think something out there
          really gives a shit about us?

@Melz: a god?

코니: no. course not. but. its just. all those people
          in korea, indochina, the philippines

@Melz: i dont know

코니: god dammit dude Im literally crying a
          waterfall over here though you cant see it

@Melz: its all right ok AHA yes ... god ... or buddha
          ... or whoever loves and cares about you its
          ok

코니: fuuuuck! for every one of those new
          foreigners: slice! one ball at a time.

@Melz: oh be nice, its prolly their first time abroad. wow ... bet they dont even know what bibiimbap is! ... can you imagine that? or samgaypsale. or dukbokgi. holy shit ... i can smell it roasting riht now ... the dukbokgi lady!

코니: gross I thought you were teaching

@Melz: kids wont mind JESUS CHRIST i want it so bad

코니: cant you just ignore it?

@Melz: impossible

ThinkTravel! Blogbook

Post Date: 2008 NOV 28

User: SkyFaralan

Confession, contempt, and roads, roads, roads. As far as you can see. When the plane reaches five-thousand feet in the air, the roads turn into rivers. At ten thousand, the rivers into jet streams.

It tows your body. The back of a polluted bus, the smell of gasoline and exhaust. The back of an airplane, watching the air conditioning steam pour from the ceiling. The back of a rickshaw, watching desiccated limbs push at the pedals of a bicycle. The back of a motorbike, feeling a stranger's hair whisk into your face. The back of the road, where you walk along paths of still-lives, now comparing them with all the others around the world; the flaneur turned critic, the dissenter turned spy, the traveler turned sedentary.

As you reach the clouds you dream of an immaculate table with hundreds of guests in their Sunday best. You all partake in a colorful feast of Dal soup, Massaman curry, roast pork belly, fried bullfrog, and live squid squirming in red pepper sauce. After prayer you pass the collection plate, for manifest destiny, for the aid and the influence, the maids and the crops, for the oil that keeps us all transgressing. The priest ejaculates into the plate, shrieking in fury. You pass the plate along, and try the new dishes: fish amok, chicken rice, bun cha, char kuey teow, nasi goreng, lechon. Some cut open their wrists and drain themselves until all the blood has spilled out. Some toss in skulls of strange enemies. Some give their fortunes, the deeds to their houses. Some their children. But most give blood, especially those who travel. They have nothing but blood. Carving knives cut their ankles like apple slices.

On the road I invented you, and you joined me. But your only purpose, really, was to verify my sojourn, to give me an excuse to go deeper into places I could not venture through alone. So together we learned to share the disease, to populate every territory with it. Every road became an artery to shoot up. Every river a Rubicon to cross. And when there were no rivers left, our blood created rivers, until every eye saw in American black and white.

So when the plate comes to us, we are ready. We have prepared a saw with a serrated edge. Our right hand, the hand that holds our wallet, goes first. Then the left, the hand that clutches our documents. Then the legs that run. Then the mouth that dares call it running away. We dip our head, let the blood seep into our hair, and cut at the veins on our neck. This blood we give in the name of the nation. Let it be seen. There is no escape.

You wake in the airplane cabin. It's night. You hear her breathing next to you. You feel her dark hand squeezing your own, grasping you like a ballast, weighing you even when gravity cannot. With your free hand you crack open the window shade and peer into the dark black ocean, its terrible acid decaying all life, breaking it down to float weightless in its empty space. You watch until the sun begins to rise. Purple, pink and yellow streaks appear splashing across the waves, each curve bathed in a shimmy of sparks. The colors foam with strange delights.

Acknowledgments

Kawika is not a name but a roof. There are many eager, willing, unwitting, housed within.

The fiction writers who led workshops or gave generous encouragement: Shawn Hsu Wong, Vu Tran, Peter Reme Bacho, M. Evelina Galang, Jose "Butch" Dalisay, Madeleine Thien, Michael Gonzalez, and Ken Liu. Much of this book was inspired by the magnificent and fearless works of Lawrence Chua, R. Zamora Linmark, Shirley Geok-lin Lim, Alfred Yuson, Han Ong, Jessica Hagedorn, and others.

The editors and agents who gave honest assessments and shaped the novel over time: Jason Pettus, Marshall Moore, Jessie Kindig, and Paul Lai.

The readers whose candid feedback pushed the novel in more focused direction: Michael James Drake, Christopher Martin, Alan Williams, and Chaya Benyamin.

The mad traveling artists and thinkers whose personalities warmed these quarters: Phanuel Antwi, Soyi Kim, Doretta Lau, Michael Zibelman, Tina Farias, Collier Nogues, Donald Goellnicht, Alvy Wong, Mary Tsoi, Anida Yoeu Ali, Thy Phu, Sophie Scott, and Valerie Soe.

The long-distance friends whose candid language animated these walls and gave voice to the spacechats: Noah Tierney, Bob Hodges, Evan Poncelet, Allen Baros, and Pat Budiman.

My twin brother, Cameron Patterson, who joined me in my first travels, has been a bottomless well of brazen and bold ideas. So too with my challenger, editor, and lover, Y-Dang Troeung, who read every word of this book, multiple times. Any accolades to Kawika must include these two as its strongest pillars.

Finally, this novel would not have been possible were it not for the many traveling companions I encountered in Asia and North America from 2005–2017. Many of you I still talk to, some I remain attached to only through social media, and a few of you have become family. But most of you, the nameless vast majority, will never know how much your quiet proximity rescued me from my darkest plunges; when the pressures of self-hate would have overtaken me, you were there.

Author Note

Kawika Guillermo's stories can be found in *The Cimarron Review*, *The Hawai'i Pacific Review*, *Word Riot*, *Drunken Boat*, and many others. He is an Assistant Professor of Humanities and Creative Writing at Hong Kong Baptist University, and he is the author of *Transitive Cultures: Anglophone Literature of the Transpacific* (Rutgers University Press, 2018).

Made in the USA
San Bernardino, CA
24 July 2019